UNFORE-SEEN

Also by Molly Gloss

MOLLY GLOSS

UNFORE-SEEN

Stories

SAGA PRESS

LONDON SYDNEY **NEW YORK** TORONTO NEW DELHI

SAGA PRESS

AN IMPRINT OF SIMON & SCHUSTER, INC.

1230 AVENUE OF THE AMERICAS, NEW YORK, NEW YORK 10020

Text copyright © 2019 by Molly Gloss

Jacket illustration copyright © 2019 by Jeffrey A. Love

SAGA PRESS and colophon are trademarks of Simon & Schuster, Inc.

For information about special discounts for bulk purchases, please contact Simon & Schuster Special Sales at 1-866-506-1949 or business@simonandschuster.com.

The Simon & Schuster Speakers Bureau can bring authors to your live event. For more information or to book an event, contact the Simon & Schuster Speakers Bureau at 1-866-248-3049 or visit our website at www.simonspeakers.com.

Interior design by Vikki Sheatsley

The text for this book was set in Cormorant Garamond.

Manufactured in the United States of America

First Edition

10 9 8 7 6 5 4 3 2 1

CIP data for this book is available from the Library of Congress.

ISBN 978-1-4814-9850-0

ISBN 978-1-4814-9852-4 (eBook)

CONTENTS

Interlocking Pieces   1

Eating Ashes   11

Personal Silence   23

Downstream   53

Dead Men Rise Up Never   67

Wenonah's Gift   85

The Presley Brothers   97

Seaborne   121

A Story   159

Little Hills   171

Unforeseen   181

Lambing Season   203

The Visited Man   221

The Blue Roan   243

The Everlasting Humming of the Earth   257

Joining   281

The Grinnell Method   297

UNFORE-SEEN

Interlocking Pieces

AFTER THE LAST REFUSAL—THE East European Minister of Health sent Teo his personal explanation and regrets—it became a matter of patience and readiness and rather careful timing.

A uniformed policeman had been posted beside her door for reasons, apparently, of protocol. At eight thirty, when he went down the corridor to the public lavatory, she was dressed and waiting, and simply walked out past the nurses' station. It stood empty. The robo-nurse was still making the eight o'clock rounds of the wing's seventy or eighty rooms. The organic nurse, just come on duty, was leaning over the vid display in the alcove behind the station, familiarizing herself with the day's new admissions.

Because it was the nearest point of escape, Teo used the staircase. But the complex skill of descending stairs had lately deserted her, so she stepped down like a child, one leg at a time, grimly clutching the metal banister with uncooperative hands. After a couple of floors she went in again to find a public data terminal in a ward that was too busy to notice her.

They had not told her even the donor's name, and a straightforward voice request met a built-in resistance: DATA RESTRICTED***KEY IN PHYSICIAN IDENT CODE. So she asked the machine for the names of organ donors on contract with the regional Ministry of Health, then a list of the hospital's terminal neurological patients, the causes and projected times of their deaths, and the postmortem neurosurgeries scheduled for the next morning. And, finally, the names of patients about whom information was media-restricted. Teo's own name appeared on the last list. She should have been ready for this but found she was not, and she sat staring until the letters grew unfamiliar, assumed strange juxtapositions, became detached and meaningless—the name of a stranger.

The computer scanned and compared the lists for her, extrapolated from the known data, and delivered only one name. She did not ask for hard copy. She looked at the vid display a moment, and then punched it off and sat staring at the blank screen.

Perhaps not consciously, she had expected a woman. The name, a man's name, threw her off balance a little. She would have liked a little time to get used to the sound of it, the sound it made in her head and on her lips. She would have liked to know the name before she knew the man. But he would be dead in the morning. So she spoke it once, only once, aloud, with exactness and with care. "Dhavir Stahl," she said. And then went to a pneumo-tube and rode up.

In the tube there were at first several others, finally only one. Not European, perhaps North African, a man with eyebrows in a thick straight line across a beetled brow. He watched her sidelong—clearly recognized her—and he wore a physician's ID badge. In a workplace as large as this one the rumor apparatus would be well established. He would know of her admission, maybe even the surgery that had been scheduled. Would, at the very least, see the incongruity of a VIP patient, street-dressed and unaccompanied, riding up in the public pneumo-tube. So Teo stood imperiously beside him with disobedient hands clasped together behind her back and eyes focused on the smooth center seam of the door while she waited for him to speak, or not. When the tube opened at the seventy-eighth floor he started out, then half turned toward her, made a stiff little bow, and said, "Good health, Madame Minister," and finally exited. If he reported straightaway to security, she might have five minutes, or ten, before they reasoned out where she had gone. And standing alone now in the pneumo-tube, she began to feel the first sour leaking of despair—what could be said, learned, shared in such little time?

There was a vid map beside the portal on the ninety-first floor. She searched it until she found the room and the straightest route, then went quickly, gripping the handrail for support, along the endless corridors, past the little tableaux of sickness framed where a door here or there stood open, and finally to the designated room, a closed door.

She would have waited. She wanted to wait, to gather up a few dangling threads, reweave a place or two that had lately worn through. But the physician in the pneumo-tube had stolen that possibility. So she took in a thin new breath and touched one wobbly thumb to the admit disk. The door opened, waited for her, closed behind her. She stood just inside, stood very straight, with her hands hanging open beside her thighs.

The man whose name was Dhavir Stahl was fitting together the pieces of a masters-level holoplex, sitting on his bed, cross-legged under a light sheet, with the scaffolding of the puzzle in front of him on the bed table and its thousands of tiny elements jumbled around him on the sheets. He glanced at Teo from under the ledge of his eyebrows while he worked. He had that vaguely anxious quality all East Europeans seemed to carry about their eyes. But his mouth was good, a wide mouth with creases lapping around its corners—creases where his smile would fit. And he worked silently, patiently.

"I would speak with you," Teo said.

He was tolerant, even faintly apologetic. "Did you look at the file, or just the door code? I've already turned down offers from a priest and a psychiatrist and, this morning, somebody from narcotics. I just don't seem to need any deathbed comforting."

"I am Teo."

"What is that? One of the research divisions?"

"My name."

His mouth made nearly a smile, perhaps embarrassment, or puzzlement.

"They hadn't told you my name, then," she said.

And finally he took it in. His face seemed to tighten, all of it pulling back toward his scalp as the skin shrinks from the skull of a corpse, so that his mouth was too wide and there was no space left for smiling.

"They seem to have a good many arbitrary rules," Teo said. "They refused me this meeting, your name even. And you, mine, it appears. I could not—I had a need to know."

She waited raggedly through a very long silence. Her palms were faintly damp, but she continued to hold them open beside her legs. Finally Dhavir Stahl moved, straightened a little, perhaps took a breath. But his eyes stayed with Teo.

"You look healthy," he said. It seemed a question.

She made a slight gesture with one shoulder, a sort of shrugging off. "I have lost motor skills." And in a moment, because he continued to wait, she added, "I am losing ability to walk. To use my hands. The cerebellum is evidently quite diseased. They first told me I would die. Then they said no, maybe not, and they sent me here."

He had not moved his eyes from her. One of his hands lightly touched the framework of the puzzle as a blind man would touch a new face, but he never took his eyes from Teo. Finally she could not bear that, and her own eyes skipped out to the window to the dark sheets of rain flapping beneath the overcast.

"You are not what I expected," he said. When her eyes came round to him again, he made that near smile and forced air from his mouth—not a laugh, a hard sound of bleak amusement. "Don't ask! God, I don't know what I expected." He let go the puzzle and looked away finally, looked down at his hands, then out to the blank vid screen on the wall, the aseptic toilet in the corner. When he lifted his face to her again, his eyes were very dark, very bright, she thought he might weep. But he said only, "You are Asian." He was not quite asking it.

"Yes."

"Pakistani?"

"Nepalese."

He nodded without surprise or interest. "Do you climb?"

She lifted her shoulders again, shrugging. "We are not all Sherpa bearers," she said with a prickly edge of impatience.

There was no change at his mouth, but he fell silent and looked away from her. Belatedly she felt she might have shown more tolerance. Her head began to ache a little from a point at the base of the skull. She would have liked to knead the muscles along her shoulders. But she waited, standing erect and stiff and dismal, with her hands hanging, while the time they had together went away quickly and ill used.

Dhavir Stahl raised his arms, made a loose, meaningless gesture in the air, then combed back his hair with the fingers of both hands. His hair and his hands seemed very fine. "Why did you come?" he said, and his eyelashes drew closed, shielding him as he spoke.

There were answers that would have hurt him again. She sorted through for one that would not. "To befriend you," she said, and saw his eyes open slowly. In a moment he sighed. It was a small sound, dry and sliding, the sound a bare foot makes in sand. He looked at the puzzle, touched an element lying loose on the bed, turned it round with a fingertip. And round.

Without looking toward her, he said, "Their computer has me dead at four-oh-seven-fourteen. They've told you that, I guess. There's a two percent chance of miscalculation. Two or three, I forget. So anyway, by four thirty." His mouth was drawn out thin.

She thought, *You will not have time to finish your puzzle.*

She said, "They would have given you another artificial heart."

He lifted his face, nearly smiled again. "They told you that? Yes. Another one. I wore out my own and one of theirs." He did not explain or justify. He simply raised his shoulders, perhaps shrugging, and said, "That's enough." He was looking toward her, but his eyes saw only inward. She waited for him. Finally he stirred, turned his palms up, studied them.

"Did they—I wasn't expecting a woman. Men and women move differently. I didn't think they'd give a man's cerebellum to a woman." He glanced at Teo, taking her in, all of her. "And you're small. I'm, what, twenty kilos heavier, half a meter taller? I'd think you'd have some trouble getting used to the way I move. Or anyway the way my brain tells my body to move." He was already looking at his hands again, rubbing them against each other with a slight papery sound.

"They told me I would adapt to it," Teo said. "Or the new cerebellum could be retaught."

His eyes skipped up to her as if she had startled or frightened him. His mouth moved too, sliding out wide to show the sharp edge of his teeth. "They didn't tell me that," he said from a rigid grin.

It was a moment before she was able to find a reason for his agitation. "It won't they said it wouldn't reduce the donor's sense of self."

After a while, after quite a while, he said, "What word did they use? They wouldn't have said 'reduce.' Maybe 'correct' or 'edit out.'" His eyes slid sideways, away from her, then back again. His mouth was still tight, grimacing, shaping a smile that wasn't there. "They were at least frank about it. They said the cerebellum only runs the automatic motor functions, the skilled body movements. They said they would have expected—no, they said they would have liked—a transplanted cerebellum to be mechanical. A part, like a lung or a kidney. The 'mind' ought to be all in the forebrain. They told me there wouldn't be any donor consciousness, none at all, if they could figure out how to stop it."

In a moment he was able to drop his eyes from Teo. He sat with his long, narrow hands cupped on his knees and stared at the scaffolding of his puzzle. She could hear his breath sliding in and out, a contained and careful sound. Finally he selected an element from among the thousands around him on the bed, turned it solemnly in his hands, turned it again, then reached to fit it into the puzzle, deftly finding a place for it among the multitude of interlocking pieces. He did not look at Teo, but in a moment he said, "You don't look scared. I'd be scared if they were putting bits of somebody else inside my head." He slurred the words a little, and just at the end and jumped his eyes to her and away.

She made a motion to open her hands, but then, irresistibly, turned her palms in, chafing harshly against her pants legs.

She chose a word from among several possible. "Yes," she said.

Dhavir's eyes came up to her again with something like surprise. And then something like tenderness. The door behind Teo opened and three security people stepped inside, diminishing the size of the room with their small crowd, their turbulence. One of them extended her hand but did not quite touch Teo's arm. "Minister Teo," she said. Formal. Irritated.

Dhavir seemed not to register the formal address. Maybe he would remember it later, maybe not, and Teo thought probably it wouldn't matter. They watched each other silently, Teo standing carefully erect with her hands, the hands that no longer brushed teeth nor wrote cursive script, the hands she had learned to distrust, hanging open beside her thighs, and Dhavir sitting cross-legged amid his puzzle, with his forearms resting across his knees. Teo waited. The security person touched her elbow, beginning to draw her firmly toward the door. Her legs, her entire body, resisted this movement, whether from disability or from stubborn opposition she could not have said. Dhavir spoke her name. "Teo," he said. She pulled her arm free and stiffened her spine to turn, to face him.

"I run lopsided," he said. "Like a duck, I guess. "I throw my toes out or something. I'm sorry." His slight smile was wry, apologizing for something else.

In a moment, she said, "I scuff my feet on the ground when I walk. I haven't run in years. You and I, perhaps we will learn new ways, together." And with infinite, excruciating care, she lifted her palms to him as if holding out a gift.

Eating Ashes

B. J. WASN'T OLD, HE was seventy-four. That wasn't old, but old enough to die. He'd smoked all his life and he always had liked to get drunk—if those habits had killed him they didn't say. They said his heart stopped, which meant they didn't know, probably. They asked Josephine if she wanted an autopsy but she didn't. He was dead, suddenly. What good would it do to take his heart out and look for the reason?

From the phone in the hospital lobby she called her eldest granddaughter, because her son was in Reno pulling the one-armed bandits and her nearest daughter never had a car that would run. "Grampa is dead," she said without her teeth: she had gone in the ambulance without the time to put her teeth in. The granddaughter came with her husband, in their big, cold van, and picked her up from in front of the hospital. "Gramma," the girl said, and put her arms around Josephine and cried. "His heart quit," Josephine said.

It had been late, ten o'clock or eleven, she'd been asleep

awhile, when B. J. had come into her bedroom and told her he had a pain; now it was two o'clock. She had used to stay up all night when she did the cannery work, she went on shift after supper and off at five with the sunrise, but she'd been retired from that for eight years, and needed her sleep at night, now. She wanted to go on home and lie down the rest of the night on her own bed, but the granddaughter said, "Oh, Gramma, you can't sleep there alone," and took her on to their own house, where they put her on a daveno bed in their extra room. They went to bed too, the granddaughter and her husband. It was Josephine who saw no point in calling people in the middle of the night—what could they do about it but wait for daylight, to start life without B. J.? If she had used her head, she'd have called a taxi to take her home, instead of her granddaughter. Let the two of them go on sleeping too.

She lay restlessly on the unfamiliar bed and thought about things. Her insides sounded, and finally she had to get up and find their bathroom in the darkness. It was a wet, sour stool, which didn't surprise her. Nerves made her bowels loose. Sitting on the toilet, she heard the granddaughter and her husband whispering. She couldn't remember when she and B. J. had ever whispered to each other, though surely they must have, early in their marriage when they'd shared the same bed. After their fourth child was born, Josephine had moved his things out of their bedroom, and B. J., when he was drunk-angry and full of his sex, sometimes had flaunted to her that he used prostitutes, which was a thing between him and God. Between her and God there was peace, because she had had enough children—that was all there was to it. From the other side of the bathroom door, the granddaughter called to her,

"Gramma, are you okay?" and she answered truthfully, "Yes I am, I've just got the runs."

She never did sleep, and as soon as there was some light through the curtains she went in to her granddaughter's telephone and called B. J.'s sister-in-law, Doris, the only number she could think of right now without her little address book. "B. J. passed away last night," she told Doris, who had been married to B. J.'s brother until that brother had been killed by cancer of the throat. Doris said, "Oh, Josie, my God, they're all dying!" Which was true, there was only Fred left now, of that family of six boys.

The granddaughter came out of the bedroom while Josephine was still on the phone, and stood there in her nightie with her eyes puffy, her hair a wild crown. She didn't look a bit like Margaret, her mother, Josephine's daughter; she had her father's falling-away chin and long build. Margaret had divorced that husband after twenty-two years, and now she lived in Arizona with a new husband. Josephine never had liked Margaret's first husband—he had a loud mouth and he thought he knew everything. But if you made a mistake in your marriage you ought to just live with it, that was what God said, it was what Josephine believed. It hadn't been any surprise to her when Margaret married a man no better than the first one: God had his own justice.

She had more strength for arguing, now that it was daylight, and when she hung up the phone from Doris, she said to her granddaughter, "I want you to take me on home now."

Her house was cold and shadowy, but the EMTs had picked up after themselves so the only evidence B. J. had died on the living room rug the night before was his undershirt lying where it had fallen. Josephine picked that up and put it in the hamper, opened the draperies and turned up the furnace. Then she put in her teeth and got out her little address book and sat down at the kitchen table.

She called everybody in the book, telling each one, "B. J. passed away last night." The first two or three times, her voice broke a little on the words, but after that she got used to saying it, and heard herself sound mournful and steady.

She called her daughters as she came to them in the little book, Margaret in Arizona, and Barbara in Eugene one hundred twenty miles away, and finally the last-born, Betty, who lived on Forty-Fourth Street not more than fifteen blocks from this house, though it was just the coincidental, alphabetic nature of their husband's names that caused her to call her daughters from farthest to nearest, oldest to youngest. She tried her son's number too, when she came to it, and let it ring and ring, knowing he was in Reno. He wouldn't be home until Friday, at least, and later than that if his wife held on to her notion of seeing the Grand Canyon.

Josephine and B. J. when they went to Reno always stayed at the Sands, it was their lucky casino. B. J. had won on keno there, a thousand-dollar pot, and he had split it with her—she'd bought a solid maple china hutch. So when she got to the S's she called the Sands and asked if Donald Lambuehl was staying there, but he wasn't. The house had begun to fill up by that time, and she said, "He isn't at the Sands," to the five or six women standing around her in the kitchen.

"Call the state police," Mary Tulare said. "Won't they look for him, in a case like this, a death? I believe they'll check with the hotels, and if you know his car license they'll look for the plate, on the highway." They talked about this possibility. How many hotels were in Reno? What highway ran between there and the Grand Canyon? Jack Amato would know Donnie's car license, they were friends from the old St. Ignatius parish; Jack had Donnie's insurance, the car and house both. Josephine's granddaughter said, "Gramma, you should eat something, let me call Jack Amato and the Nevada Police," and took the phone out of her hands.

She wouldn't eat, her bowels still weren't settled, but she got up and worked in the kitchen, she and Opal Breese and Dorothy Haines, scrubbing potatoes and putting them on to boil, chopping up onions and celery. She put the dry skins of the onions and the empty paper sack in the little trash-burning stove that stood alongside the electric range. It was as old as the house, that stove, she'd kept it when they'd remodeled the kitchen in 1955, though B. J. had wanted to take it out. Their children liked to poke around in the stove when they were little and lick the cold ashes from their fingers, that was what B. J. kept bringing up. But they were big kids by 1955, through with eating ashes, and anyway the ashes satisfied some lack in their bodies—this was what she'd been told by the old doctor they all were seeing in those days. So she had dug in her heels about keeping the stove. The kitchen was her territory—the kitchen and the laundry—and B. J. knew it.

She got hamburger out of the freezer and set it on the drainboard so when it thawed they'd be able to make up some meatballs to have with the potato salad. Dorothy made radish roses and Josephine and Opal snapped up the late beans B. J. had picked the day before from the garden they grew in the side yard. She dug some bacon out of the meat keeper in the icebox, because B. J. always liked bacon on his green beans, and then she stood up straight and said, "Tuh," in annoyance at herself, when she remembered he was dead. She didn't believe in ghosts but it felt to her as if B. J. must be in the next room, swapping lies with Dorothy's husband, Paul. How could he be dead? She wasn't sure she believed in death.

Her daughter Betty came into the house, her eyes red, her husband and their youngest child trailing her. She put her arms around Josephine heavily and wailed like a child, "Mom, oh Mom, is Pop really dead?" This was too close to what Josephine had just been thinking.

"I told you he is," she said, annoyed beyond reason. Betty was a cross Josephine carried, for sins only God knew about, she'd been a slow baby, her talking hard to get, tongue-twisted still today, and she was an ugly girl besides, her mouth small and lopsided, her teeth too big in that little mouth. Her husband, Dewey, wasn't a prize—he had a consumptive look to him, he never had held a steady job, he wasn't Catholic. But he was better than none, and Betty had come home pregnant when she was fourteen. Dewey was already thirty then, and B. J. had privately sworn to Josephine that he'd throw Dewey's ass in jail if he didn't make right by his mistake. Josephine had to say this much for Dewey, he had married Betty without a whimper and they were still married twenty years later. Betty, and Dewey too, drank worse than B. J. ever had; her red eyes might have been from that. Those three grandchildren had grown up badly, no fault of their own. The oldest girl took welfare for her fatherless babies; it was the heartbreak of Josephine's life.

About the time the potatoes reached a boil, Barbara came. She had driven up from Eugene in two hours, but without her husband, without their three children. They would all come for the funeral, she said. The children had cried for their Poppy, Paul was sorry too. Paul was the husband, he owned a hardware business. Josephine had approved of the marriage when it first happened, but the business was 120 miles south, and Barbara and her husband came up to Portland only two or three times a year. They would stay at the house an hour or two and then go on to the husband's mother's house. Those grandchildren called Josephine "Nanny," B. J. "Poppy"; it was the husband's mother who was Gramma, the husband's father who was Grampa. B. J., more so than Josephine, had blamed Paul for taking those three grandchildren away from him. "Well I guess it's too much trouble for them to come, even now that he's dead," she said to Barbara, and people got between them with a lot of words and smoothed it over.

Someone met Margaret at the airport, she came in while people were eating meatballs and potato salad in the living room. Margaret had always been B. J.'s favorite. He would get her to rub his neck for him, or walk up and down his back when he had a kink from bending over the tables all day. He'd been a pattern cutter until he'd retired, guiding the heavy cutting machinery around pieces of work shirts, overalls, uniforms, five dozen thick. B. J. had taken Margaret's side of it in her divorce, and whenever Margaret came up from Arizona to see them, at Mass he would give Margaret a little nudge, trying to get her to go up and take Communion, as if he wanted her to spite the Church. Margaret cried on Josephine's neck, her mouth in Josephine's hair, "Oh Pop, oh Pop," and Josephine patted her and said, "He loved you girls."

Josephine and her granddaughter and Marvell Johnston did

up the dirty dishes. It was nine o'clock by then and Josephine was tired, she wanted to go to bed, but she set her feet solidly before the sink when other women tried to take over the work from her. "She likes to keep busy," someone said. "Let her go ahead, it's better if she stays busy."

"It's got nothing to do with staying busy," Josephine said angrily, but what did it have to do with . . .?

People touched her arms, her back. "Oh now, Josie," someone said.

The house emptied out swiftly around ten o'clock. Margaret and Barbara sat on in the living room. They put on the TV and talked low enough so Josephine couldn't hear their words from the bathroom, where she put her teeth in a glass and unpinned her hair, brushing slow through it from the scalp. When the phone rang she stayed in the bathroom—she was washing her face, the creases of her neck, with a soapy washcloth. After a while Barbara came and said through the bathroom door, "Mother." Josephine didn't care about Barbara's husband but she wished the three children had come. She couldn't remember the last time they had slept overnight in this house. "They've found Donnie," Barbara said. "He and Linda and the boys will be here in the morning."

Donnie and his wife had two sons Josephine used to get along with. They were fourteen and sixteen now; they'd become sullen, she didn't know who they were anymore. On New Year's Day, B. J. had slapped the older one for his smart mouth, in front of Donnie and Linda, and there'd been a terrible explosion of yelling and tears. Josephine had yelled too, at B. J., at Donnie. It had blown over slowly. That grandson, when he came in the house, still wouldn't talk to B. J., hadn't spoken to him in almost ten months. Never would, now.

She rinsed her teeth off and put them in her mouth again and went out in the hall for the phone book. She sat down in the kitchen to call the Doves Mortuary, the night number. "We've got hold of my son now," she said into the phone. "I want to go ahead and set a day for the rosary and the funeral." The girls came into the kitchen while she was still on the phone. Barbara stood behind Josephine and kneaded her neck with her long strong fingers. Josephine couldn't hear the TV anymore; they might have turned it off when the phone rang. They were good girls, both of them, she didn't blame them for having husbands she couldn't love. "They want me to bring Pop's clothes over tomorrow, to bury him in," Josephine said when she hung up the phone.

B. J.'s bedroom smelled of cigarettes. Smelled like B. J. She opened a drawer of his dresser and got out a pair of socks, an undershirt, boxer shorts. They were stiff and clean. Josephine still used a Monkey Wards wringer washer and hung her laundry on a line in the backyard. Even in this stinking room she could smell the hot water and lavender soap. She got out his navy blue suit, the suit he wore to Mass, and to funerals and weddings. It was thirty years old, at least. She laid it on the bed and stood and looked at it. All his children had finished taller than him, Josephine stood over him an inch herself, but she never had thought he was small. He was wiry, strong, even in his seventies, he never had put on a soft belly, he could still dig up the garden himself with a heavy fork, and he still mowed his own lawn, even the front that was so damn steep. She never had thought he was small. But she saw suddenly that the shoulders of the suit were narrow, the trousers no bigger than Barbara's twelve-year-old son's. On her tongue, she found a dry flake of something, not ash, tooth powder, she brought it back into her throat and swallowed, and her eyes burned suddenly with tears. When she had washed his clothes—all these years, fifty-two years, wringing his pants through the washer and pinning his shirts, his underwear on the line—why hadn't she seen how small he was? Small as a boy. She never had noticed it until this moment.

Personal Silence

THERE WAS A LITTLE FINGER of land, a peninsula, that stuck up from the corner of Washington State pointing straight north at Vancouver Island. On the state map it was small enough it had no name. Jay found an old Clallam County map in a used bookstore in Olympia, and on the county map the name was printed the long way, marching northward up the finger's reach: Naniamuk. There was a village near the tip, and this was named too: Mizzle. He liked the way the finger pointed at Vancouver Island. Now he liked the name the town had. He bought a chart of the strait between Mizzle and Port Renfrew and a used book on small boat building, and when he left Olympia he went up the county roads to Naniamuk and followed the peninsula's one paved road all the way out to its dead end at Mizzle.

It was a three-week walk. His leg had been broken and badly healed a couple of years ago when he had been arrested in Colombia. He could walk long-strided, leaning into the straps of the pack, arms pumping loosely, hands unfisted, and he imagined anyone watching him would have had a hard time telling, but if he did more than eight or ten miles in a day he got gimpy and that led to blisters. So he had learned not to push it. He camped in a logged-over state park one night, bummed a couple of nights in barns and garages, slept other nights just off the road in whatever grass and stunted tress grew at the edge of the right-of-way.

The last day, halfway along the Naniamuk peninsula, he left the road and hiked west to the ocean, through the low pines and grassy dunes and coils of rusted razorwire, and set his tent on the sand at the edge of the grass. It was a featureless beach, wide and flat, stretching toward no visible headlands. There were few driftlogs, and at the tide line just broken clamshells, dead kelp, garbage, wreckage. No tidepools, no offshore stacks, no agates. The surf broke far out and got muddy as it rolled in. When the sun went down behind the overcast, the brown combers blackened and vanished without luminescence.

The daylight that rose up slowly the next morning was gray and damp, standing at the edge of rain. He wore his rubber-bottom shoes tramping in the wet grass along the edge of the road to Mizzle. The peninsula put him in mind of the mid-coast of Chile, the valleys between Talca and Puerto Montt—flat and low-lying, the rain-beaten grass pocked with little lakes and bogs. There was not the great poverty of the Chilean valleys, but if there had been prosperity up here once, it was gone. The big beachfront houses were boarded up, empty. The rich had moved in from the coasts. Houses still lived in were dwarfish, clinker-built, with small windows oddly placed. People were growing cranberries in the bogs and raising bunches of blond, stupid-faced cattle on the wet pasturage.

At the town limit of Mizzle a big, quaintly painted sign-board stood up beside the road. "Welcome to Mizzle! Most Westerly Town in the Contiguous United States of America!" Jay stood at the shoulder of the road and sketched the sign in his notebook for its odd phrasing, its fanciful enthusiasm.

The town was more than he had thought, and less. There had been three or four motels—one still ran a neon vacancy sign. An RV park had a couple of trailers standing in it. The downtown was a short row of gift shops and ice cream stores, mostly boarded shut. There was a town park—a square of unmown lawn with an unpainted gazebo set on it. Tourists had gotten here ahead of him and had gone again.

He walked out to where the road dead-ended at the tip of the peninsula. It was unmarked, unexceptional. The paving petered out and a graveled road kept on a little way through weeds and hillocks of dirt. Where the graveled road ended, people had been dumping garbage. He stood up on one of the hillocks and looked to the land's end across the dump. There was no beach, just a strip of tidal mud. The salt water of the strait lay flat and gray as sheet metal. The crossing was forty-three nautical miles; there was no seeing Vancouver Island.

He went back along the road through the downtown, looking up the short side streets for the truer town: the hardware store, the grocery, the lumberyard. There was an AG market. The computerized checkout that was broken, perhaps had been broken for months or years—a clunky mechanical cash register sat on top of the scanner, and a long list of out-of-stock goods was taped across the LED display.

Jay bought a carton of cottage cheese and stood outside eating it with the spoon that folded out of his Swiss Army knife.

He read from a free tourist leaflet that had been stacked up in a wire rack at the front of the store. The paper of the top copy was yellowed, puckered. On the first inside page was a peninsula map of grand scale naming all the shallow lakes, the graveled roads, the minor capes and inlets. There was a key of symbols: bird scratchings were the nesting grounds of the snowy plover, squiggly ovoids were privately held oyster beds, a stylized anchor marked a public boat launch and a private anchorage on the eastern, the bayside shoreline. Offshore there, on the interior strait, the mapmaker had drawn a non-specific fish, a crab, a gaffrigged-daysailer, and off the ocean-side, a long-necked razor clam and a kite. He could guess the boat launch was shut down: recreational boating and fishing had been banned in the strait and in Puget Sound for years. There was little likelihood any oysters had been grown in a while, nor kites flown, clams dug.

Bud's Country Store sold bathtubs and plastic pipe, clamming guns, Coleman lanterns, two-by-fours and plywood, marine supplies, teapots, towels, rubber boots. What they didn't have they would order, though it was understood delivery might be uncertain. He bought a weekly paper printed seventy miles away in Port Angeles, a day-old copy of the Seattle semi-daily, and a canister of butane, and walked up the road again to the trailer park. "Four Pines RV Village" was painted on a driftwood log mounted high on posts to make a gateway. If there had been pines, they'd been cut down. Behind the arch was a weedy lawn striped with whitish oyster-shell driveways. Stubby posts held out electrical outlets, water couplings, wastewater hoses. Some of them were dismantled. There was a gunite building with two steamed-up windows: a shower house, maybe, or a laundry, or both. The trailer next to the building was a single-wide with a tip-out and a roofed wooden porch. "Office" was painted on the front of it in a black childish print across the fiberglass. There was one other trailer parked along the fence, somebody's permanent home, an old round-back with its tires hidden behind rusted aluminum skirting.

Jay dug out a form letter and held it against his notebook while he wrote across the bottom. *I'd just like to pitch a tent, stay out of your way, and pay when I use the shower. Thanks.* He looked at what he had written, added exclamation points, went up to the porch, and knocked, waiting awkwardly with the letter in his hand. The girl who opened the door was thin and pale; she had a small face, small features. She looked at him without looking in his eyes. Maybe she was eleven or twelve years old.

He smiled. This was always a moment he hated, doubly so if it was a child—he would need to do it twice. He held out the letter, held out his smile with it. Her eyes jumped to his face and then back to the letter with a look that was difficult to pin down—confusion or astonishment and then something like preoccupation, as if she had lost sight of him standing there. It was common to get a quick shake of the head, a closed door. He didn't know what the girl's look meant. He kept smiling gently. Several women at different times had told him he had a sweet smile. That was the word they all had used—"sweet." He usually tried to imagine they meant peaceable, without threat.

After a difficult silence, the girl seemed to come awake and remember him standing there. She finally put out her hand for the letter. He hated waiting while she read it. He looked across the trailer park to a scraggly line of Scotch broom on the other side of the fence. In a minute she held out the paper to him, again without looking in his face. "You have to ask my dad." Her voice was small, low.

He didn't take the letter back yet. He raised his eyebrows in a questioning way. Often it was easier from this point. She would be watching him for those kinds of nonverbal language. He was "keeping a personal silence," he had written in the form letter.

"Over in the shower house," she said. She had fine brown hair that hung straight down to her shoulders, and straight bangs she hid behind. Jay glanced toward the gunite building with deliberate, self-conscious hesitation, then made a helpless gesture. The girl may have looked at him from behind her scrim of bangs. "I can ask him," she said, murmuring.

Her little rump was flat, in corduroy pants too big for her. She had kept his letter, and she swung it fluttering in her hand as he followed her to the shower house. A man knelt on the concrete floor, hunched up at the foot of the hot-water tank. His pants rode low, baring some of the shallow crack of his buttocks. He looked tall, heavy-boned, though there wasn't much weight on him now, if there ever had been.

"Dad," the girl said.

He had pulled apart the thick fiberglass blanket around the heater to get at the thermostat. His head was shoved inside big loose wings of the blanketing. "What," he said, without bringing his head out.

"He wants to put up a tent," she said. "Here, read this." She shook Jay's letter.

He rocked back on his hips and his heels and rubbed his scalp with a big hand. There were bits of fiberglass, like mica chips, in his hair. "Shit," he said loudly, addressing the hot-water heater. Then he stood slowly, hitching up his pants above the crack. He was very tall, six and a half feet or better, bony-faced. He looked at the girl. "What," he said.

She pushed the letter at him silently. Jay smiled, made a slight, apologetic grimace when the man's eyes finally came around to him. It was always a hard thing trying to tell by people's faces whether they'd help him out or not. This one looked him over briefly, silently, then took the letter and looked at it without much attention. He kept picking fiberglass out of his hair and his skin, and afterward looking under his fingernails for traces of it. "I read about this in *Time*," he said at one point, but it was just recognition, not approval, and he didn't look at Jay when he said it. He kept reading the letter and scrubbing at the bits of fiberglass. It wasn't clear if he had spoken to Jay or to the girl.

Finally he looked at Jay. "You're walking around the world, huh." It evidently wasn't a question, so Jay stood there and waited. "I don't see what good will come of it—except after you're killed you might get on the night news." He had a look at his mouth, smugness, or bitterness. Jay smiled again, shrugging.

The man looked at him. Finally he said, "You know anything about water heaters? If you can fix it, I'd let you have a couple of dollars for the shower meter. Yes? No?"

Jay looked at the heater. It was propane-fired. He shook his head, tried to look apologetic. It wasn't quite a lie. He didn't want to spend the rest of the day fiddling with it for one hot shower.

"Shit," the man said mildly. He hitched at his pants with the knuckles of both hands. Jay's letter was still in one fist and he looked down at it inattentively when the paper made a faint crackly noise against his hip. "Here," he said, holding the sheet out. Jay had fifty or sixty clean copies of it in a plastic ziplock in his backpack. He went through a lot of them when he was on the move. He took the rumpled piece of paper, folded it, pushed it down in a front pocket.

"I had some bums come in after dark and use my water," the man said. He waited as if that was something Jay might want to respond to. Jay waited too.

"Well, keep off to the edge by the fence," the man warned him. "You can put up a tent for free, I guess, it's not like we're crowded, but leave the trailer spaces clear anyway. I got locks on the utilities now, so you pay me if you want water, or need to take a crap, and don't take one in the bushes or I'll have to kick you out of here."

Jay nodded. He stuck out his hand, and after a very brief moment, the man shook it. The man's hand was prickly, damp.

"You show him, Mare," he said to the girl. He tapped her shoulder with his fingertips lightly, but his eyes were on Jay.

Jay followed the young girl, Mare, across the trailer park, across the wet grass and broken-shell driveways to a low fence of two-by-fours and wire that marked the property line. The grass was mowed beside the fence but left to sprout in clumps along the wire and around the wooden uprights. There was not much space between the fence and the last row of driveways. If anybody ever parked a motor home in the driveway behind him, he'd have the exhaust pipe in his vestibule. The girl put her hands in her corduroy pockets and stubbed the grass with the toe of her shoe. "Here?" she asked him. He nodded and swung his pack down onto the grass.

Mare watched him make his camp. She didn't try to help him. She was comfortably silent. When he had everything ordered, he looked at her and smiled briefly and sat down on his little sitz pad on the grass. He took out his notebook, but he didn't work on the journal. He pulled around a clean page and began a list of materials he would need for beginning the boat. He wrote down substitutes when he could think of them, in case he had trouble getting his first choice. He planned to cross the strait to Vancouver Island and then sail east and north through the Gulf Islands and up through the inland passage to Alaska. He hadn't figured out yet how he would get across the Bering Strait to Siberia—whether he would try to sail across in this boat he would build, or if he'd barter it up there, to get some other craft, or a ride. It might take him all winter to build a skipjack, all summer to sail it and go up the west coast of Canada and Alaska, and then he would need to wait for summer again before crossing the Bering Strait. He'd have time to find out what he wanted to do before he got to it.

The girl after a while approached him silently and squatted down on her heels so she could see what he was writing. She didn't ask him about the list. She read it over and then looked off toward her family's trailer. She kept crouching there beside him, balancing lightly.

"Do you think it's helping yet?" she asked in a minute. She whispered it, looking at him sideward though her long bangs.

He raised his eyebrows questioningly.

"They're still fighting," she murmured. "Aren't they?"

His mother had written to the Oklahoma draft board pleading Jay's only-child-of-a-widow status, but by then the so-called Third World's War was taking a few thousand American lives a day and they weren't exempting anyone. Within a few weeks of his eighteenth birthday, they sent him to the Israeli front.

The tour of duty was four years at first, then extended to eight. He thought they would extend it again, but after eight years they sent him home on a C31 full of cremation canisters. He sat on the toilet in the tail of the plane and swallowed all the pills he had, three at a time, until they were gone. The illegal-drug infrastructure had come overseas with the war, and eventually he had learned he could sleep and not dream if he took Nembutal, which was easy to get. Gradually after that he had begun to take Dexamyl to wake up from the Nembutal, Librium to smooth out the jitters from the Dexamyl, Percodan to get high, Demerol when he needed to come down quickly from the high, Dexamyl again if the Demerol took him down too far. He thought he would be dead by the time the plane landed, but his body remained inexplicably, persistently resistant to death. He wound up in a Delayed Stress Syndrome Inpatient Rehab Center that was housed in a former prison. He was thirty years old when the funding for the DSS Centers was struck from the war budget. Jay was freed to walk and hitchhike from the prison in Idaho to his mother's house in Tulsa. She had been dead for years, but he stood in the street in front of the house and waited for something to happen, a memory or a sentiment, to connect him to his childhood and adolescence. Nothing came. He had been someone else for a long time.

He was still standing on the curb there after dark when a man came out of the house behind him. The man had a flashlight, but he didn't click it on. He came over to where Jay stood.

"You should come inside," he said to Jay. "They'll be coming around pretty soon, checking." He spoke quietly. He might have meant a curfew. Tulsa had been fired on a few times by planes flying up to or back from the Kansas missile silos, out of bases in Haiti—crazy terrorists of the crazy Jorge Ruiz government. Probably there was a permanent brownout and a curfew here.

Jay said, "Okay," but he didn't move. He didn't know where he would go anyway. He was cold and needing sleep. There was an appeal in the possibility of arrest.

The man looked at him in the darkness. "You can come inside my house," he said, after he had looked at Jay.

There was a daybed in a small room at the front of his house, and Jay lay on it without taking off his clothes. The next morning he sat on the bed and looked out the window to his mother's house across the street.

The man who had taken him in was a Quaker named Bob Settleman. He had a son who was on an aircraft carrier in the Indian Ocean, and a daughter who was in a federal prison serving a ten-year sentence for failure to report. Jay went with him to a First Day Meeting. There was nothing much to it. People sat silently. After a while an old woman stood and said something about the droughts and warm weather perhaps reflecting God's unhappiness with the state of the world. But that was the only time anyone mentioned God. Three other people rose to speak. One said he was tired of being the only person who remembered to shut the blackout screens in the Meeting room before they locked up. Then, after a long silence, a woman stood and expressed her fear that an entire generation had been desensitized to violence, by decades of daily video coverage of the war. She spoke gently, in a trembling voice, just a few plain sentences. It didn't seem to matter a great deal, the words she spoke. While she was speaking, Jay felt something come into the room. The woman's voice, some quality in it, seemed to charge the air with its manifest, exquisitely painful truth. After she had finished, there was another long silence. Then Bob Settleman stood slowly and told about watching Jay standing on the curb after dark. He seemed to be relating it intangibly to what had been said about the war. "I could see he was in some need," Bob said, gesturing urgently. Jay looked at his hands. He thought he should be embarrassed, but nothing like that arose in him. He could still feel the palpable trembling of the woman's voice—in the air, in his bones.

Afterward, walking away from the Meeting house, Bob looked at his feet and said, as if it was an apology, "It's been a long time since I've been at a Meeting that was Gathered into the Light like that. I guess I got swept up in it."

Jay didn't look at him. After a while, he said, "It's okay." He didn't ask anything. He felt he knew, without asking, what Gathered into the Light meant.

He stayed in Tulsa, warehousing for a laundry products distributor. He kept going to the First Day Meetings with Bob. He found it was true, Meetings were rarely Gathered. But he liked the long silences anyway, and the unpredictability of the messages people felt compelled to share. For a long time, he didn't speak himself. He listened without hearing any voice whispering inside him. But finally he did hear one. When he stood, he felt the long silence Gathering, until the trembling words he spoke came out on the air as Truth.

"I wonder, if somebody could walk far enough, or long enough, if they'd have to come to the end of the war, eventually."

He had, by now, an established web of support: a New York Catholic priest who banked his receipts from the journal subscriptions, kept his accounts, filed his taxes, wired him expense money when he asked for it; a Canadian rare-seeds collective willing to receive his mail, sort it, bundle it up, and send it to him whenever he supplied them with an address; a Massachusetts Monthly Meeting of Friends whose members had the work of typing from the handwritten pages he sent them, printing, collating, stapling, mailing the ten thousand copies of his sometimes-monthly writings. He had, as of last count, a paid subscription list of 1,651, a nonpaid "mailing list" of 8,274. Some of those were churches, environmental groups, cooperatives; many were couples, so the real count of persons who supported him was greater by a factor of three or four, maybe. Many of them were people he had met, walking. He hadn't walked, yet, in the Eastern Hemisphere. If he lived long enough to finish what he had started, he thought he could hope for a total list as high as fifty or sixty thousand names. A Chilean who had been a delegate at the failed peace conferences in Suriname had kept a yearlong public silence as a protest of Jay's arrest and bad treatment in Colombia. And he knew of one other world-peace-walker he had inspired, a Cuban Nobel chemist who had been the one primarily featured in *Time*. He wasn't fooled into believing it was an important circle of influence. He had to view it in the context of the world. Casualties were notoriously underreported, but at least as many people were killed in a given day, directly or indirectly, by the war, as made up his optimistic future list of subscribers. It may have been he kept at it because he had been doing it too long now to stop. It was what he did, who he was. It had been a long time since he had felt the certainty and clarity of a Meeting that was Gathered into the Light.

. . .

On the Naniamuk peninsula, he scouted out a few broken-down sheds, and garages with overgrown driveways, and passed entreating notes to the owners he could locate. He needed a roof over the boat project. He expected rain in this part of the world about every day. One woman had a son dead in India and another son who had been listed AWOL or MIA in the interior of Brazil for two years. She asked Jay if he had walked across Brazil yet. *Yes,* he wrote quickly, *eight months there.* She didn't ask him anything else—nothing about the land or the weather or the fighting. She showed him old photos of both her sons without asking if he had seen the lost one among the refugees in the cities and villages he had walked through. She lent him the use of her dilapidated garage, and the few cheap tools he found in disarray inside it.

He left the garage door raised to let some light in on his work. The girl Mare came unexpectedly after a couple of days and watched him lofting the deck and hull-bottom panels onto plywood. It had been raining a little. She stood under her umbrella a while, without coming in close enough to shelter under the garage roof. But gradually, studying what he was doing, a look rose in her face—distractedness as before on the porch of her trailer, and then fear, or something like grief. He didn't know what to make of these looks of hers.

"You're building a boat," she said, low voiced.

He stopped working a minute and looked at the two pieces of plywood he had laid end to end. He was marking and lining them with a straightedge and a piece of curving batten. He had gone across the Florida Strait in a homemade plywood skipjack, had sailed it around the coast of Cuba to Haiti, Puerto Rico, Jamaica, and then across the channel to Yucatán. And later he had built a punt to cross the mouths of the Amazon. A Cuban refugee, a fisherman, had helped him build the Caribbean boat, and the punt had been a simple thing, hardly more than a raft. This was the first time he had tried to build a skipjack without help, but he had learned he could do about anything if he had time enough to make mistakes, undo them, set them right. He nodded, yes, he was building a boat.

"There are mines in the strait," Mare said, dropping her low voice lower.

He smiled slightly, giving her a face that belittled the problem. He had seen mines in the Yucatán Channel too, and in the strait off Florida. His boat had slid by them, ridden over them. They were triggered for the heavy warships and the armored oil tankers.

He went on working. Mare watched him seriously, without saying anything else. He thought she would leave when she saw how slowly the boat making went, but she stayed on, and when he began lofting the deck piece she came into the garage and put down her umbrella and helped him brace the batten against the nails when he lofted the deck piece. At dusk she walked with him up the streets to the Four Pines. There was a fine rain falling still, and she held her umbrella high up so he could get under it if he hunched a little.

In the morning she was waiting for him, sitting on the porch of her trailer when he tramped across the wet grass toward the street. Since Colombia, he had had difficulty with waking early. He had to depend on his bladder, usually, to force him out of the sleeping bag, then he was slow to feel really awake, his mouth and eyes thick, heavy, until he had washed his face, eaten something, walked a while. He saw it was something like that with the girl. She sat hunkered up on the top step, resting her chin on her knees, clasping her arms about her thin legs. Under her eyes, the tender skin was puffy, dark. Her hair stuck out uncombed. She didn't speak to him. She came stiffly down from the porch and fell in beside him, with her eyes fixed on the rubber toe caps of her shoes. She had a brown lunch sack clutched in one hand and the other hand sunk in the pocket of her corduroys.

They walked down the paved road and then the graveled streets to where the boat garage was. Their walking made a quiet scratching sound. There was no one else out. Jay thought he could hear the surf beating on the ocean side of the peninsula, but maybe not. He heard a dim continuous susurration. They were half a mile from the beach. Maybe what he heard was wind moving in the trees and the grass, or the whisperings of the snowy plover, nestings in the brush above the tidal flats on the strait side of the peninsula.

He had not padlocked the garage—a pry-bar would have got anybody in through the small side door in a couple of minutes. He pulled up the rollaway front door to let light in on the tools, the sheets of plywood. Mare put her lunch down on a box and stood looking at the lofted pieces, the hull bottom and deck panels drawn on the plywood. He would make those cuts today. He manhandled one of the sheets up off the floor onto the sawhorses. Mare took hold of one end silently. It occurred to him that he could have gotten the panels cut without her, but it would be easier with her there to hold the big sheets of wood steady under the saw.

He cut the deck panel slowly with hand tools—a brace and bit to make an entry for the keyhole saw, a ripsaw for the long outer cuts. When he was most of the way along the straight finish of the starboard side, on an impulse he gave the saw over to Mare and came around to the other side to hold the sheet down for her. She looked at him once shyly from behind her long bangs and then stood at his place before the wood, holding the saw in both hands. She hadn't drawn a saw in her life, he could tell that, but she'd been watching him. She pushed the saw into the cut he had started and drew it up slow and wobbly. She was holding her mouth out in a tight flat line, all concentration. He had to smile, watching her.

They ate lunch sitting on the sawhorses at the front of the garage. Jay had carried a carton of yogurt in the pocket of his coat, and he ate that slowly with his spoon. Mare offered him part of her peanut butter sandwich, and quartered pieces of a yellow apple. He shook his head, shrugging, smiling thinly. She considered his face, and then looked away.

"I get these little dreams," she said in a minute, low voiced, with apple in her mouth.

He had a facial expression he relied on a good deal, a questioning look. *What? Say again? Explain.* She glanced swiftly sideward at his look and then down at her fingers gathered in her lap. "They're not dreams, I guess. I'm not asleep. I just get them all of a sudden. I see something that's happened, or something that hasn't happened yet. Things remind me." She looked at him again cautiously through her bangs. "When I saw you on the porch, when you gave me the letter, I remembered somebody else who gave me a letter before. I think it was a long time ago."

He shook his head, took the notepad from his shirt pocket, and wrote a couple of lines about déjà vu. He would have written more, but she was reading while he wrote and he felt her stiffening, looking away.

"I know what that is," she said, lowering her face. "It isn't that. Everybody gets that."

He waited silently. There wouldn't have been anything to say anyway. She picked at the corduroy on the front of her pants leg. After a while she said, whispering, "I remember things that happened to other people, but they were me. I think I might be dreaming other people's lives, or the dreams are what I did before, when I was alive a different time, or when I'll be somebody else, later on." Her fingernails kept picking at the cord. "I guess you don't get dreams like that." Her eyes came up to him. "Nobody else does, I guess." She looked away. "I do, though. I get them a lot. I just don't tell anymore." Her mouth was small, drawn up. She looked toward him again. "I can tell you, though."

Before she had finished telling him, he had thought of an epilepsy, *le Petit absentia*, maybe it was called. He had seen it once in a witch-child in Haiti, a girl who fell into a brief, staring trance a hundred times a day. A neurologist had written to him, naming it from the description he had read in Jay's journal. Maybe there was a simple way to tell, a test, a couple of things to look for. Of course, maybe it wasn't that. It might only be a fancy, something she'd invented, an attention-getter. But her look made him sympathetic. He reached out and pushed her bangs back from her smooth, solemn brow. *It's okay,* he hoped to tell her with this small gesture, his hand lightly brushing her bangs. *I won't tell.*

There hadn't been a long Labor Day weekend for years. It was one of the minor observances scratched from the calendar by the exigencies of war. But people who were tied in with the school calendar still observed the first weekend of September as a sort of holiday, a last hurrah before the opening Monday of the school year. Some of them still came to the beach.

The weather by good luck was fair, the abiding peninsula winds balmy, sunlit, so there were a couple of small trailers and a few tents in the RV park, and a no-vacancy sign at the motel Saturday morning by the time the fog burned off.

Jay spent both days on the lawn in front of the town's gazebo, behind a stack of back issues of his journal and a big poster-board display he had pasted up, with an outsize rewording of his form letter, and clippings from newspapers and from *Time*. He put out a hat on the grass in front of him with a couple of seed dollars in it. His personal style of busking was diffident, self-conscious. He kept his attention mostly on the notebook in his lap. He sketched from memory the archway at the front of the RV park, the humpbacked old trailer, the girl Mare's thin face. He made notes to do with the boat, and fiddled with an op-ed piece he would send to *Time*, trying to follow up on the little publicity they'd given the Cuban chemist. The op-ed would go in his October journal, whether *Time* took it or not, and the sketches would show up there too, in the margins of his daybook entries, or on the cover. He printed other people's writings too, things that came in his mail—poetry, letters, meeting notices, back-page news items pertaining to peace issues, casualty and armament statistics sent at rare intervals by an anonymous letter writer with a Washington, DC, postmark—but most of the pages were his own work. On bureaucratic forms he entered *writer* as his occupation without feeling he was misrepresenting anything. He liked to write. His writing had gotten gradually better since he had been doing the journal—sometimes he thought it was not from the practice at writing, but the practice at silence.

Rarely, somebody stopped to read the poster, or stooped to pick up a journal, or put money in his hat, or all three. Those people he tried to make eye contact with, smiling gently by way of inviting them in. He wouldn't get any serious readers, serious talkers, probably, on a holiday weekend in a beach town, but you never knew. He was careful not to look at the others, the bypassers, but he kept track of them peripherally. He had been arrested quite a few times, assaulted a few. And since Colombia, he suffered from a chronic fear.

Mare came and sat with him on Sunday. He didn't mind having her there. She was comfortable with his silence; she seemed naturally silent herself, much of the time. She read from back issues of his journal and shared the best parts with him as if he hadn't been the writer himself. Not reading the lines aloud but holding a page out for him silently and waiting, watching, while he read the part she pointed to, and then offering her terse opinion: "Ick," or "I'm glad," or "I'd never do that."

He had written about a town in the Guatemala highlands where he had herded goats for a couple of months, and when she pushed that page toward him she said in a changed way, timid, earnest, "I lived there too. But it was before. Before I was me. I was a different person."

He had not gotten around to writing anyone about the epilepsy after he'd lost that first strong feeling of its possibility. His silence invited squirrels, he knew that, though it made him tired, unhappy, thinking of it. He was tired now, suddenly, and annoyed with her. He shook his head, let her see a flat, skeptical smile.

"Mare!"

Her father came across the shaggy grass, moving swiftly, his arms swinging in a stiff way, elbows akimbo. Jay stood up warily.

"I'm locked out of the damn house," the man said, not looking at Jay. "Where's your key?"

Mare got up from the grass, dug around in her pockets, and brought out a key with a fluorescent pink plastic keeper. He closed his fingers on it, made a vague gesture with the fist. "I about made up my mind to bust a window," he said. "I was looking for you." He was annoyed.

Mare put her hands in her pockets, looked at her feet. "I'm helping him stop the war," she said, murmuring.

The man's eyes went to Jay and then the posterboard sign, the hat, the stacked-up journals. His face kept hold of that look of annoyance but took on something else, too, maybe it was just surprise. "He's putting up signs and hustling for money, is what it looks like he's doing," he said, big and arrogant. For a while longer he stood there looking at the sign as if he were reading it. Maybe he was. He had a manner of standing—shifting his weight from foot to foot and hitching at his pants every so often with the knuckles of his hands.

"I got a kidney shot out, in North Africa," he said suddenly. "But there's not much fighting there anymore, that front's moved south or somewhere, I don't know who's got that ground now. They can keep it, whoever." He had a long hooked nose, bony ridges below his eyes, a wide lipless mouth. Strong features. Jay could see nothing of him in Mare's small pale face. It wasn't evident, how they were with each other. Jay saw her now watching her dad through her bangs, with something like the shyness she had with everyone else.

"Don't be down here all day," her dad said to her, gesturing again with the fist he had closed around the house key. He looked at Jay, but he didn't say anything else. He shifted his weight one more time and then walked off long-strided, swinging his long arms. He was tall enough that some of the tourists looked at him covertly after he'd passed them. Mare watched him too. Then she looked at Jay, a ducking, sideward look. He thought she was embarrassed by her dad. He shrugged. *It's okay.* But that wasn't it. She said, pulling in her thin shoulders timidly, "There is a lake there named Negro because the water is so dark." She had remained focused on his disbelief, waiting to say this small proving thing about Guatemala. And it was true enough to shake him a little. There was a Lago Negro in just about every country below the US border; he remembered that in a minute. But there was a long startled moment before that, when he only saw the little black lake in the highlands, in Guatemala, and Mare, dark-faced, in a dugout boat paddling away from the weedy shore.

He had the store rip four long stringers out of a fir board and then he kerfed the stringers every three inches along their lengths. With the school year started, he didn't have Mare to hold the long pieces across the sawhorses. He got the cuts done slowly, single-handed, bracing the bouncy long wood with his knee.

Mare's dad came up the road early in the day. Jay thought he wasn't looking for the garage. There was a flooded cranberry field on the other side of the road, and his attention was on the people getting in the crop from it. There were two men and three women wading slowly up and down in green rubber hip waders, stripping off the berries by hand into big plastic buckets. Mare's dad, walking along the road, watched them. But when he came even with the garage, he turned suddenly and walked up the driveway. Jay stopped what he was doing and waited, holding the saw. Mare's dad stood just inside the rollaway door, shifting his weight, knuckling his hips.

"I heard you were building a boat," he said, looking at the wood, not at Jay. "You never said how long you wanted to camp, but I didn't figure it would be long enough to build a boat." Jay thought he knew where this was headed. He'd been hustled along plenty of times before this. But it didn't go that way. The man looked at him. "In that letter you showed, I figured you meant you could talk if you wanted to. Now I hear your tongue was cut off." He lifted his chin, reproachful.

Jay kept standing there holding the saw, waiting. He hadn't been asked anything. The man dropped his eyes. He turned part-way from Jay and looked over his shoulder toward the cranberry bog, the people working there. There was a long stiff silence.

"She's a weird kid," he said suddenly. "You figured that out by now, I guess." His voice was loud; he may not have had soft speaking in him anywhere. "I'd have her to a shrink, but I can't afford it." He hitched at his pants with the backs of both hands. "I guess she likes you because you don't say anything. She can tell you whatever she wants and you're not gonna tell her she's nuts." He looked at Jay. "You think she's nuts?" His face had a sorrowful aspect now, his brows drawn up in a heavy pleat above the bridge of his nose.

Jay looked at the saw. He tested the row of teeth against the tips of his fingers and kept from looking at the man. He realized he didn't know his name, first or last, or if he had a wife. Where was Mare's mother?

The man blew out a puffing breath through his lips. "I guess she is," he said unhappily. Jay ducked his head, shrugged. *I don't know.* He had been writing about Mare lately—pages that would probably show up in the journal, in the October mailing. He had spent a lot of time wondering about her, and then writing it down. This was something new to wonder about. He had thought her dad was someone else, not this big sorrowful man looking for reassurance from a stranger who camped in his park.

A figure of jets passed over them suddenly, flying inland from the ocean. There were six. They flew low, dragging a screaming roar, a shudder, through the air. Mare's dad didn't look up.

"She used to tell people these damn dreams of hers all the time," the man said, after the noise was past. "I know I never broke her of it, she just got sly who she tells them to. She never tells me anymore." He stood there silently, looking at the cranberry pickers. "The last one she told me," he said, in his heavy, unquiet voice, "was how she'd be killed dead when she was twelve years old." He looked over at Jay. "She didn't tell you that yet," he said, when he saw Jay's face. He smiled in a bitter way. "She was about eight, I guess, when she told me that one." He thought about it and then he added, "She's twelve now. She was twelve in June." He made a vague gesture with both hands, a sort of open-palms shrugging. Then he pushed his hands down in his back pockets. He kept them there while he shifted his weight in that manner he had, almost a rocking back and forth.

Watching him, Jay wondered suddenly if Mare might not put herself in the path of something deadly, to make sure this dream was a true one—a proof for her dad. He wondered if her dad had thought of that.

"I don't know where she gets her ideas," the man said, making a pained face, "if it's from TV or books or what, but she told me when she got killed it'd be written up, and in the long run it'd help get the war ended. Before that, she never had noticed we were even in a war." He looked at Jay wildly. "Maybe I'm nuts too, but here you are, peace-peddling in our backyard, and when I saw you with those magazines you write, I started to wonder what was going on. I started to wonder if this is a damn different world than I've been believing all my life." His voice had begun to rise, so by the last few words he sounded plaintive, teary. Jay had given up believing in God the year he was eighteen. He didn't know what it was that Gathered a Meeting into the Light, but he didn't think it was God, or not the God they talked about in most churches. It occurred to him, he couldn't have told Mare's dad where the borders were of the world he, Jay, believed in.

"I don't have a reason for telling you this," the man said after a silence. He had brought his voice down again so he sounded just agitated, defensive. "Except I guess I wondered if I was nuts, and I figured I'd ask somebody who couldn't answer." His mouth spread out flat in a humorless grin. He took his hands out of his pockets, hitched up his pants. "I thought about kicking you on down the road, but I guess it wouldn't matter. If it isn't you, it'll be somebody else. And"—his eyes jumped away from Jay—"I was afraid she might quick do something to get herself killed, if she knew you were packing up." He waited, looking off across the road. Then he looked at Jay. "I've been worrying, lately, that she'll get killed all right, one way or the other, either it'll come true on its own, or she'll make it."

They stood together in silence in the dim garage, looking at the cutout pieces of Jay's boat. He had the deck and hull-bottom pieces, the bulkheads, the transom, the knee braces cut out. You could see the shape of the boat in some of them, in the curving lines of the cuts.

"I guess you couldn't taste anything without a tongue," the man said after a while. "I'd miss that, more than the talking." He knuckled his hips and walked off toward the road. All his height was in his legs. He walked fast with a loose, sloping gait on those long legs.

In the afternoon Jay took a clam shovel out of the garage and walked down to the beach. The sand was black and oily from an offshore spill or a sinking. There wasn't any debris on the low tide, just the oil. Maybe on the high tide there would be wreckage, or oil-fouled birds. He walked along the edge of the surf on the wet black sand, looking for clam sign. There wasn't much. He dug a few holes without finding anything. He hadn't expected to. Almost at dusk he saw somebody walking toward him from way down the beach. Gradually it became Mare. She didn't greet him. She turned alongside him silently and walked with him, studying the sand. She carried a denim knapsack that pulled her shoulders down: blocky shapes of books, a lunch box. She hadn't been home yet. If she had gone to the garage and not found him there, she didn't say.

He touched the blade of the shovel to the sand every little while, looking in the pressure circle for the stipple of clams. He didn't look at Mare. Something, maybe it was a clam sign, irised in the black sheen on the sand. He dug a fast hole straight down, slinging the wet mud sideways. Mare crouched out of the way, watching the hole. "I see it!" She dropped on the sand and pushed her arm into the muddy hole, brought it out again reflexively. Blood sprang bright red along the cut the razor-edged clamshell had made. She held her hands together in her lap while her face brought up a look, a slow unfolding of surprise and fear and distractedness. Jay reached for her, clasping both her hands between his palms, and in a moment she saw him again. "It cut me," she said, and started to cry. The tears maybe weren't about her hand.

He washed out the cut in a puddle of salt water. He didn't have anything to wrap around it. He picked up the clam shovel in one hand and held onto her cut hand with the other. They started back along the beach. He could feel her pulse in the tips of his fingers. *What did you dream?* he wanted to say.

It had begun to be dark. There was no line dividing the sky from the sea, just a griseous smear and below it the cream-colored lines of surf. Ahead of them Jay watched something rolling in the shallow water. It came up on the beach and then rode out again. The tide was rising. Every little while the surf brought the thing in again. It was pale, a driftlog, it rolled heavily in the shallow combers. Then it wasn't a log. Jay let down the shovel and Mare's hand and waded out to it. The water was cold, dark. He took the body by its wrist and dragged it up on the sand. It had been chewed on, or shattered. The legs were gone, and the eyes, the nose. He couldn't tell if it was a man or a woman. He dragged it way up on the beach, on the dry sand, above the high-tide line. Mare stood where she was and watched him.

He got the clam shovel and went back to the body and began to dig a hole beside it. The dry sand was silky; some of it slipped down and tried to fill the grave as he dug. In the darkness, maybe he was shoveling out the same hole over and over. The shovel handle was sticky from Mare's blood on his palms. When he looked behind him, he saw Mare sitting on the sand, huddled with her thin knees pulled up, waiting. She held her hurt hand with the other one, cradled.

When he had buried the legless body, he walked back to her, and she stood up and he took her hand again and they went on along the beach in the darkness. He was cold. His wet shoes and his jeans grated with sand. The cut on Mare's hand felt sticky, hot, where he clasped his palm against it. She said, in a whisper, "I dreamed this, once." He couldn't see her face. He looked out but he couldn't see the water, only hear it, a ceaseless numbing murmur on the dark air. He remembered the look that had come in her face when she had first seen his boat building. *There are mines in the strait.* He wondered if that was when she had dreamed this moment, a pale body rolling up on the sand.

"I know," he said, though what came out was shapeless, ill-made, a sound like Ah woe. Mare didn't look at him. But in a while she leaned in to him in the darkness and whispered against his cheek. "It's okay," she said, holding on to his hand. "I won't tell."

He had seen a lot of dead or dying children, had often written about them. Even on this remote coast, far from any battlefield, he could easily imagine the myriad ways a child might die. Harder to imagine what manner of death, any death, could bring an end to war. But he had sent off the pages for his October journal already and Mare was in them, and Lago Negro, and her father standing shifting his feet, not looking up as the jets screamed over him. She had dreamed her own death, and he had written that down, and when she was dead he would write that down too. He didn't know why, suddenly, his mouth was full of the remembered salt taste of tears, and blood, and the sea.

Downstream

WHERE THE RIVER RAN ACROSS the waist of the city it was edged in by piers and dikes and seawalls, and places where boulders had been trucked in to hold embankments along the back sides of warehouses and old millworks. It wouldn't have been entirely true, though, to say there was no riverbank. There were still a few vacant lots, places where a building had been torn down or it had never been appropriate to build one—under the piers of bridges, for instance—where the ground was allowed to slant out gradually to the muddy water, and weeds grew doggedly in the crazed soil among broken bricks, rusted iron, cast-off tires.

It was at one of those places, where there was still that kind of meager riverbank inclining down from Macadam Avenue between the tiers of warehouses, that Anne saw the man and the horse standing out in the water. The late sun was behind them so there was no detail, just their burnished red silhouettes. The man was washing down the horse, lifting water in his cupped hands and sluicing it over the animal's back and shoulders and flanks.

"Look," Anne said.

Mel was driving. The rush-hour traffic on the old Ross Island Bridge was clotted and slow; the sun shone flat in his eyes below the edge of the sun visor. He drove with both hands gripping the steering wheel. "What?" he said, without turning his head.

"There's a man down there with a horse. In the river."

"You're kidding," Mel said. He was still watching the narrow road. He might not have been able to see over the concrete parapet anyway from his side of the car.

Anne held both hands above her bangs and peered against the sun. The man leaned into the shoulder of the horse and bent to run a palm down along the animal's foreleg. As the car slid finally into the shadow of the Tualatin Hills, the figures, no longer backlit, deepened suddenly so she could see that the horse was not red but chestnut brown. She could see too that the man's shirt was faded almost colorless, the long sleeves folded carelessly above the elbows. His canvas jeans were worn almost white at the thighs. Bent over washing mud from the leg of the horse, he tipped his head back and seemed for a moment to look right at Anne. Then he straightened, still looking up toward the car, toward Anne, and lifted one hand in greeting. She had lifted her own hand to return the gesture when she realized he was reaching to comb his wet fingers through his hair. She swiveled her head to watch him—stooping again, continuing to wash his horse in the gray water there at the riverbank—until the corner of a building closed them off.

"Where?" Mel said, turning his own head belatedly.

"Back there. You can't see them now."

He blew out a little sound of incredulousness. "What would a guy be doing with a horse down there?"

"They were washing. In the river."

He made another small sound—annoyance. "You know what I mean. There's nothing but warehouses and crap down there." He glanced at Anne, waiting for another answer. They had been together almost ten years, and a lot of things had gradually built up between them. Anne turned her head and looked out the side window; she felt she had answered his question.

While they dined with friends—or not exactly friends, they were some sort of acquaintances of Mel's—she thought of mentioning the man she had seen along the riverbank but then decided not to, for reasons she couldn't quite make out, something vaguely to do with Mel and with horses, how she had used to love horses and how, since she'd been with Mel, she had forgotten how much she had once loved them. It was Mel who said, "We saw the damn stupidest thing driving over here. Some guy was trying to swim a horse across the river, down there under the Ross Island Bridge."

"You're kidding," the other man said. His name was David. Mel had done some work for his company or David had done work for Mel's company, something like that.

"He wasn't swimming," Anne said. Her cheeks burned as if Mel had said something private about their sex life—as if what she had seen along the bank of the river was profoundly personal.

He may not have heard her. Without looking up from the cigarette he was lighting, he said, "Christ, I wouldn't take a swim in that river if you paid me. You ever see those old guys down there fishing? All those Koreans or whatever, and the old bums hauling in bottom fish. Begging for cancer. And a guy rides a horse out into that shit."

"He wasn't riding," Anne said, and then, "You're the one begging for cancer."

Mel put his weight back in the chair and looked at her. He had started smoking again on his last trip to Thailand, which they hadn't talked about at all. "So you tell it," he said. "You got a better look than I did."

"You didn't see him," Anne said savagely.

After a long moment of silence, David's wife Kay laughed and said, "It's all industrial along there. What a place to keep a horse."

Mel, who had been looking at Anne, turned his head deliberately toward Kay. "Well, nobody'd be keeping a horse around there, Kay, not in that neighborhood. The guy must have trailered it in." He spoke to her softly, as if they were alone in the room.

"There wasn't any trailer," Anne said. She remembered that she had seen the prints of horses' hooves among clumps of weed and wracks of shattered wood on the slick clay slope going down to the water.

"Maybe from Mountain Park," Kay said, glancing once at Anne and then back to Mel. She had a long, narrow chin and she seemed to point it at each of them. "There's a stable up there, isn't there? An arena and riding trails and all of that. Maybe he rode down from there. How far would that be? Three or four miles?"

"More than that," Mel said, shaking his head.

Kay's husband made a big gesture with both hands, trying to get between the two of them, get back in the game. "He'd have to come down along Taylors Ferry Road or all the way out from West Linn along Macadam. I don't see how anybody could ride a horse through there and not get run over. He must have trucked it in."

Anne looked out the window to the dark street while the others went on debating. Later, while they sat at the dining room table talking about the stock market and eating osso buco from square white plates, Anne began to remember that the man under the bridge had had a beard: a bony face sunburnt above a crescent of reddish beard. It was a plain face, completely guileless in that way you seldom saw on men anymore, and the top half of his forehead stark white where his hat had cast a shadow. He must have set the hat down somewhere, set it on a stone or a log while he sleeved the sweat from his face before walking the horse downhill to the river.

When Mel drove them back over the bridge that night, the sky was ruddy above the glare of the neons, and much of the city itself was clear yellow below the shine of the streetlights, but there was a pocket of darkness along the riverbank where the man had stood with his horse. Before she had met Mel, Anne had been with a man who taught history at the community college. A few times driving down with him from the Tualatin Hills, looking out at the city straddling the river, he had unsuccessfully tried to get her to imagine the landscape and the riverbank as it must have been when the Lewis and Clark party camped there, or when the trapper William Johnson hewed the logs for his little cabin, the one that was believed to have stood just about under the piers of the Ross Island Bridge on what would later, very much later, be Macadam Avenue. Tonight, without any effort at all, she could imagine trees in ranks down close to the water, and clean stones along the river edge, and little worn paths in the grass where animals came down to drink or to bathe in the shallows under the eaves of firs.

Mel had had three or four martinis and he drove with exaggerated caution, all his attention apparently focused on the bridge lanes and the late, light traffic, but he said without looking toward her, "Gone?"

She'd been thinking about William Johnson and how, when he had built his cabin there in the 1840s, there were no other white men or women known to be living for several miles in either direction along the banks of the river, and how later an Indian woman had come by and the two of them had married and lived there together until a town began to grow up around them and then they'd moved somewhere else, somewhere less crowded. At least that was the nostalgic legend she remembered Tom Kline—was that his name?—telling her.

"What?"

"The guy with the horse. Look and see if he's gone." Once, Anne would have seen this as a sign of how well Mel knew her, knew the things that interested her. Now it was a dig, or a way to reopen their half-voiced argument.

She turned in the seat, twisting all the way around to look back through the rear window. In the darkness above the silvered edge of the river she was not surprised to see a small stuttering light. It was the campfire he had kindled after he and the horse had finished their work, after the two of them had gone tiredly together up through the ferns and salal brush, under the cool shadow of the trees.

"It's dark. They're gone."

In the slow, precise voice Mel used when he was showing

her how little he was affected by a couple of drinks, he said, "I think there's a horse show at the Expo Center. The guy must be a stupid shit, though, to let a show horse get out in that stinking water."

She didn't bother to argue. It wasn't a show horse, she might have said but didn't. By now she had remembered the way the horse looked, patiently standing, trailing harness—its thick neck and homely sloping flanks. The horse and the man had been pulling out stumps to widen a clearing, hauling peeled logs up the slope to a cabin site. She looked at Mel, the whole cast of his face slightly greenish in the light thrown from the dashboard, and she made a brief, unsuccessful attempt to imagine him with a beard.

She had, in the recent past, had more luck imagining him dead. It was a benign sort of fantasy, absent the dead body, the coffin, blood, illness. In the daydream, she was surrounded by solemn-faced friends who supported her, and when Anne wept she was solemn too and her nose didn't run. Afterward, with the insurance money, she put up a log house in the wooded foothills behind Newberg or Yamhill on a lively little year-round creek that never flooded, and she grew a giant garden and began painting landscapes in watercolors and chalk, drove into Portland to sell her produce and paintings at the Saturday Market. She was prone to daydreams furnished with elaborate details, and this particular one felt easier to her, felt purer, than the dream that began with divorce.

In the morning she awoke thinking of the fact that people used to grow everything they ate. She had a two-year-old seed catalog, and she leafed through the pages while she drank her coffee, then hunted up a pad of paper and began to lay out a garden plan. She would have to have forty acres, she decided—room to pasture horses, grow raspberries, bell peppers, potatoes. She planned an orchard, its neat rows of apple and prune trees hedged by old roses. When she heard Mel come in from washing the car she folded the papers—the list of seeds and rootstock, and the diagram—and put them inside the seed catalog and put the seed catalog carelessly back in the drawer where they kept the directions for all their appliances, because if she tried to hide it, he might suspect there was something to hide and might open to the sugar-pod peas and find the list and think Anne had a screw loose, because of course he wouldn't know about the log house in the Yamhill Valley, and would probably think the plan and the list were for the corner behind the garage where she had turned under the sod and set out three tomato plants.

She went out to the yard and laid a hose among the tomatoes and stood watching the water run out to darken the clods. The leaves of the plants were hairy and yellowish, the limbs spindly. There were five or six grass-green tomatoes, hard and round and small as marbles, on each of the bushes. She squatted and spent a few minutes pulling out the grass that had come up around the plants. The grass broke off in her hand, leaving the stripped white stems standing up in the dirt. It would be hot later in the day, but above the edge of the garage the sun was not much more than a smudge behind a yellowy haze. In the summer whenever they went out of the city—up into the mountains or over to the coast where the sky was clean and blue—when they came back to town she would always notice the jaundiced sky for a day or two until it became, if not the correct color, the ordinary one, and she stopped seeing it. There seemed no particular reason why she was aware of it today—unable not to see it.

She left Mel on the phone talking to someone in Hong Kong, and drove to the garden nursery on Stark Street. She bought sacks of sterilized manure and compost, and a tall clay pot, its wall pockets planted with strawberry starts. The clerk helped her load the pot into the trunk of her car and brace it with the sacks of manure. She didn't have far to drive, she told him, but when she left the parking lot she turned west on impulse, away from the house. Above the edge of the railing on the Ross Island Bridge, when she slowed the car she wasn't surprised to see a small clearing in the trees, and smoke rising up from a brush pile. Along the west bank of the river on both sides of the bridge, shaley steps and blue pools of water stepped down from the hillside. She turned north onto Barbur Boulevard to circle back toward home, and in the rearview mirror caught sight of the man coaxing his laboring horse up a grassy path through the woods. They were hauling a load of mud and stones on a canvas drag.

She didn't ask Mel to help her with the strawberry pot. She lugged it out of the trunk herself and set it on the patio. The sacks of manure and compost she carried over one by one and piled up at the corner of the garage. It was steer manure—the nursery didn't carry horse manure, the clerk had told her. She split open one of the sacks with the edge of her rose clippers and dumped the dry fertilizer out at the feet of the tomato plants, worked it into the dirt, and turned the hose on to water it in.

She had been sleeping in the guest bedroom for the last few weeks, but after midnight she took a blanket out to the back deck and curled up on the chaise. There was too much highway noise to hear crickets or birds, but she could smell the mown grass. The night air, unconditioned, felt alive to her, felt real.

Occasionally she heard a dog barking. Neither she nor Mel had ever wanted children, but they used to talk about getting a dog. She didn't know when they had stopped talking about it, or which of them had decided it was too much trouble.

In the morning, she took the car downtown without saying anything to Mel. When she crossed the bridge, she was not surprised to see several horses browsing the knee-high grass along the bank of the river. In the clearing, the man was on his knees, setting rocks into mud slurry for the foundation of a fireplace. The ground had been plowed in crooked furrows between the stumps, and corn was beginning to sprout there.

The central library was a Carnegie building from the 1910s and lately renovated in classic style, though there were no longer card catalogs, just banks of computers where the oak cupboards with their long, skinny drawers had used to stand. She found a new book about the early history of the city, one that must have come out after she had stopped trying to impress Tom Kline by reading about such things—after she and Mel had gotten together—and books about subsistence farming, home veterinary remedies, "anachronistic" crafts.

Crossing the bridge again, facing into the morning sun, she could see in glimpses through the railing blue spruce draped with lichen, and candle-spire firs, and a fringe of red-twig willow ranging up and down both sides of the river. Above the east bank an osprey worked the shore, looking for spawning salmon. The man, as he crouched washing his muddy hands in the water at the river's edge, lifted his head and watched the bird for a moment.

She spent the rest of the morning reading how to notch the low side of a tree before sawing through from the high side, and how to lever up the logs of a cabin single-handedly with long poles and a rock fulcrum. Some of the books had copyright dates from the sixties and early seventies, when everybody she knew had been thinking about homesteading, or joining a farming commune. She had spent one summer living in a tent on Whidbey Island, picking strawberries and raspberries and Blue Lake green beans, one crop after the other. Her boyfriend back then was an architecture student at the University of Oregon, and in the fall when he went back to school she followed him. She had thought briefly about staying behind on the island—she had liked living in a tent, doing farm work, being dirty a lot of the time, the smell of her own body so much like the smell of earth in a strawberry field. Now she thought: *My life might have been entirely different.*

Late in the afternoon she was in the bathtub when a great noise sprang suddenly high up like a fountain and then down and then up again in a new shape, booming and wordless—Mel was playing around with the wiring on the stereo. She had been almost asleep. In her dream, the world had folded in on itself and she was on another page: The tub was tin and she had carried water to it in kettles heated on a cast-iron stove. She sank her body in the green water until her ears flooded.

Years earlier she had bought a denim tote bag, a shapeless cheap thing with two looping handles, to carry books back and forth from the library, a swimsuit when she went to the Y. There was an unopened can of racquetballs in the bottom of the bag. She took that out and put in the library books and her own barely read gardening books—not all of them, not the ones about patio gardens and landscape design, but one about organic methods of pest control and another about vegetables and fruits. She looked through her clothes and put a flannel nightgown and a wool shirt and two pairs of insulated ski socks in the sack with the books. Then she dressed in jeans and a cotton shirt and her old leather-and-shearling lace-up boots and stood in front of the bathroom medicine cabinet, staring at the little boxes and jars and tubes on the glass shelves. Finally she took toothpaste and moleskin and aspirin and a leftover prescription bottle of antibiotic and the old-fashioned red Merthiolate that Mel sometimes used to paint a wart, and put them in the tote bag with the other things. In the basement on a shelf above the electric dryer there were several little packets of seeds—broccoli and peas, snap beans, zucchini, little flat packages with the corners torn out and crumbs of dirt stuck to the colored photos on the fronts. Tokens of earlier seasons of brief optimism. She put them in the bag, inside one of the socks, and carried the bag out to the car. She left the unused sacks of manure and compost piled up by the garage, but she dug the strawberry starts out of the clay pot, put them in a cardboard box, and put the box in the trunk of the car. When she drove away from the house, Mel was still playing with the fine tuner on the stereo.

The sun was low by then, just above the brim of the hills, shining flat in her eyes when she crossed the Ross Island Bridge. It would have been perilous to look away from the lanes. She could just see from the edge of her eye the clearing behind the screen of old trees, and a wisp of smoke rising from the stone chimney of the cabin.

She drove off the bridge onto Macadam and parked the car on the graveled shoulder, took out the tote bag and the box of strawberry starts and walked downhill across a dry weedy ditch and into the shade of three-hundred-year-old firs and cedars and hemlocks. Through the manzanita and huckleberry a narrow trail trodden by animals wound downhill toward the river's edge. In low places where the ground was still damp, unshod horses had left their tracks. Anne shifted the weight of the cardboard box to her other hip. He would be interested in bartering for the strawberries, she felt—strawberries, a rare and fine thing in his valley, while horses were easy to get and cheap. Although she didn't think she needed the man, she had a plan that included a horse.

Dead Men Rise Up Never

THESE DAYS, HE'S FAMOUS. YOU pick up a magazine and there's a story he's written, you open a newspaper and he's covering the Russo-Jap war or sailing around the world, escaping cannibals in the South Seas. But when I first knew him he was just a kid, a "work beast" he liked to call himself, on account of he was up every morning at three o'clock delivering newspapers, out again with the late papers after school, working Saturdays on an ice wagon, and Sundays setting up pins in a bowling alley. Then a couple of years later—this would have been '90 or maybe '91—he was an oyster pirate, hanging around the Oakland waterfront and pretty often drunk. But I was there too, stealing oysters and becoming pretty thoroughly alcohol soaked, so don't take any of this as judgment.

We were school chums, Johnny and me, which you wouldn't have thought. You'd have thought he was a sissy and a bookworm, owing to the fact he'd plant himself on a bench in the schoolyard every recess and stick his nose in a book, which was a long mile from my own practice, shooting squirrels with a pellet gun and collecting cigarette coupons, trading them for picture cards of racehorses, prizefighters, stage actors and such. But one time this big kid Mike Pinella ground his boot into my best set of Indian Chieftain cards, and Johnny just popped off the bench, lit into the kid, and bloodied his nose, which redeemed him in my mind. Then it turned out he collected cards too, so after that we started hanging around together. When his afternoon papers were finished, we'd go after mud hens on the Oakland Estuary with homemade slingshots, or rent a rowboat, pull out onto the bay and fish for rock cod, or just stroll along the waterfront watching ships sail through the Golden Gate. And I visited him at home a few times, which was how I first got acquainted with Plume and the rest of that spiritist realm.

His mother's name was Flora, though she wasn't any pretty flower. She was dwarfish with a skimpy head of dark hair, black squinty eyes, a thin mouth always set in a hard straight line. I wouldn't say she was ugly, although she came near to it, and she had a savage glare verging on madness. But she advertised herself as a medium holding séances and planchette readings, and in that field of work, odd looks were the wonted thing, an inkling of her profession.

I had the idea that the furnishings in Johnny's house might be tattooed with mystical configurations and puzzles cabalistic, but they were living in a dingy little cottage on Pine Street near the estuary in West Oakland, and the front room had just a coal stove, some plain chairs and bare floors, and a drop-leaf table covered with newspaper in lieu of a tablecloth—the only time I saw a good linen cloth on that table was when Flora was holding a seance. You wouldn't know you were in an uncanny house except for the half-dozen Mason jars lined up on a shelf in the kitchen. Johnny said the dark shapes in each one, small as wrens and slowly turning in milky plasma, were the corpses of dybbuks and poltergeists his mother had taken captive. He said this offhanded, with a sidelong glance at me, so I didn't know whether to take it for truth or mockery. Looking back, I think maybe he hadn't made up his mind himself.

Flora had been born to luxury—she'd had an education in music and elocution and social graces, all of which she'd lost when her mother died and she couldn't get along with her step-mother. She was always looking for ways to get back to that fancy life, but when I knew the family, she was married to a man who wasn't Johnny's daddy, a part-time carpenter and farmer without prospects for improving their situation. Her knack for the occult brought in, at most, a middling income, so she was always hectoring her husband into unsupportable ventures and money-losing schemes one after the other, while betting the household budget on Chinese lottery games. The Work Beast turned over nearly every cent he made to his mother, who had always to be bailed out of some financial hole or other.

Flora communicated with several kinds of spirits—ghosts, wraiths, sprites, even jinn. She'd walk around the house talking with one or another of them, asking their advice, listening to their secrets, whispering hers, and it was those pneumae that she called on for the seances and planchette readings that made up most of her business.

Plume, in particular, occupied Flora's body whenever she conducted a seance. All the clients in those days were set on Indians, and Plume, so Flora said, had been a Blackfoot war chief in his temporal life. Plume spoke English in a growly low voice, and he punctuated every seance with wild war whoops. He could get the people holding hands around the table to moan and chant and whoop as if they, too, were Indians gathering for a war dance, and more than anything else this was what brought Flora her trade.

Johnny liked to put on an air of disdain for his mother's ghosts, but not from misbelief. It was his opinion that none of the spirits she talked to, even Plume, were better than third-rate. They might tell a woman that her uncle had a goiter—information of no particular use to her—or that a man's peach crop would come down with canker, which anybody could guess from the wet winter, but none of the spirits who hung around Flora's house could tell a man where he might nail a job or find a gold mine. When any of them gave advice to Flora herself, what numbers to bet in the Chinese lottery, for instance, the numbers would always be off by one or two. And if the messages they sent to her clients weren't outright worthless, they were usually cryptic, damn near impossible to make sense of, which Flora promoted as mysterious, but Johnny thought was their canny way of hiding ignorance.

"I don't know why she listens to any of them," he told me. "They never come across with any goods." But it galled him that Flora kept the planchette and her whispered correspondence to herself. In spite of his low regard for Plume and the others, he couldn't help thinking if he ever had the chance to slip a question into their world, he might learn the truth of his parentage.

His father had died before Johnny was born, or so Flora had always said, but in one telling it was a tragic accident in a lumber mill, another time a heroic death, saving his pregnant wife from desperadoes. Yet again, he'd been run over by a wagon in the street. Her vague and shifting accounts left Johnny plenty of room for his own lively notions. He liked to imagine he was the natural-born child of a famous man—it was Muir or Roosevelt, usually—stolen from his rightful family as an infant, while his true parents (Flora not his actual mother) were even now searching the world for him. But I suppose he knew this was fanciful; what he really wanted from his mother's spirits was to be put in touch with his father's ghost.

My folks moved us up to Auburn right after Johnny and I graduated Grammar School. In the letters we passed back and forth after that, he said he was working for Hickmott's Cannery, stuffing pickles into jars for ten cents an hour, which was long hours and filthy work. But he was squirreling away the small change, finding the gumption finally to keep some of his wages out of the hands of his mother, and when he had enough saved up, he planned to buy a boat.

He could sail, Johnny could, having taught himself by the time he was twelve, navigating in rented boats across those forty miles of open water thronged with commercial traffic, and up the northern end of the bay through all those estuaries and inlets, swift-current narrows and treacherous shallows. He was a natural sailor, and it was his idea to quit the cannery and be an oyster pirate.

The oyster beds all up and down the bay were owned by the railroad. Armed guards protected the beds, and pirating was a felony, so the California Fish Patrol was also on the lookout. But a daring pirate could earn a month's factory wages from one good night's haul, and the way Johnny thought of it, oyster pirates were folk heroes fighting the Octopus. The railroad monopoly kept the prices high, and when pirates undersold to saloons and stores along the waterfront, everybody but the railroad came out the winner. It was dangerous business—every nighttime raid was an invitation to get shot or arrested—but that wasn't any discouragement to Johnny, just the opposite. He was a bookish kid who had learned to hide that side of his nature behind a front of nerve and daring. He wrote to me that prison would be an easier life than working at the cannery.

Well, every pirate needed a crew, a fellow or two to drop from the boat and fan out across the mud flats, gathering up the plunder; so after he bought his boat, a decked-over fourteen-footer with a centerboard, he wrote and offered me a one-third split. I left the factory job I had in Auburn, came down to Oakland, and moved in with Johnny, into his little slant-roofed bedroom tacked onto the side of the kitchen. I told my parents I was taking taxidermy lessons in San Francisco.

We went out only on the darkest nights when the tide was low. Some nights were so dark I couldn't see the boat a couple of yards away, and more than once, reaching down into the black water to grab slippery oysters off the seabed, I'd feel something greasy, something cold as ice, brush through my hands. I guess it was Flora's influence that led me to think this wasn't any fish or eel. She had never said there were wraiths or ghosts in the drink, but I knew there were drowned men aplenty, and the hardest part of pirating, for me, was reaching down into that oily wet darkness, not knowing what I might touch, and imagining the worst. I never admitted a bit of this to Johnny; I guess I was working up a front of nerve and daring myself, when it came to ghosts and suchlike.

We ran oysters for a couple of years without getting shot. We had some close calls, but Johnny had a thoroughgoing knowledge of the water's depth everywhere along that shore-line, and his boat had a shallower draft, was frailer but faster than the patrol boats, plus he had a gift for sailing in absolute silence over still water, where any knock or bump could make a shocking loud noise.

Whenever the moon was too bright or the tide too high for pirating, we hung around the Oakland waterfront with the rest of the hoodlums and drunkards and became fairly much drunks ourselves, which I have already mentioned. And we might have gone on like that until we finally got ourselves killed or thrown in the pen—that was the path we were on. But one night after a couple of hours of blind drinking, Johnny had the idea we ought to steal the planchette from his mother's cupboard and try to get in touch with his dead father. I was too drunk to put up an argument, so we stumbled back to his house and he snuck the planchette into the little bedroom we slept in. And the way his life unfolded after that, the whole adventure path he followed—and my life too, as far as that goes, the unhappy, insolvent path I've followed—was more or less on account of that night.

I don't know if you've seen a planchette—in modern times it's gone out of use in favor of Ouija boards. The one Flora used was a heart-shaped piece of African blackwood supported by two wheeled casters carved of bone, with an aperture at the apex to hold a pen, the needle-sharp tip of the pen being the heart's third support. Flora always pretended to poke the nib into the palm of her hand so the planchette's words would be written in blood, but the truth was, her palm hid a tiny vial of red ink. Johnny didn't want to fake it; he wanted the answers to be real, written in his own real blood. So we spread a sheet of newsprint flat on the floor and set the planchette in the middle of it, and Johnny pierced his hand with the nib of the pen. He could be quiet as death when we were out pirating, but he was pretty drunk that night and not seeming to care how much noise he made, which I suppose was why Flora came into the room in her nightdress just as the pen had pulled his blood up into its tip. A few drops fell on the newspaper as she fixed her mad, glittering black eyes on each of us in turn, and I don't know when I've felt such a cold fear. But I'll say this for Johnny, he put on a solemn face and made up a lie on the spot.

"One of the fellows at the docks got killed dead tonight, killed by the Fish Patrol. We weren't with him when he died. We were just hoping the planchette will have some last words for us, something from our pal, to guide us in the earth-life."

This went well with her. She knew his low opinion of Plume and the others, and it must have surprised her that he would wish to ask the planchette a question. She may have taken it as a sign that her son had finally come around to respecting her occult gift. In any case, she pulled her brows together over her nose, considering, and then just gathered up her gown and sat right down on the floor with us and placed her fingertips on the wooden heart.

"You should touch the board very lightly but firmly, and do nothing of your own volition," she said, in a hoarse whisper.

I had spied on her readings a few times, but I'd never

touched a planchette myself. There was a little electrical shiver when I touched the board, which maybe was my own nerves, but when Johnny placed his hands on the board, the whole thing trembled. And after a long moment, the wooden heart went skating across the paper. We all leaned in, watching the pen trace a line of red words. Then Johnny straightened up and threw me a look. "Oh, that's Herbert's hand," he said. "Isn't it, Frank? I would know his fist anywhere. It's Herbert's, I'm sure of it. Isn't it?"

Well, there wasn't anybody down at the docks named Herbert, dead or alive, but I said, "That's his hand, all right," and Flora nodded solemnly.

"You may ask the board a Question Unspoken," she said, in a spectral voice. "That is, with your mind only. Your friend or his kindred spirit will bring word from him."

So we kept our hands lightly on the board and closed our eyes, and I guess Johnny asked his Question Unspoken. For myself, I asked the planchette for a bit of information about the Fish Patrol, and what haul we could expect from the next low tide. The planchette twitched under our fingers and began to write. When the heart ceased moving, Flora pulled her arms into her lap with a sigh, and seemed to wake from half sleep, and then Johnny and I leaned in to read what was written on the paper: *for the youthful inquirer after truth dead men rise up never seducer astrologer Carquinez* and then a scratchy line unreadable as the blood-ink ran dry.

To my mind the message was just about worthlessly opaque, but it seemed to mean something to Johnny. His face colored up and he threw a wild look at his mother, who appeared flustered, her squinty eyes blinking and blinking.

"Not dead!" Johnny said. "He's some damn astrologer or horoscopist living over on the Carquinez Strait and I'm his bastard child!"

Johnny, of course, had asked the planchette to put him in touch with his father's ghost, and he sure as hell knew what the answering message meant: he was the bastard son of a living philanderer. I expected Flora to argue the planchette's meaning, and she briefly did. "Now, do not mind this message, Johnny, such a strange message must not be meant for you, something from an abnormal imagination, a strange zodiacal voice to be sure, and not to be credited." She babbled on, and all the while she caught up the paper from under the planchette and crumpled it.

But as Johnny went on shouting—"You're a damned liar! Quit playing tricks!"—she grew boiling mad, and gave up all pretense. Her defense became a lurid tale about a faked horoscope and a clever seduction, attempted suicides, a thwarted abortion. She stormed and raved, shouting down her son with the anthems of a sufferer: "Innocent! Abandoned! Destitute! Cast on the mercy of friends! You might never have been born!"

Flora was famous for her temper, and Johnny was no match for her outrage, never had been. They wrangled back and forth a while and then he just took off from the house, cracking along so fast I had to jog-trot to catch up to him. We headed for the Heinold's Saloon, a cracker box of a bar built on pilings over the water at the end of Webster Street, and open all night. Heinold knew our likes, and we were already half-drunk when we came in, so before long we were thoroughly plastered.

Johnny railed against his mother a good long while and then began pouring scorn on the son of a bitch who had fathered him, and in the late middle of the night he asked me, "How many astrologers can there be in that damn town?" meaning Benicia on the Carquinez Strait. He didn't have the man's name, only that his trade was horoscopy.

"We oughta go on over there and smoke the skunk out," I told him.

So we stumbled down to the wharf and put out in Johnny's skiff. We were somewhere at the upper end of San Pablo Bay, where the current runs pretty fast out of Carquinez, when Johnny in a drunken stupor missed his footing and fell overboard. There was nothing but a fingernail moon; it was so dark I could only just make out his wan face bobbing on the water, receding from me as the boat sailed on. We shouted back and forth while I fumbled to get the boat turned around, but by the time I got back to where he'd gone over, there was nothing to see but a dark glimmer on the water. My shouts went unanswered.

He wrote up the story afterward, the whole account; maybe you have read it yourself. He was thoroughly under alcohol's sway, and when the current took him down the strait, the shore lights slipping farther and farther into the distance, he decided this drunken exploit was a perfect closure to his imperfect life. "A romantic rounding off of my short but daring career."

He was in the water a good four hours, alternately floating and swimming, thinking he might die or wishing to, and then falling into dreams, long disquiet dreams, he said, and when the effects of the liquor began to fade, it dawned on him that he didn't in the least want to be drowned. But a stiff breeze had sprung up, choppy little waves were lapping into his mouth, and he was beginning to swallow salt water. He was cold and miserable and utterly done in. And then Plume came roaring into his head, into his whole body, and kept him alive.

"The game is worth the candle"—that's what he remembered Plume saying. "I was ready to cash in my chips, but I felt like those were the magic words that banished all the irks and riddles of existence. Those hours in the water, it was one of those agelong nights that embrace an eternity of happening."

A Greek fisherman running his boat into Vallejo pulled him out of the water sometime in the early morning hours, and right after that he signed on with the *Sophia Sutherland*, a schooner headed to Japan and the Bering Sea to hunt seals. He wrote me later that he had given up using the name Johnny and begun calling himself Jack. He said he liked the tougher sound of it.

In 1906, I was living in Santa Rosa, which, after the big earthquake, was a smoking ruin every bit as much as San Francisco. I hadn't seen Johnny in a few years. He was famous by then and there were plenty of people asking for his time, but I would send a letter, and every so often he'd write back. After the quake he surprised me with a note, in some concern as to whether I had made it through or was burned out. He was living on a ranch up in Sonoma Valley by then, but he came down to Oakland, and I took the ferry over, and he met me at the landing. We spent the day at Heinold's Saloon, knocking back more than a few. Heinold's had always been the place for off-season seamen, and draymen hauling loads across the estuary bridge, as well as hoboes and other assorted down-and-outers. A few of them happened into the place while we were there, and I saw Johnny slip a dollar into more than one hand.

I asked after his life, and he told a few stories, but he was modest about it, leaving out the perils and escapades. He'd been an able seaman in the Japan Sea, had been a hobo for a while, had gone up to the Klondike with the rest of the gold diggers, that was all he said. Well, he was a big celebrity by '06, and in the stories I'd read, he'd saved a crewman who went overboard in a typhoon out of Yokohama. He'd been jailed and beaten up when he was marching to Washington with General Kelly's hobo army. He'd climbed through the Chilkoot Pass under a heavy load and then hiked from Deep Lake to Lake Lindeman three or four times a day carrying 150 pounds of gear each time. Survived on scant rations through a bitter winter in the Klondike and canoed out through the roughest water any man had ever paddled.

When he asked after my life, I told him, "I'm a taxidermist with a wife and five children, that's the short story. The only adventure I ever had was palling around with you." I guess he could see that my shoes and trousers had known better days.

We went on drinking into the night, and then he walked me back to the ferry landing. We leaned on the railing along the harbor front, smoking stogies and looking out at the dark water, and after a while he said, "You remember that night we snuck the planchette into my room?"

I remembered it. "The planchette told you the truth and you took it hard."

He gave me a look and shook his head. "Hell, Frank, it wasn't the planchette. I was moving the pen so it'd write something close to what I wanted. My cousin had told me the truth, and I just couldn't work up the nerve to front my mother. I figured I'd get the planchette to bring it up. I don't know what the hell the pen would have written if I hadn't been moving it around.

"But I hadn't figured on my mother blowing her stack like that. I thought she'd cry and beg me to forgive her." He slid me a half smile. "I never planned it, but it sure gave her a good scare, me rising up from the dead like a drowned ghost, and when I said it was Plume who saved me, that did the job. She couldn't quit wailing and asking pardon for lying to me all those years."

I wasn't sure what to make of this. "You always said it was Plume who took over your body and kept you alive."

He looked at me sidelong. "She claimed the chief never conversed with anybody but her. That's the whole reason I said it was Plume. To shake her."

I don't know if he had started out that night planning to tell me the truth, but once he got started, he just went ahead. He said when he went overboard he wasn't thinking he might die nor wishing to, he was too drunk out of his wits to hold that kind of a thought. He said he just drifted on the cold current, and after a short while washed up on the north shore. Nothing of strange dreams and never a word from Plume. When the sun came up, he swam out from the beach far enough to fake the need of rescue.

I guess it should have burned me up, hearing all this about the planchette, and the night he went overboard in the bay. But I just felt myself becoming someone old and feeble, bent under a weight of years.

Nobody in my own family had ever put much faith in spiritism. My mother was firm in her Methodist beliefs, firm in the knowledge that souls abided after death, but equally sure that spiritism might open a channel to the devil. I had come into Johnny's house unacquainted with the spiritist world, and somewhat in fear of it. But after the planchette told us the story of Johnny's parentage, and after Plume kept Johnny alive all those hours in the cold waters of the bay, well, I swung around to trust in mediums, and the spirit world, and in the years afterward I had more or less lived my life by their advice. The truth is, I hardly ever got counsel from them that did me any good. It would be something I already knew, or purely bad information, or else something so murky I couldn't make sense of it. But once in a blue moon one of the spirits at a seance or a planchette reading would let loose with something shrewd, something bona fide, which kept me on the hook, and I would take another run at it, hoping the answer this time might improve my fortune. Hoping one of them might one day quit playing tricks and do me a modest good turn.

Before we split up for the night, I asked if he'd ever looked up the astrologer in Carquinez who might have been his father. He took a while to answer. "Dead men rise up never," he said, in old Plume's spectral voice, which was just the sort of murky answer I was accustomed to hearing from the spirits.

Johnny had inherited a touch of the occult gift himself, being the son of a medium and a horoscopist—that's what I used to think. I always figured his luck, his fortunate career, all the close calls and heroism he'd written about, and the daring escapes from calamity, had come about with help from the spirits.

I never told him that while he'd been sleeping off his drunken stupor on a north shore beach, I'd been searching the dark water in a widening eddy of guilt and despair. The water in that bay was so damn cold nobody overboard ever lasted long; this was something we all knew. When I tacked back to the Oakland docks at sunrise, I was shaking so hard from grief and hopelessness I couldn't get up the strength to walk over to Flora's to bring her the news. I told Heinold the story and he sent someone off to the house, and I just sat down on the pier and wept. And it was hours before we got word that Johnny'd been pulled from the drink alive. Hours more before he told us all about Plume and "the game is worth the candle."

I took every word he said for truth. And believed all he wrote afterward. You might say my troubles are due to my own foolishness, and I might not disagree.

Wenonah's Gift

IN THE SPRING OF THE year, in the days that are known as The Assuaging, the girl Dulce built her house beneath the limbs of a great cedar, climbing first, straddle-legged, to hang wind-bells in the lowest branches so when the air moved against the shards of glass the delicate unstructured music would speak to her while she worked. Two rills ran together near there, with the tree standing in the crotch between. The sound the waters made, sliding turning and rubbing against stones, and the wind stroking the glass bells and shaking the high boughs of the cedar, seemed to her to weave a complex song, a finely textured chorus, which was her reason for choosing that place where the house would stand.

She had already thrown the pottery, all the bowls, pitchers, and jugs heavy and brown speckled bright berry color, before she began the laying of the foundation. She had pieced and tied a quilt, thick batted and nappy, had braided a sleeping mat from rags dyed hazelnut brown, all this before she began the building of a place where they would see use. And she had fashioned a narrow oaken trunk carved in bears and branches of spruce, made it specially for Guy, and soon as it was finished had traded it for one of Guy's great curving windows made specially for her, a wide arch hung with pendulous glass ropes of wisteria. She had traded to Enid a long stool with knuckled feet so she might have a sun-saver to heat her house and impel her woodworking tools. All this first. And only then, with everything in readiness, did she begin the dwelling itself, setting the stones for the foundation, laying the notched and planed floorboards, raising the squared-log walls from trees she had felled and stacked to dry two seasons earlier.

Often, she did not work alone. One or another of the people would come along the path between the rills and stay to talk and to work, asking, Shall I do it this way? or Is this the place to make the notch? so that the work and the house remained hers, though shared.

Finally on the last day Wenonah came, pushing lean-legged through the pea vines that bloomed beside the water. The old woman did not put her hands to the work. She squatted on the grass in the stippled shade and from her seamed walnut face, from those deeply lidded eyes, simply watched while the girl built the house of her majority.

When Wenonah had been there a long time and Dulce's sweat had darkened her shirt at the neck, the old woman said, "I've brought a cheese," and they sat together on the thin spiky grass and ate cheese and passed a jug of very cold cider. Dulce let the soles of her feet rest on stones in the creek. She looked sideways at her house. She was a little afraid to look at Wenonah.

Finally, carefully, she said, "It's small," so the old woman might say, *No, girl, no, it's a house of good size.*

But Wenonah moved with faint impatience, pushing the palm of one hand through the air. "Yes, it's small." And then, puckering her mouth, shifting her buttocks against the ground, "Who needs more? It's the right size." And after a silence, lifting her chin as if there had been argument, "This is a good place. I like the sound the waters make."

Because it was the last day before the holy days, in the afternoon several people came to work on Dulce's house. Guy's window had not yet been set, the shingling was unfinished, the door had not been hung. So they drifted in one by one and set to work. Sometimes if there was a small stillness they could hear hammer blows rung from other places among the trees—Chloe's house, and Thom's, both unfinished as Dulce's, with other groups of people lending hands there too.

When the sunlight began to fail, someone came with a sodium torch and the house was finished in that false day-brightness, with Dulce, alone, straddling the roof peak to nail the last shingles. Then they extinguished the torch and stood together silently, studying the dark bulk of the house against the trees. Finally the old woman, Wenonah, made a sound that was nearly a sigh, a sound of weariness or of sadness, and patted the girl's arm.

"Good. Good."

In small knots of twos and threes they straggled back through the scattered houses and the trees, moving gently, with the sounds of their voices and the gestures of their hands muted like the dusk. Where the woodland opened out a little, someone had made a fire in a ring of stones, a high yellow blaze, and people gathered in the glare around it, standing or squatting together, and children in bunches too, spurting round and among the adults, sending their thin shouts rising with the firesmoke.

The girl and the grandmother stood together, and while Wenonah spoke to this one or that, Dulce held her body self-consciously apart, and spoke only the few words that were necessary for courtesy. No child spoke to her, though she was often the focus of their furtive stares. There were already foods passing from hand to hand around the group, flat rounds of bread and bunches of bright red radishes, narrow-neck jugs of beer and steaming ribs of lamb, but Dulce, fasting, only handed them on.

Afterward, there was tale-telling, with first one and then another Teller standing on the hewn stump of a tree with the children sprawled closest and then the others, the adults and the three who would be confirmed as adults, sitting in a wide fan, making audience. Wenonah, who was one of the Tellers, took her turn but did not bother to push through the crowd to take the stump. She only stood where she was among the people and sent her canorous voice out over their heads, with all the faces turned up and toward her as though she were the hub of a wheel. She chose a tale of the ancient Civilized tribes, the people who had called themselves The Mare Comes.

Dulce sat beside the old woman's sandaled feet and looked out past the shoulders and faces crowded there. In the jumping firelight she glimpsed Chloe once, and later, more clearly, Thom, sitting rigid and aloof. He might have felt her watching. His eyes came round and snagged her and then lurched away.

Afterward, Dulce could not remember the tale Wenonah had told—only that it was a story of great passion and souls swollen with blood. The Civilized tales always ended in war.

There was dancing and game playing, and the minstrels brought out their stringed instruments. Dulce stayed with Wenonah, or perhaps Wenonah with her. The old woman listened to this one and that, and sometimes laughed or spoke some light thing herself, and once she shared a pipe with two clansmen, another time gambled with sticks and lost and went off grumping and disgusted. All the while Dulce was near her, standing very stiff and silent with her eyes often turning out to the darknesses of the trees.

In time there were people sleeping on the ground, fallen where they would, and the others stepping over them carefully to go on with their gaming or to find their own path home to bed, until finally more slept than celebrated. Then the old woman plucked Dulce's sleeve.

"I am too old to pillow my head on a stone."

In darkness and weariness and silence, the girl and the old woman climbed the ridge to Wenonah's house. It sat on a high shelf so the window looked out on the tips of cedars and the far edge of sky, dark as metal against the serrated line of the trees. From there, they could see pillars of pale smoke rising from the valleys, marking other villages, other bonfires celebrating the Vernal Assuaging, where there were, as here, new houses, untrodden thresholds, unproven young adults.

Wenonah was a maker of bows, and from the rafters of her house hung sheaves of wild-cherry arrow-woods and half-shaped bows of yew and ash, and raw limbs drying, rubbed shiny with grease. The floor was littered with wood shavings and peeled bark, the dark stains of spilled fat, fragments of feathers and twisted fiber bowstring. Wenonah cleared a space on the floor and unrolled a mat there and she and Dulce lay down together beneath her thin old confirmation quilt. They did not touch.

After a while Wenonah said, "You must wait." She lay on her hip and spoke the words into the darkness. "Find a place and then wait. The others will be anxious, will run to the hunt, and one will come to where you are."

Dulce lay on her back and looked at the long, straight shapes of the unfinished bows. She hugged her own shoulders under the quilt.

For a long time she listened to the old woman sleeping, and later the rain dribbling against the roof. Then she went out and stood at the edge of the bluff with the hood of her shirt thrown back so the rain purled in her hair, and she waited until the thin rim of sun made a wound against the horizon. Behind her, there was a sound of a bare foot on the grass and when she turned it was Wenonah, holding a long bow and sheaf of arrows with both her hands stretched out flat and wide so the things lay across her palms like a formal offering. The bow was very pale, a smooth double curve with the short straightness of the grip between, and the ends curving back again equally, and the bow string taut and dark. The tips of the arrows were obsidian.

The old woman sucked in the edges of her mouth. There were fine, clear beads of rain in her eyelashes. She thrust the gifts toward Dulce, pushing them hard into her hands. They did not speak. The girl made a small sound and the old woman looked away, frowning, ducking her chin. But they did not speak. And the only touch between them was the dry rasp of the old woman's hands against the girl's wrists as she gave over the bow and the arrows.

The priest, Daivid, sat hunched on the crosspaths stone with the hood of his cloak pulled high against the rain. Perhaps he had drunk too much beer or gambled too long: his eyes were faintly swollen, his mouth a thin line. Dulce squatted a little way from him. Chloe was there too, sitting on the wet grass with her knees drawn up under her shirt and her arms lapping round her shins. In the thin daylight she seemed gray faced. Her eyes touched Dulce and slid aside. A bow carved of yew lay on the grass beside her feet. The three waited and in a moment the other priests came—the tall woman named Hannah and the old man, Steev. They waited together, all of them, in silence, until at last Thom came, holding a red-lacquered longbow in the tight fist of his hand. He did not quite look in Chloe's face, and not at all toward Dulce. Perhaps it was their old childhood friendship that kept his eyes hard and narrow and turned from her. Then the priest, Daivid, stood with a little grunting sound and led them all through the rain, away from the houses.

The sky paled a little, hanging ragged in the points of the trees, but there was no hardening into daylight, just a timeless grayness so that Dulce did not know how far or how long they walked. Often she smelled the salt water of the Sound, but the way was known only to the priests and they did not speak. Dulce's new bow and sheaf rubbed a line where she carried them slung across a shoulder. The hem of her long shirt drew wetness up like a wick so it slapped stinging cold and gritty against her calves.

The sky began to darken with twilight—they had walked very far—when they came finally to a ruin of Civilization, some ancient wreckage of their many wars. Among the trees there were long hillocks of bricks and broken sheets of paving hard under the moss. And there had been a gate: part of a stone arch rose into the limbs of the cedars. Daivid stood beneath it and threw back his cowl and then Dulce saw the others who were gathered already at that place, faces she did not know, or knew a little, priests and youths of other villages. They made no sound, they only crouched or stood or lay silently, separately, under the shadows of the trees and among the fine twigs of huckleberry bush and salal. Above their heads there were enigmatic symbols gouged in the granite, U NAV L RESE.

In the darkness under the high stone arch, Dulce found a place for herself and squatted down, bunching her body against the cold. And then she simply waited for day. She could feel the others near her, crouching silent too, waiting too. Only the priests slept. She could hear, sometimes, the sounds of their dreams.

Others came in the night—one thin boy and several girls, following their priests through the darkness. They found places under the arch and made their own bodies small against the cold. Afterward, in the stillness, Dulce heard someone make a faint sound, a sigh.

Through high gaps in the trees, the sky seemed not to lighten but simply to clarify so that everything became easier to see but without brightness. Finally the old priest whose name was Steev came quietly and bent to touch Dulce's wrist. She followed him into the timber of the Proving Ground. Others had also begun to scatter. She saw Thom, following the priest Hannah, turning to cast Dulce a quick white look.

Steev led her through the darkness under the wet trees, a long walk to a small cave along a bluff with a view of the Sound. It was an old cave, Civilized, with concrete walls and unglassed windows, small and high, looking out over the gray water. They did not go into the cave's mouth.

In toneless weariness, standing beside the dark opening, Steev said, "Wait at this place for the call to start. And afterward, when you have been confirmed, you may go out through the gate where we were." He was an old man, and perhaps he had attended too many confirmations. He did not quite look into Dulce's face.

She stood out of her shirt, stood naked with her hair cold and lank against her neck, and handed the shirt to the priest. She held Wenonah's bow fisted in one hand, the sheaf of arrows across her shoulder, a thin-bladed knife strapped to her calf with a string. She stood watching the priest go back along the path toward the gate, and then she crouched with her hips against the cool flat wall of the cave and she waited. She could see her heartbeat in her breast.

At dawn, above the gray mist rose a clear, distant bell-note from a horn. Irresistibly, she ran. The haft of the knife struck hard little blows against her ankle bone, the sheaf of arrows beat against her spine. She ran until the breath and the first spurt of fear were gone out of her. Then from a high ridge she rested the heels of her hands on her knees and sucked the frigid air, panting. From this height she could see behind her the gray finger of the Sound, and ahead between distant hillocks, several priests standing in the drizzle under the arch of the gate. Through the gauze of rain, standing utterly still, they seemed faceless, bodiless, like the stone phallics that stood in small groves at the edge of some of the old ruined villages of the Civilized tribes. And seeing them Dulce remembered her grandmother's counsel.

When she had chosen a place, she crouched among the leaves and held the bow across the tops of her bent legs and simply waited. Her chest was very tight, so she took air in through her mouth. The rain beaded on the backs of her hands, her shoulders, the crown of her head. She waited a long time, squatting silently, with her naked buttocks resting against her naked heels and the foliage dripping and the wind running cold against her back, tangling the loose strands of her hair.

Finally, in twilight the color of pewter, between the long straps of the leaves there was a transient paleness, a shape sliding. She closed her mouth, lips tightening stiffly over teeth, and waited. In a moment it came toward her through the high leaves, moving soundless on fine, long-boned legs. She waited, crouching still, with the bow in her hands nocked, waiting too, and the straight shaft of the arrow pointing away from her breast. There was only a little shaking and it did not reach her hands.

She waited until she could see the smooth glide of muscle beneath the skin, until even the sharp body smell was in her nostrils, and then she made only one fluid motion rearing above the leaves with the bow lifting in her hands and the bowstring drawn taut and then freed, all of it a single wholeness, complete and seamless, with only the face startling toward her, the widened eyes, seeming separate and disconnected.

She stood afterward with the bow still poised and her heart beating behind her eyes, stood very still, staring, watching the rain puddle in the folds of the body. Then a little sound came out of her on a little breath and she let the bow down and squatted where she was in the wet fronds, hugging hands to elbows, rocking back and forth on her hips, until she was done with shaking and weeping.

It began to be dark. In a while she dipped her thumbs in the small stream of blood and marked her face and her breast with pairs of bright stripes, but in the darkness there would be no seeing the red tokens of her confirmation, so she waited for daylight, sitting alone and still. Her hair was heavy and wet and the wind brought it into her face. After a long time, she groped in the stems of grass beside the body until her hand closed on the lacquered red bow. Under her fingertips, in the darkness, its touch was cold and hard as bone—the rib of a giant. She freed the bowstring with the edge of her knife so she might tie back her hair with its stiff strand.

When there was a little light, she took the body across her shoulders and went away cautiously toward the gate of the Proving Ground. She held Thom's red bow in one fist, her own bow resting in a pale double curve low against her back.

Later, in all the valleys, there were heavy palls of smoke, and ashes dusting the trees, and where a newly-made house became a funeral pyre, there would be black cinders for a while and then, in the sweetened soil, small blooms, and tall thin trees growing.

The Presley Brothers

Recorded at the Waldorf-Astoria Hotel on the occasion of the induction of Elvis and Jesse Presley into the Rock and Roll Hall of Fame, January 23, 1986

[Sustained applause]

[Elvis Presley]: Well, the last record Jesse and I made together was twenty-five years ago now, so I wouldn't have blamed y'all if you'd forgot all about the Presley Brothers. But it's an honor to be up here with the rest of these fellows [gesturing], all these men we sung with and admired, and the ones already passed, Bob Johnson, Jimmy Yancey, who we listened to when we were kids, and took after as much as we could. [scattered applause]

They told me I'd have ten minutes, give or take, to say whatever I wanted, so I guess I'll tell you a bit about our growing up, because you know we were always singing. When we were two years old, we'd be at church and we'd slide off Momma's lap, run up the aisle to the stage so we could try to join the choir. At home, the radio was always playing—Momma loved music—and we'd join our voices to whatever we heard coming out of that Philco she kept on the kitchen table. But then I think we were ten when we gave our first public performance. This came about because one morning at school—I don't recall the reason—we stood up and sang something for our fifth-grade class and then Miss Osborne, who was our teacher at the time, encouraged us to enter a singing contest at the Mississippi-Alabama Fair and Dairy Show. Momma dressed us like cowboys and we climbed up on a chair together so we could reach the microphone. We sang Red Foley's country song "Old Shep," and I believe we placed fifth. [laughter, applause] So, for our eleventh birthday, Daddy and Momma gave me a guitar and they gave Jesse a bicycle, and we were told to share. We always had shared everything anyway, right from the start.

When we were born, Daddy was just eighteen years old and Momma was twenty-two. They were living in Tupelo back then and Daddy was working for a lumberyard. We were born in a two-room shotgun shack he built himself from lumber cadged from that yard. Jesse came out first and I was born thirty minutes later. Jesse was blue and cold—the midwife thought he was stillborn—but she blew air into him and pinched his little cheeks and slapped his little behind and just about the time Momma had quit hoping for a miracle he took in a big gasp and pinked right up. Jesse always said he remembered it all. He remembered a string of longing tightening suddenly between him and me, and the plucked note, the sacred note, calling across space, and he said it was God hearing that note who reached out and touched him and gave him life. [sustained applause]

Every walleyed uncle and yard cousin seems to make it into Tupelo. [laughter] It creates a peculiar culture, I will say that, but it wasn't a bad place for kids to grow up. We lived in a mostly black neighborhood, and we heard a lot of what we used to call "race radio"—black gospel music and blues—coming out the windows when we were walking home from school or playing out in the yard or the street. At home we listened to Mississippi Slim's radio show, which I guess you would say was hillbilly music, but we didn't hold one kind of music above the other, we were just crazy about all of it. Hank Snow and Sister Rosetta Tharpe: we admired them equally.

We learned how to play that birthday guitar from our daddy's brother and from the pastor at the Assembly of God church. We watched other people playing too, and picked up a few things that way. We hung around the record shops that had juke-boxes or listening booths—do y'all remember those? [scattered applause, whoops]—and we learned to sing harmony mostly by listening to the Delmore Brothers over and over again. Being twins, we had the same voice, you know, and "parallel thirds" is not something we had heard of back then, but we figured out for ourselves how to arrange a song so each line would stand alone as a melody line, and we took turns singing the solo bits. We both of us studied and played by ear. Jesse never did learn to read music, and I was thirty-five or better before Roy Orbison sat me down and taught me the notes. [laughter, applause]

Mississippi Slim's little brother was a classmate of ours, and after Slim heard us singing he booked us for a couple of on-air performances. Jesse wasn't shy but I was, and we weren't but twelve years old. The first time we were to sing I had such a case of stage fright that I didn't think I could go through with it. Slim said Jesse should go on the air alone, but Jesse shook his head. We had our own twin language, which they tell me is not uncommon, but ours was a language mostly without words, and Jesse that time looked over at me and he told me without words that I should not be afraid. That I was not alone in the world. And I remembered it was true: God had reached out and touched Jesse so I wouldn't have to be alone. So I went ahead and sang, and that was the first time anybody ever heard the Presley Brothers singing on the radio. [applause]

Then, just about the time we were going into high school, Daddy moved us over to Memphis, which took some getting used to. We were in rooming houses to start with and then public housing, and the high school kids teased us for that, and for liking hillbilly music and black music. When we pulled a C minus in music class [laughter], it made Jesse mad. He came in the next day with our guitar and tried to prove our teacher wrong. He sang a Rufus Thomas song, "Bear Cat," and the teacher said she just didn't care for that type of song. She said she knew better than to ask where Jesse had learned that music, or where any of it came from. We both knew what she meant: that he shouldn't be singing black music, or listening to it. But Jesse just said to her, "Ma'am, I learned it from Mr. Thomas singing it on the radio, and where it comes from"—and he tapped his chest—"is inside of me." [applause]

After a while, we made some friends in Memphis and we formed a hillbilly group with a couple of other kids from The Lauderdale Courts where we were living, and we started playing around The Courts some, for birthday parties and that sort of thing. One of those boys had a washtub bass and the other had a fiddle, and Jesse borrowed a second guitar from one of the neighbors. Me and Jesse did the vocals, singing tight harmony. We knew pretty much all of Hank Snow, and we could play Roy Acuff, Ernest Tubb, Jimmie Rogers, Bob Wills.

We split off from those boys, though, after we said we wanted to sing some blues, some R & B and black gospel ballads, and they said we were turning colored. It was after that, we took to styling our hair with rose oil and Vaseline and we grew sideburns, which was a look we had seen on blues players hanging around Beale Street. Y'all know Beale? The downtown Memphis strip? [whoops] Neon-lit shops, jazz joints, all-black nightclubs. We met B. B. King down on Beale, did y'all know that? [applause, whoops] We knew him before any of us had a name. Well, he was on the way to getting a name, and it might have been him we were trying to look like.

Everything was segregated in those days, but the blues clubs had "white nights," and after we turned eighteen we went to those shows as often as we could. We were just nuts for the sounds we heard there—screaming, shouting, wailing, reckless. The white gospel groups had monthly singings downtown too. We figured some of those fellows must have been going into the blues clubs on "white nights" just like we were, because you could hear those white groups trying to come close to the way the black groups sounded. Some of them would even jiggle their legs around like the blacks did, and they'd wear wild, flashy suits like the ones in the windows at Lansky Brothers.

In Memphis we were listening to WDIA, which played all black music, and then late at night we listened to Dewey Phillips's *Red Hot & Blue* show on WHBQ. Dewey was like us, just crazy about all kinds of music. He mixed up R & B with country boogie, he played blues and gospel, and love songs from harmony groups. LaVern Baker and then the Drifters, Big Joe Turner, Howlin' Wolf, then Ruth Brown and maybe an old gospel song from Sister Rosetta.

People have said it was the Presley Brothers who opened up the door between black music and country music, but we just saw the open door and walked on through it. We never had a music lesson or a singing lesson, it was Beale Street and the radio and all, that was our musical education.

There is a story you might have heard about our first record, how we recorded it as a gift for our mother, and how we got accidentally discovered by Mr. Phillips. [gesturing toward Sam Phillips] [whoops, applause] We told that story ourselves so many times I think we almost came to believe it, but here's the truth: if all we had wanted was to make a record for Momma for her birthday, we could have gone on down the street to the drugstore where there was a little record-making service for a lot less money. [laughter] But we went into Sun Records and paid for studio time so we could record a two-sided acetate disc because we were hoping Mr. Phillips would hear us singing. We were hoping to catch a big break and be famous: that's the real story. [laughter, applause]

Sun was mostly recording black musicians in those days and Mr. Phillips will tell you, he was particularly looking for a white man who had a black sound and what used to be called a "Negro feel." A white singer who could bring in a broader audience for that type of music. Mr. Phillips wasn't looking for close harmony when we walked in, but after he heard us, he was interested enough to bring us back to the studio a couple of times and finally we had a session with Scotty Moore on bass and Bill Black on steel string guitar [scattered applause] to see if we could come up with something. It went all day into the night with nothing much taking hold. We were tired, just about to quit, when Jesse, messing around, started belting out Arthur Crudup's old blues number "That's All Right." And I jumped in, but it wasn't any stacked harmony, I was just coming in rough, and then the others picked up their instruments and it was gritty as all get-out. But Mr. Phillips happened to have the door to the studio standing open, and he stepped in and said, "Go back and do that again," and he recorded it. [applause]

Maybe you know the rest of that story, Dewey playing the song on his radio show a bunch of times and everybody thinking we were black at first, and then playing a show at Overton Park and all the girls screaming when we shook our legs. [shouts and prolonged applause] A lot of the black groups on Beale Street shimmied around some, and it was always a natural thing for both of us, just like it was for them. Feeling the rhythm, and feeling like we just couldn't stand still, and I was nervous, besides, so in the instrumental parts I would back off from the mike and be playing and shaking and the crowd would just go wild. It wasn't a calculated thing, but as time went on we both started being conscious of what would get a reaction. One of us would do something and if it provoked the audience then we'd both take it up, and maybe take it a little farther.

Then Bob Neal signed on as our manager and we played the regional circuit for a couple of years, calling ourselves the Hillbilly Cats. [a few whoops] Some of those teenage boys in the audience got to hating us [laughter], which I guess was on account of the girls screaming. They were worried we were out to steal their girls, I guess. There were occasions in some towns in Texas when we'd have to be sure to have a police guard because somebody was always trying to take a crack at us, or get up a gang and try to waylay us. I never heard of that happening to the Everly Brothers [laughter], but I happen to know it was those squeaky-clean Everlys [gestures toward the Everlys] that the kids should have been worried about. It was always Phil and Don who were out to steal the girls. [applause, laughter]

We were making records for Sun, ten sides or so by then, but not getting much radio airplay, which Bob always said was because our music was hard to pin down, put a name to. The country music disc jockeys said we sounded too much like black singers, and the R & B guys said our blues had too much hillbilly sound. Rockabilly was what everybody called it later, but there just wasn't a name for it right then.

We were a bit too wild for the Grand Ole Opry, but Bob got us a regular Saturday night gig on the Louisiana Hayride, and then Colonel Parker come along [scattered boos, Mr. Presley's hand rising to quiet them], and he got us signed with RCA. Well, we were still minors, just twenty years old, so it was our daddy who signed for us.

The first song we did with RCA was "Heartbreak Hotel" [applause], and they put some money behind it, promoted it pretty heavy, got us some radio airplay, which is what we'd been needing, and I guess you could say that song did fairly well for us. [applause] Everything went pretty crazy after that. I don't know if y'all remember, but we had ten number one hits, I think it was, and did all those TV shows—Milton Berle, Steve Allen, Ed Sullivan—and that silly movie, *Double Trouble*, all of it in those first couple of years. Not even two years, it was twenty-one months from when "Heartbreak" hit the charts to when I went off to the Army, just twenty-one months, and we were touring all that time when we weren't recording or making a movie or flying off to do some TV show. Amazing to think about, even now, how much happened in such a short time.

Well now I think I'd better wrap this up. I wanted to talk about those early times, the way we started, because the rest of it, the last twenty-five years and what all, has been talked just about to death.

We were a couple of poor dumb Southern country boys who got lucky, that's what folks used to say. [boos] But luck is just life coming together, working itself out the way it will do, this is what Momma always said.

So I will finish up by telling you this one time life worked itself out. It was after we did the first Milton Berle show and we were flying back to Nashville, flying over Arkansas, when one of the engines died and the plane heeled over pretty hard and started to drop. Now this was 1956, and we were just getting started—there was just the one album and it had just come out. So I think of that sometimes, that if that plane had gone on and crashed y'all would have "Blue Suede Shoes" and "Heartbreak Hotel," but that'd be all of it. We'd have been nothing but a foot-note to the history of rock and roll, not anybody you'd think of voting into the Hall of Fame.

All our lives Jesse and I wondered about the way he was born, which was a kind of miracle and a mystery. We both of us had these dreams where we were separated but we went on believing in each other even though each of us was sure that the other must be lost. We dreamed we were in a place all dark and without shape, and we were waiting there for the other one to show up. And this felt like it was only part dream and the rest was part memory.

We were both always interested in the spiritual side of things, the meaning of life, those soulful questions, which was on account of our dreams and the way Jesse was born. And we were readers, both of us, we carried around a trunk full of books when we were on the road, and we'd read certain parts to each other out loud. While we had been waiting to go on the Milton Berle show, he had read to me something about the Buddhist way of thinking—how people have all these lifetimes, and how the dead meet up in this place called the Bardo, which is some kind of state of existence between two lives on earth. You meet up there with the ones you love, and you talk things over before being born again. Or anyway that's how he understood it, and he thought our dreams might be some memory of being in the Bardo, each of us waiting for the other one to get there.

So that time over Arkansas, when the plane looked to be going down, there was a minute when we thought this might be it, this might be all of this lifetime we were going to get. I looked over at Jesse and he just smiled and said, "Look for me, Elvis. I'll be waiting."

And I said to him, "I will, Jesse. I'll look for you."

And now he's gone I think often about how he used to say he would be the one to go first—that he had been the one to go first in all our lifetimes. So I think of him waiting for me. And I know when I get there I will go looking for him and when we find each other, the string that joins me to him will play such a note, y'all will hear it all the way up here in the world.

[silence]

[sustained applause]

Excerpted from citations for the Presley Brothers on the occasion of their induction into the Rock and Roll Hall of Fame

The Presleys reshaped [those] old R & B songs—infused them with their own vocal character—but they never softened the wailing, reckless edges, as so many white artists were doing in the 1950s. And it was the cover image of their first album, *Elvis and Jesse!*—the brothers' faces transformed by the music, their guitars lifted high—that crucially placed the guitar, not the piano, at the center of this new music known as rock and roll.

　　—*Music critic Robert Rodman*

The Presleys, more than anyone else, gave the young a belief in themselves as a distinct and somehow unified generation—the first in America ever to feel the power of an integrated youth culture.

　　—*Historian Marty Jezer*

Their early recordings, more than any others, contain the seeds of what rock and roll was, has been, and most likely what it may foreseeably become.

　　—*Critic Dave Marsh*

Hall of Fame Series Interview. Recorded in the Foster Theater, Rock and Roll Hall of Fame, Cleveland, Ohio, February 22, 1997

John Halliman: Welcome, Mr. Presley. Thank you for being here.

Elvis Presley: It's my pleasure.

JH: You yourself—that is, Elvis, the singer-songwriter—were inducted into the Rock and Roll Hall of Fame last year, twenty-nine years after your first solo album [applause] but I want to start by talking just a bit about you and your brother, about the Presley Brothers. As a duo, you were in that very first group of musicians inducted into the Hall of Fame in 1986. Bob Dylan, speaking at your induction, said when he first heard the Presley Brothers, "it felt like busting out of jail." Fats Domino, also in that first group, called you and your brother "the Kings."

EP: I'll tell you who the kings of rock and roll are, it's those guys we heard growing up, those black singers we took after. It's Arthur Crudup, and all the rest.

JH: Arthur Crudup was a well-known black musician in Memphis, is that right? You heard him sing in the blues clubs there?

EP: Yes sir, we did. If I ever got to the place where I could feel all that old Arthur felt, I'd be a rocker like nobody ever saw.

JH: Little Richard, who was inducted in that same group with you and your brother, has said that the Presley Brothers opened the door for black music, allowed black musicians to make it into the mainstream. But there have been a few critics over the years who've accused you and your brother of "stealing" black music.

EP: Well, we did steal it, I guess. It was the music we liked to listen to, and we liked to sing it, if that's stealing. Rock and roll is just rhythm and blues, or it sprung from that, mixed up with old-timey country music, hillbilly music, and we always tried to show respect for all those artists we listened to when we were kids.

JH: The Everly Brothers were also inducted into the Hall of

Fame that year. You and your brother are most often compared to the Everlys, and I wonder what you think of that comparison, what differences or similarities you see.

EP: Well, it's what they always used to say, we were the rowdy boys and they were the good boys. [laughter] No, all of us come out of the country tradition some way or other, but I would say Don and Phil stayed closer to it than we did. They could get to rocking pretty hard, but it was always with a steel-string guitar, strumming or fingerpicking, kind of a bluegrass instrumentation, and that tight, melodic vocal harmony. I guess we took it more toward a backbeat-heavy R and B. We got away from stacked harmonies into kind of a raw, slurred vocal style. And we always jiggled around a bit more than they did. [laughter, applause] But you know, rock and roll is a big old tent and there's plenty of room in it for all of us. We were big fans of the Everlys.

JH: After you were discharged from the Army, you and your brother only briefly performed as a duo and then split up. Would you talk about that?

EP: Well, that's been talked about till the cows come home.

JH: But if I may say so, not very often by you. You spent two years in the Army, which some of your biographers have said was the beginning of your split. I wonder if you could start by just saying a little about that, about being out of the music business for so long, separated from your brother both musically and physically for the first time in your lives.

EP: Well, you know, I got a draft notice and Jesse didn't. The Memphis Draft Board had a lot of leeway in those days, and people say they were trying to split us up, that they thought we were a bad influence on their children. We never did see how any type of music could have a bad influence on people when it's only music, but we did think maybe my going into the Army would be the end of our career. RCA had us into the studio to record some songs to put onto the radio while I was gone, and then Jesse kept on touring, paired up with different fellows, Little Richard, Bill Haley, Jerry Lee Lewis, which the Colonel billed as Jesse Presley and Friends. So it worked out all right.

JH: Ten of the songs you recorded together before you went into the Army hit the top of the charts while you were away.

EP: Well, you know Jesse had some hits too, singing solo. "Hard-Headed Woman," that was his. And he had made that one picture while I was over there in Germany—

JH: *King Creole.*

EP: Yes sir. And a couple of hits came from that.

JH: And when you came out of the Army you and Jesse made only the one album together before you each went off to separate careers.

EP: Well, he enjoyed making that picture, and he wanted to get into making more movies. There's not much call for identical twins in the movies [laughter], and I guess we had used up about all the ideas they had for it when we made that first one.

JH: *Double Trouble.*

EP: Yes sir, that's the one. So Jesse started making movies, and sometimes, you know, it would interfere with our recording schedule and our touring schedule. So after a while we just each of us went our own way.

JH: It was amicable?

EP: Yes sir, it was.

JH: Is there anything more you're willing to say about the breakup?

EP: No sir, that's pretty much all I want to say about it.

JH: Nothing about Priscilla or—

EP: No sir, that's all I will say.

JH: You broke up in 1961. Your brother made twenty-seven movies in the 1960s, almost three a year, which most critics have said were no more than vehicles for soundtrack albums. There were some good songs in the first few movies but it seemed like they were more and more a watering down of the music that had made the Presley Brothers so famous. And in those same years, you were out there playing small town clubs and fairs, very small venues. Colonel Parker had to stop managing your career to focus on your brother, and you weren't recording at all. So each of you in your different ways had fallen from the heights, so to speak. Were you in touch with Jesse during that time?

EP: We were in touch, yes sir. But I want to say something else about Jesse's movies, and about his not being at the heights. You know they offered him Jon Voight's part in *Midnight Cowboy*, but Fox was making quite a bit of money off those other pictures, and they had him locked into them.

JH: I didn't know that.

EP: *West Side Story* is another one that was offered to him, back when we first split up. But he had that contract with Hal Wallis and he couldn't get out of it.

JH: Did you and Jesse talk about the track your careers were on? Did you talk about getting back together? Jesse's movies were making money, but was he concerned about what had happened to his music? And were you concerned that you might never have a solo song make it onto the charts?

EP: Jesse always said, "I'm making these silly movies so you can go off and be a poet."

JH: A poet?

EP: I had started to write songs, that's what he meant by being a poet.

JH: He said he was making movies so you could write songs?

EP: It was something like that, yes sir. It seemed like everybody was focused on him, and they were pretty much leaving me alone, and he'd say, well, you need the quiet so you can work on your writing.

JH: Of course eventually he did get away from, as you say, those silly movies. He started touring, he had a whole other career in the seventies, filling those big arenas, and by then you were beginning to record again, singing your own songs, you went down a very different path from your brother's. And you are now, along with Bob Dylan, Paul Simon, maybe Leonard Cohen, often mentioned as one of rock and roll's first generation of singer-songwriters.

[silence]

EP: I don't know if you're asking me a question. [laughter]

JH: [laughing] I guess I'm not. Well, I will just say that "poetry" is not a bad way to describe the songs you write. Even when the melodies are simple the lyrics are complex; sometimes, to my ear, opaque. You've written quite a lot about loneliness and separation, death and loss, about drug use, about faith and religion, you've written about the toll taken by celebrity. I don't want to say all your songs are dark, but even your love songs are shaded with something I would call worry, or maybe yearning, or regret.

EP: That's the blues, I guess. There's joy in the blues, but it's always a little bit sad, a little bit shaded—that's a good word—with worry, with regret. That's where my music comes from, the blues. That's where we started, Jesse and me.

JH: The "white nights" in blues clubs, as I've heard you say in interviews. But I want to get back to how things changed for you when you became Elvis, just Elvis. You made a comeback as a solo act and then you won several Grammys—

EP: We both did. Jesse had three.

JH: He did, yes. Not for rock and roll, but he did win in the spiritual category.

EP: It was gospel that we loved before anything, growing up. He was always proud of those albums.

JH: I think you know Dave Hilbrun? I heard him saying the other day that Jesse Presley was the greatest white gospel singer of his time. That he was the last rock and roll artist to make gospel a vital part of his music. But let's shift gears now, and before we run out of time I want to ask you about who is on your list of favorite singers. You have often talked about the old blues singers, but who is it you admire among your peers, your contemporaries?

EP: Oh, that's a long list. A real long list. [pause] Well, I'll just tell you to listen to Roy Orbison. He gets up there on those high notes and he doesn't back off, he doesn't go soft like most of us do, he takes it high and sings it stronger than he does in his natural voice. Nobody else does that. And he writes some great songs, great storytelling, so much nuance of emotion.

JH: You've sung with Roy Orbison.

EP: I met Roy the first time back in 1955 when Jesse and I were just getting started, when we were all just kids. And later on, when Roy and I were both living in Tennessee we hung out some. He had lost his wife and two of his kids, you know, in terrible accidents, different accidents, his boys drowned in a swimming pool and his wife was in a motorcycle crash. This was after Jesse had passed, and we were both interested in spiritual matters, we talked quite a bit about what it all means, the purpose of our lives and all, what death means, we were both trying to find some insight, I guess you could say. And then I hooked up with Roy again in the late eighties, and one time we were jamming in his basement with George Harrison when Bob Dylan come by and he wanted to sing with us but he had left his guitar over at Tom Petty's, so we trooped over there to get his guitar and Tom came back with us. We had a pretty good time singing each other's songs, so then we made a record together and did a little bit of touring—

JH: The Traveling Wilburys.

EP: Yes sir. Roy died just about the time we were bringing out our second album. So that was it for the Wilburys.

JH: Well, now I have to ask: Where do you go from here? When you're at the top, what does the future look like to you?

EP: My brother always said there wasn't any such thing as the future really, it was just now and now and now. He got that from the Buddhists. And I know there's no top to any of it, to life or to music. So I'm just trying to be here now. Trying to stay sane. Trying to be a decent husband and father. Trying to make good music. But I know that's not what you're asking me, you want to know what I'm doing these days. I guess what I've been doing is reading through some letters Jesse wrote to me. You were saying earlier, about the two of us being separated from each other that first time, but we wrote back and forth every day while I was over there in Germany. The only day we didn't write is the day we buried Momma. And after I got back we just went on writing, we wrote even on the days when we were sitting right there in the same room.

JH: It's hard to picture what you'd find to write about when you were both in the same room.

EP: We wrote just as if the other one wasn't there. I would write, "Jesse sounded good at rehearsal today," and he'd write, "Elvis is sitting here fixing a broken string on his guitar."

JH: Like keeping a diary almost.

EP: It was. And we copied down things we were reading, things we wanted to share with each other. When I started writing songs I'd send them to him and ask him what he thought. And he'd do the same.

JH: Jesse was writing songs?

EP: He said he was just writing what was in his mind. But sometimes I'd take what he was saying, put in some line breaks and maybe take out the little words, you know, to show him how he was writing poems, same as me. But he never thought so.

JH: Have you saved them all? You have twenty years of letters in a box somewhere?

EP: I still write to Jesse every day, so I guess it's more than forty years of letters now, and I know he's still writing to me, from wherever he is. I just haven't seen those yet.

JH: That's astonishing. Forty years, writing every day. That's a lot of letters.

EP: I've been reading through them, which I can tell you is taking quite a while. [laughter] I want to put some of them into a book.

JH: How are you choosing which ones to include? Will you be telling the story of your lives?

EP: No, no, it'll be Jesse's poems, that's what I'm doing. I'm looking for the ones where he's talking about what's in his mind, and then I'm trying to put them on the page so you can see they're poems.

JH: Have you thought of putting any of them to music? Making them into songs?

EP: I have thought of it. We'll see what happens.

JH: Well, Elvis, thank you. I would like to keep on talking. I feel like there's a lot we haven't touched on, but we always want to have a Q and A session with the audience before we finish, and I'm afraid we've already gone on so long, we've only got time for three or four questions. Those of you with questions for Mr. Presley, there's microphones up front here, at the top of both aisles, so come on up and we'll get started.

Q1: Hello, Mr. Presley.

EP: Hello.

Q1: Mr. Presley, would you talk about your interest in karate?

EP: I met up with karate in the Army. I liked what it had to say about tapping into your inner strength. The preciousness of the *chi* life force, the power of restraint, of stillness and concentration. I felt like I could apply some of that to my singing, and later on to my song writing and recording. I still practice it. And tai chi. I do tai chi on the days when I'm feeling too old and crackly for karate. [laughter]

Q2: Mr. Presley, I love your song "Losing You." But honestly, I don't know what it means. Could you say what it means?

EP: [singing softly] Only when I think past memory, past distance, in all the ways I learned to miss you, call to you beneath my breath, whisper in the language of children, then I think you can hear me, silence recognizes the silence it calls to, this grammar of longing, a book lying open as twilight deepens, and shadows cover the gray pages.

[silence] [applause]

EP: I'm sorry, honey, what was your question now? [laughter]

Q2: I just wondered what it means. It's just so sad.

EP: Well, I guess it just means that. It means sad.

Q3: Hey. Thanks for taking my question, Elvis.

EP: Sure. Have I heard it yet? [laughter]

Q3: Well, not to be mean or anything, but your brother pretty much went downhill there at the end, he had all these fans but they were like all these blue-haired grand-mothers, like he was Liberace or something, he was bloated and drugged, a joke. And then there's you, with this serious reputation and all. Do you feel like commenting on how two men with the same DNA wound up so different, having these different lives?

EP: No sir, I don't feel like commenting on that at all.

Q3: If you—

JH: Well, I think we just have time for one more question. Miss? Over on the left.

Q4: Mr. Presley, I guess I have two questions. Do you have a title for the book, the one with Jesse's letters? And could you tell us one of the poems you made from his writing, if you can remember any?

EP: I guess I've been calling the book *The Foreseeable Future*, from something he wrote to me once. I won't tell you that one, but here's one I think I can remember:

> I come awake this morning
> So damn early
> Barest gray between the blinds

Heard geese calling
Wild, unruly, keen.
This is January.
Are they going south so late
Or already turning north?
Afraid to know
Which it was
I went on lying still
Didn't open the blinds
Listened to my heart in my ears.
If there is a purpose
To me being Jesse Presley
I wonder what it is.
Then I had this worn old thought:
That time is a river
The past not finished yet.
I once was lost
But still upstream
My absence
Not yet met.

[silence]

EP: I think always of you waiting, brother. I will look for you
when I get there.

[prolonged applause]

*From Annie Leibovitz at Work, discussing her iconic photograph
of the Presley Brothers—last known photo of the brothers together—
taken the evening of August 11, 1977, five days before Jesse Presley's
death at age forty-two:*

This was taken while I was on assignment for *Rolling Stone*, shooting Elvis Presley at the start of his "Way Down in the Heart" tour. We were backstage before the first concert at the Keller Auditorium in Portland, Oregon, when his brother Jesse came in unannounced. He had flown up from Memphis on a momentary impulse just to wish his brother a good show, and he flew back the same night. He usually went around with a large entourage but that night there were just two men with him, and they stood back and watched us all in silence. (Their shoes are dimly visible at the left edge of frame.)

I took several dozen shots that night during the few minutes the brothers were together. While I was shooting, I was struck by how different the brothers looked from each other, not like twins, certainly not identical twins, and I thought I was capturing the different ways they had lived their lives, and how it showed in their faces. But afterward, I saw what the camera had seen: how alike their expressions were—a kind of tender regard, as if each thought the other was the one needing safeguarding.

Seaborne

THERE WERE TWO PEOPLE WORKING from a raft near the breakwater, and although Neye thought they could see him come over the dune and now could see him standing against the skyline, they made no greeting and certainly made no move to come in.

It was all low sand hills along that coast, with a tough umber-colored salt grass trying to stitch everything down against the wind. Finally Neye just sat on the last seaward rise of the dunes—high enough there to see across the roofs of the buildings to the cove—and waited, watching them.

They took turns. When one's head bobbed up beside the raft, the other would pitch over the side, then the one who had come up would sit on the raft or lie on it until the other diver came up again. They were down four or five minutes at a time. From this distance, he couldn't tell which of them might be male, which female; their bodies were both brown and narrow and naked above the waist. He couldn't see a power source either, but the

raft moved gradually south, self-directed, beside the elbow bend
of the breakwater.

He waited quite a while. It was hot and there was no shade,
and the grass scratched through his sleeves whenever he leaned
back on his forearms. The sun fell behind him, and the rounded
shadows of the dunes spread out flatter and began to darken
the water. When the edge of shade touched the raft, the divers
quit. Both of them lay awhile, stretched on their backs on the
fiberglass decking, and then they took the little motor skiff
that was tied alongside and came in with it, sliding silently
past the big two-masted bylander lying at anchor in the deeps
of the cove. Gradually, as Neye watched, one began to show the
long, thin back muscles of an adolescent boy. And the other
became a woman. Her breasts were small and high as a girl's,
but her hair, which must once have been black, was grizzled.
She wore her hair—both of them did—clipped short in a manner common to offshore farmers, so short it looked like a tight
little cap.

When the bottom of the skiff bumped the beach, Neye had
already started down toward them. His knees were a little stiffened from the long walk and then the long wait, so he was careful how he set his feet, pushing his boots heel-down through
the long straps of grass to the sand. He kept his eyes, though,
on the woman. She went over the side and hauled in the boat
while the boy was still at the tiller, and then she stood a moment
with the sea lapping her ankles, stood flexing her back with
both hands kneading some ache there above the tailbone. She
was small, her hands, her shoulders, the narrow bones of her
face, small. But there was lean muscle in her arms and in the
bare calves that showed below her knee pants.

She steadied the boat a little with both hands while the boy climbed out, and then they dragged the skiff up the sand toward the tide line. Neye was near enough by that time, so he came down and grabbed hold of the gunwale and helped them with it the last little way. The boy shot him a look, curious at least, or maybe guardedly friendly, but the woman neither looked toward him nor said anything. When they pulled the boat up to the edge of the grass, she reached in for what could have been a sack bunched up below one of the seats. She shook it out and pulled it over her head: a long loose tunic the color of the sand. Against that paleness her throat and wrists seemed nut-brown. She dragged out a couple of boxes of gear, too, while the boy was pulling on his own shirt, and then she simply walked away, from Neye and from the boy as well, without a word or a look, just grasping the boxes by their handles and starting up the slope toward the buildings.

Neye thought to follow her. But he could feel the boy looking at him straightforward, now that the woman was gone, and so he waited. It seemed to him, among other things, that this would be an easier place to start.

"You walked in?" the boy said.

Neye had left the Osprey in Bedyn. Maybe there would have been room to land it here, maybe not, but most of these offshore farmers affected a sort of contempt of aircraft. When they could not go by boat, they went by foot. And he hadn't wanted to provoke her by setting down in her front yard in a big government flyer.

"Yes," he said. "I walked."

"From Bedyn?"

"Yes." It was supposed to be about nine or ten kilometers.

It had seemed a little more than that to Neye, but fairly easy walking: low rises and a smooth beaten track and—for a while at least—the shade of the seaward dunes to break the sun.

The boy lifted his head up a little and sideways, as though he had looked away, but in fact he kept his eyes on Neye. He had a wide face, large-pored and reddish brown, like terra-cotta. His hair was reddish too, or maybe the sun had colored it so. Though he was very young, there were little pleats in the skin beside his eyes. There was nothing about him that was like Cirant, only the boyish thinness, yet looking at him, Neye thought of his own son. And he was aware briefly of his own chronic loneliness.

"She doesn't like itinerants much," the boy said, with that disarming sideways stare. "If you want to spend more than a day or so, you'll do better farther up the coast. Even there you might not find anything steady. We've all had three shitty years in a row."

It would have been easy to play it that way—to pretend to be what he was not. But he doubted it would get him any further than the truth. So he said, "I'm not looking for work. I'm with Registry."

It had been more than five years since anyone from the department had come out here. But somebody had told the boy. Lisel herself, or somebody. Because he looked at Neye straight this time, with a hardened, narrow expression, and then he just walked off after the woman, going barefoot along the path that was worn down between the cove and the farm buildings.

Neye wasn't much surprised and didn't try to stop him. He went back for his duffel, to the place he'd dropped it on the beach when he had helped them push the skiff up. And then he followed where the two of them had gone.

All the buildings were cheap extruded dobes, so they looked like big stones or terrapins hunched down among the dunes. Through the wall of the largest, he could feel a slight vibration as if it housed a freezer silo, or, more likely, a set of nursery tanks. He stood beside it a moment, delaying, because he wasn't sure which building they'd gone into. The air was cooler now and darkening, and he was alone. Then the woman came from a small dobe at his right, no longer carrying the boxes of gear, her hands pushed in a pouch pocket in the front of her shirt.

He could see that she meant to walk by him without speaking. He did not reach out a hand nor make any motion to stop her, only said, "I'm not looking for work. I'm with the Registry department."

She kept going. There was only a little surprise in the side-long look she gave him. "You should have done some checking before you walked all the way out here. Jin is legally psy-blind."

To her retreating back, he said, "I didn't come to talk to Jin."

She didn't stop, didn't turn, but she made a loud nasal sound of amusement. "You still need to do some research. I've never scored higher than eight hundred on any of your many head tests."

He had been standing in one place watching her walk away from him, but she had said enough to set him in motion. He followed her through the brown dusk to the house. "Not everything gets picked up in those neurological tests."

She made only that sound again, that small hard sound like a laugh. When she stooped into her house, the light came up dim yellow. There was one round room with a bite out of it where the bathroom took up space along the outer wall. The room was crowded and cluttered. Neye stood just outside the doorless air-portal, waiting, while she went out of sight into the lavatory. And after a while, still waiting, he squatted down in the open doorway.

Probably she showered. Her hair was wet again and combed down smooth against her scalp when she finally came out.

He thought if he had not been there watching from her doorstep, she would have eaten now. But she would not offer him food, and could not prepare and eat it before him. So, stubbornly, she began to pick at the room, making incomplete, indifferent tidying motions among the remains of her breakfast.

There was no point in waiting. "In Bedyn, they say you are a healer."

She was turned more than halfway from Neye, so he could see only a part of the side of her face. He could see the small muscles of her jaw, but they did not tighten at all. After a long time, with a slight sideways glance of disgust or impatience, she said, "Then the people of Bedyn are imbeciles."

"You deny it?"

She turned her head all the way round to him, gave him an unwavering stare. "In Bedyn they say people who work for Registry can read minds." And then she was the one who waited, watching him. If there was any fear under there, it was damn well secured. He could feel only the smooth, hard shimmer of her armor.

He smiled just a little, as though he was faintly tired of an old canard. "I don't read minds," he said. "Your scores are almost as high as mine. So you'll have to tell me if you are or are not a healer, I won't be able to pick it out of your brain."

There was no change in her face. But after a while he could feel her deciding to believe him. She looked away a little and said, "I've never seen anyone healed of anything just by the laying on of hands."

It was not a lie, only a careful choosing of words.

"I'm asking if you are a healer."

Without hesitation, but also without looking toward him, she shook her head, one hard, hostile denial. "No," she said. "I cannot heal."

"There's a scar on the inside of Jin's wrist." He had thought that would make her look round again. But she picked up a dish, scraped a bit of flat cake—shellfish, he thought, or seaweed— and the rind of a tiwit fruit into the garbage before she looked in his direction. She'd had time, he thought, to discover that look of weary impatience.

"A banguii ripped him with a pincer." That was all she said.

"The scar is very clean. Did you take him to Bedyn, to one of the meds there?"

"It closed up well," she said, and then for the second time looked straight at Neye with that sort of daring stare. "I gave him an antibiotic and a pressure bandage. That was the only magic."

Deliberately she looked around the room. But she made no move toward the two or three dirty plates or the cherar, gelled and cold in a dish on the table. Instead, in a moment, she kicked a pallet out flat and dimmed the light and then stood a moment above her bed, looking toward him in the near darkness. "I don't suppose you plan to walk back in the dark. But don't try to sleep in any of my buildings. I'm up before dawn and I expect you to be gone by then."

"I'll stay a little longer than that," Neye said. He tried to say it gently, without much defiance.

She straightened but for a while said nothing. Then: "You have a permit to trespass."

"Yes."

"I want to see it."

"It's not case-specific. It's inclusive."

"I want to see it."

He did not argue. He said, "You'll have to show me to a comp."

She went past him out into the yard, and he followed her to another dobe, an office, where she waited behind him while he sat and wrote his request into the desk. His number and his name came silently on the screen, and then the permit codes one after the other, blinking on in rows. In a moment she said, "There is evidently little that you have not permission to do." She said it with no surprise, just a kind of sourness that was not directed at him.

He did not turn toward her.

"I want a hard copy of the permit to trespass," she said. She made it sound simple, straightforward, without the whine of its barren gesture. He touched a key and a thin leaf of paper pushed out of the slot below the screen. She reached to take it, folded it once, and then, without interest, laid it on the desktop.

He was watching her now, sitting in the office chair but half-turned from the comp and leaning back on one elbow.

She said, "I don't know what you intend. To catch me in the act? You could wait years here and not see a medical emergency, we both know that, and I don't think Registry has that kind of perseverance. You could make your own emergency, but I don't think they'd let you cut somebody's throat just to test me." She waited, as if the last part had been a question.

He said, "I'll just try to persuade you to stop hiding a scarce gift."

She seemed careful not to frown, to speak without even much curiosity. "You are so certain, then, that I'm lying."

He dipped his chin a little and in a moment raised it so he was looking at her squarely. "Pretty certain," he said, but again gently, without malice.

She stared at him. Finally she said, "I won't feed you. I won't let you sleep in any of my buildings. I have that right."

"Yes."

She looked at him a little longer and then turned and went out ahead of him, back to her house. When he reached the doorway, she already lay on her side on the pallet with her back to him. He waited several minutes. He could hear her breathing and he was certain she was not sleeping, but when he spoke to her, when he said, "Lisel," there was no reply. So finally he left.

In the late dusk, now that Lisel had put out hers, there was only one light showing. He went to it. The boy, Jin, made his quarters there in a toolshed behind a stack of plastic shipping crates. Unlike Lisel's, this space was bare and clean and the light was clear. If he had eaten, the dishes were already picked up, because now he sat on his pallet leaning back to the dobe wall with a sheaf of hard copy pressed against his updrawn thighs. He raised his face to Neye as he came round the edge of the crates, then rather pointedly turned his attention back to the papers.

"I'd like to talk to you."

The boy didn't look up. But in a moment he said, "You need to talk to Lisel, I think. I'm only an apprentice."

"I want to talk to you, too. Can I sit down?"

He kept reading. After quite a while he said, "Suit yourself."

Neye put his duffel on the floor and sat beside it. For a while he watched the boy read from the bundle of thin pages. It was a slow way to take in information, but there was no sign of an auvid here, and he hadn't seen one in Lisel's place either. All their money was tied up in good farm equipment—the big computerized raft, the late-model bylander, the rearing tanks humming inside that largest dobe. It was a fairly common set of priorities among the ruralists. If there was money left over, they bought food—seaweed cakes and tewit maybe—certainly not auvids.

"How long have you worked for Lisel?"

The boy kept his eyes on the print. "Four years."

"You were pretty young, then."

"I was twelve."

"How far did you get with the EDT?"

He glanced up at Neye. "I didn't drop out. I finished early."

"At twelve?"

"Yes."

"Marine husbandry?"

"Invertebrate biology."

Neye let his eyebrow slide up a little, let the boy see he was surprised, impressed. Hell, he was impressed.

"So how come you're here? There's a lot more money in research. And less risk."

"There are risks in the lab, they're just different. The wages are good out here too, just a different currency." It ought to have been a cliché. But the boy spoke quietly, matter-of-factly, so that it sounded only true. And it was at that point Neye began to take him more seriously. He may have been young and psy-blind, but apparently he wasn't simple.

In a moment Neye said, "You'll Master within the year, then. By that time Teath should be opened up to homesteaders. There's some good coastline there, I've seen the prospectus."

Jin smiled, holding up the pages in his hand, shaking them as they spread and fluttered winglike over his grip. "I've seen it too," he said. "Lisel got me the hard copy." And in a moment, with a slight lifting of his chin, "It doesn't look that good to me."

Neye thought, before he said, "You seem to work well together. You and Lisel. Will you just stay here? Partner?"

Jin made a wordless grunting sound that was not yes or no. He pretended again to read the papers.

"You must be pliant. Working with her even this long. She strikes me as pretty rock-ribbed."

"You don't know anything about it." Jin didn't look up and there was no anger in his voice, just a faint raspy impatience.

Neye waited briefly. "She's a healer," he said then, without making it quite a question.

Now Jin's head came all the way up. There was a horizontal crease at the bridge of his nose, joining his brows in a single line. "Those people in Bedyn are harassing her again." His wasn't a question either.

Neye was neutral, patient, persistent. "Registry says they get eight or ten complaints every year. They're not all from Bedyn."

The boy's face had reddened. "They're all from hypochondriacs and neurotics."

There was a weighted silence. Neye could feel the boy grappling with his agitation. It wasn't quite anger, or at least that wasn't all of it.

"The rumors started somewhere," Neye said.

"Sure. Her grandmother was a healer." Jin gave him that

shying sideward look of his. "You'd know that," he said, so there was no place to fit a denial. "It's supposed to skip generations, right? And Lisel is"—his eyes jumped down, then up again—"a private person. So every time some kid sticks a hand in a reaper and bleeds to death before the ambulance can get there, somebody says that damn reclusive bitch, Lisel, could have saved him."

No blood had been spilled when Cirant died. But something in what Jin had said, maybe just "kid" and "death" together in the same line, made Neye see suddenly, fleetingly, the face of his son. And raised in him an obscure irritability.

He let Jin sit silently for quite a while. Then finally he said, "There's only one clinic in Bedyn. You must know that. Two medics and one apprentice and one ambulance with an out-dated robomed. Over a hundred thousand square kilometers of farmshore and inland ranches. Eight thousand people—"

"I know what you're getting at," Jin said, shifting his weight on the pallet, looking impatiently at Neye and then away again.

Neye stiffened his tone of voice slightly. He said, "Just a minute. I want to finish this," and then he was silent while he waited for the boy's eyes to come around to him. "If Lisel has a healing gift, she's required by law to register it with the local Med team. Maybe someplace else, or under other circumstances, it wouldn't be very important. Probably Registry wouldn't have sent anybody out the first time, let alone the third. But here, yes, it's important. And there's something more at stake than just compliance with the law. That is what I'm getting at."

He fell silent again, briefly, but he was still looking at Jin. Then he said, "Did she heal your wrist?"

The boy put both hands in his lap so the rise of his knees hid them from Neye. Maybe he was rubbing the white scar along the inside of his wrist. He was steady now, not restless anymore, but there was, again, a deep crosswise crease at the bridge of his nose, a frown. "She dressed it, yes," he said. "There was no laying on of hands, if that's what you mean. I'm sorry for it, but those people won't find any help for their problem here." And then with only a little shift of tension to betray him, the earnest lie: "Because Lisel isn't gifted. She's not a healer."

She came silently and alone from her house into the thin darkness before sunrise. The sky hung down in shaggy ribbons, low and lead-colored and damp. She pulled her arms inside the sleeves of her shirt and padded soundlessly to the nursery building with her breath pluming out white in front of her and then scattering around her shoulders as she walked through it. Neye watched her from the rise of dune behind the house, sitting hunched on the grass where it had been beaten down under his little khirtz tent. There was no light yet in the shed, no sign of Jin, and it occurred to him that Lisel had reserved the cottony quiet, the grayness, the solitude of these dawns for herself.

When she came out again from the nursery, the sky had lightened but the opaque fog filled all the distances. There was no seeing the rocky headlands of the cove nor even the bylander anchored between those fleshless arms. She stood a moment looking out toward the smoky water and then went over the rise toward the tide pond. She went in bare feet, bare calves, through the grass that was bent over heavy with wet and chill. The tide was out, the pond a dark smudge, muddy, crosshatched with posts and rails, maybe waiting for a new batch of young mollusks to graduate from the settling tank in the nursery.

Neye watched her take tools from a little cachebox near the

ingress pipe and squat on her heels in the mud in front of the orifice. She was retiling around the opening. He watched her quite a while. She worked slowly, with care, chipping out the broken pieces round the mouth and then fitting the new ones, mortaring them in carefully so there was a smooth, clean lip at the opening. When she finished, she stepped back to the edge of the wet sand and looked across at her work. In some places there had been no tiles broken at all, at others one or two or three deep into the conduit. The older tiles were dark, the new ones stark white, so even from his distance Neye could see the abstract pattern, the notching line going around the circle of the opening. Lisel stepped back across the mud, squatted again, and felt all around the aperture with the tips of her fingers. Watching her, Neye could almost feel with his own hands the utter smoothness. The only irregularity would be the one presented to the eye, light butting against dark. Under her fingertips the tiles would make a seamless whole, a ring.

She stood again and stowed away the tools and then wiped her damp palms on her trousers. He would like to have seen her face, to know if the tiling—both doing it and seeing it done—had softened the lines around her mouth.

She walked out along the sunken mark of the conduit between the crouching dunes to the shoreline of the cove. With the tide out, the cobb racks stood above the water, algae-dark, crusted and knobby with adult mollusks. Jin was there on the dark mud flats beside the piers. He had come down, with his shoulders hunched and his face bleary with sleep, while Lisel worked at the pond ingress. Now he had the mop lying on its face with the back off, was tightening or untightening something in the motor.

Lisel said a couple of words. From a distance they were only blurred sounds, indistinct, but they had not the inflection of a greeting. Perhaps a question. Jin spoke a wordless grunting sound in reply. He didn't lift his head. Lisel went past him to the cobb racks, began to stride up and down between the vertical rows of lattice. They ranged parallel to the shore so the first row had its footings in the mud, the last knee-deep in the sea. She went between them, one after the other, wading finally to her hips in the water along the far rack. Probably, while the tide was low, she looked for the little infectious shell lesions that could bring a cobb crop to ruin.

She began to wade back along the ends of the racks, pushing long-legged through the water so it raised a white surf against her thighs. Jin was standing now, watching the mop move up the first row to scour the bottom sand for predators and parasites, but she did not look toward him or the machine. She lifted her face so that she seemed to look up straight and sudden to Neye. He was too far from her to see her eyes. In a moment she looked away.

He spent a good part of the morning working his way along the rocks on the southern headland to its point, and from there he could see the bubblefence that closed the mouth of the cove. Evidently that was what they were inspecting or repairing, diving as before, alternately, from the raft just inside the fence line.

The wind was cold and wet and there was no seeing the north end of the breakwater through the rags of low fog. Cautiously, he went a little way out on the jetty, stepping with care along the top of the narrow wall and then finally sitting on it with his feet hanging on the inland side and his back to the open ocean. The raft crept steadily from the north end of the fence toward the southern, and if he stayed where he was they would eventually work within a few meters of him. For now, from where he sat, he could see the first stroke or two of their arms, the scissoring of their legs, when they went into the water.

The two of them seemed not to notice that the weather had changed. They wore again only their knee pants and lay alternately on the raft as though the sun warmed its plastic decking. The water would be temperate, but Neye found little solace in that: he sat uncomfortably on the breakwater, hunching his back against the chill overspray of surf breaking high and white on the seawall behind him.

Neither Jin nor Lisel looked toward him. But if there was annoyance or furtiveness in the woman, he could not see it. They simply, steadily worked south along the fence line as if he were not there above them, watching. Infrequently they spoke, but only to one another. There would have been no hearing it anyway, over the noise of the surf, but sometimes from the shape of their mouths he knew a word or two, knew they spoke of the perforated pipe strung below them on the seafloor, the red keefish, one tool or another. He did not see his own name spoken. Once, maybe, Jin asked if she was hungry and she shook her head, spraying beads of water from the bristly ends of her hair.

Probably it was close to the way they worked when they were alone. But they did not smile, never touched except to clasp hands hauling one another up onto the raft. And he had a sense of that much being false, a closed face they were turning to him. They were not lovers, but there was comfortableness between them, a familiarity that was love, or at least affection, and he thought Lisel was trying to protect that from him. As if it were a frailty he would exploit. Maybe it was Jin's throat she thought he would cut.

There was no shadow of the sun this time to end their day. In a smoky dusk they worked until they finished, following the fence line all the way to the rocky headland. When the raft bumped its nose against the crags, they quit and lay together as they had the day before, stretched on their backs, while the flatboat rocked under them in a wet wind.

Neye climbed back along the seawall to the point of the cape and stood just above the raft awhile, watching them. But he was cold and stiff and finally he started back, picking a way along the stony foreland to the beach. He was careful. In the wet darkening, among the broken rocks, he found a place for each step before he let his weight down on it.

Once, he stood a moment and looked back at Lisel, while he waited for some of the tautness to go out of his shoulders. She and the boy were stowing gear in the skiff now. From this distance, in the vague light, they both seemed frail and young, their movements thickened by weariness. He imagined he saw a little of Cirant, again, in the boy's thin shape silhouetted against the water.

He began again to climb down and in toward the beach, toward the dark curve of sand where the tide, withdrawing, had left an erratic line of spume and seaweed. He steadied himself with his hands. The stones under his palms were cold and slick.

He didn't fall until he was at the edge of the beach. He jumped the last little way from the rock, and his heel came down flat and then skewed sideways off some turtleback stone there under the skin of sand. There was a blur of darkened shapes and the sky sliding high up, tinted red through the lens of his pain, and then the grit of sand in his mouth. He held his knee with both hands, curling around it on his side with his cheek against the ground. He lay staring out at the sea, breathing carefully and holding his body very still and staring out at the low sky and the water under it, leaden in the darkness. He held his knee tightly with both hands.

After a while someone came. He felt the slight rasp of feet on the sand, saw a bare foot and then Jin, bending to see him.

"You fell." Not a question. In the darkness, the wind raised the boy's hair so it made a soft russet crown around his head.

Neye pushed sand out of his mouth with his tongue. When he could, he said, "Okay. Be okay. Minute."

Jin squatted near him. His hand reached for Neye's knee.

"Don't! Touch!"

The boy rocked back on his haunches, folded his arms on his chest, across the long yellow tunic blotched with wetness. "You might have broken something."

"No. Did'n' break." He had slipped the knee once before. He thought he should say that. To explain. But it was too many words to push out of his chest. He wanted to close his eyes. But the boy was still there, watching.

"You look pretty pale," Jin said, and inside his skull Neye could feel the light wordless sing of the boy's compassion.

He held his knee tightly and pushed himself with his left arm to sit. With his teeth clamped down hard against the sound he might have made. In a while he was able to say, "Go on back. I'm okay." He thought he said it all right. The faint high whine was in the front of his head, behind his eyes.

The boy made no move to go. He squatted watching, with his eyebrows cramped together. Behind him, the skiff was drawn up a little way on the sand. And beyond that, a hundred meters back along the rock shore, Lisel squatted waiting on the raft. She did not look toward them. She sat on her heels with her arms clasped round her knees while she looked out at the water.

Maybe the boy saw him looking. He said, "She thought maybe it was . . . a ruse or something. You understand?"

Neye squeezed his hand carefully against his leg and then bent the knee slightly, testing, putting a little weight on the heel of his foot. Then he swung his good leg under him and rose to that knee, with the other leg extended stiffly out.

"Can I help you?" Jin was standing again, but bent over him with his palms on his thighs.

"No."

He pushed up hard on the good knee, with the heel of his other foot braced against the ground. He almost made it up. But the dark sky slipped off sideways and he felt Jin's hands taking hold of him, buttressing him as he tottered. Neye leaned against the boy and waited until the line of the sea came level.

"Thanks," he said, when his breathing had leveled out too. He made as if to stand away, but the boy's hands gripped him tightly.

"I'll help you to the boat."

He took in a breath carefully, so it made no sound. "No. I just slipped the knee. It'll loosen up. If I walk on it."

Jin let go with one hand so he could push the wet red hair back from his forehead. With his other hand he continued to hold Neye's arm. "You're in a lot of pain," he said. "Don't let Lisel . . ."

"Go on back," Neye said. He looked down at the beach, past

the skiff and the raft and the woman, to the headland bulking dark against the horizon.

Jin let his hand drop from Neye. "I'm sorry about her. She just . . ." He made a loose gesture as if, with that, he explained something.

"Go on back." Neye was squeezing his thigh with one hand but he thought he was standing pretty straight. He just did not quite put all his weight on the leg. Not while the boy was there.

After a while Jin said, "Okay." But it was a little while more before he went away, pushing the skiff so it grated quietly off the sand.

Neye took a step. And again. He was sweating softly, grinding his teeth. Behind him, he heard Jin and then Lisel, no words, just the hissing sounds of their argument. He pushed his leg out and out and out, stepping along the dark sand. Then he heard the skiff, the faint slip of it going through the water, slanting across the cove toward the buildings grown suddenly more distant. He did not look that way. Not at the boat. Not at the buildings. He watched his feet, the prints they made in the sand. He squeezed his leg high above the pain and pushed it out and out, following the strand of pale beach that went away ahead of him into the darkness.

He had not had the strength to drag the khirtz tent out of his duffel and inflate it, so he'd lain on the grass on the lee side of Jin's shed and pulled a plastex sheet about him and slept that way, curled around the pain. At dawn Jin came and stood over him. He did not hear the boy's feet in the grass, only felt him there suddenly and opened his eyes to the narrow shape he made against the sky, against the colorless morning.

"You're okay?" Jin said.

"Yes."

The boy shifted his weight. Finally he squatted down beside Neye with his palms together, pressed between his knees. "I heard you come up from the beach last night." There was something he wanted to say, maybe another apology on behalf of Lisel. But while Neye waited for him to push it out, she came toward them up the path from the cobb racks, and when the boy saw her, he stood and pushed his hands into the pocket of his shirt. He and Lisel were both stiff-faced. She looked at him once, glancingly, and then dropped her eyes to Neye.

"Registry must have come on hard times," she said, so it was harsh and scoffing. "Or have they always taken the lame and halt into their service?"

He was almost too tired for anger. In a little while he made a sound, a slight release of air, and pushed against his hands to sit up. He was very careful. He did not think there was any change in his face that she would be able to detect; but his hair had come free of its clasp and when it swung forward across his cheeks in a dark, loose drape, he didn't push it back. He braced one leg out stiffly, pushing up on the other to stand. He had thought he might need to put his hand against the wall of the shed to prop himself, but he stood unsupported, straight, and he looked straight at her from beneath the thick forelock of his hair. "If it becomes a chronic problem, they will probably ask me to get a plastic knee. In the interim, I'll try to be more careful." He looked at Jin and then back at Lisel. "No one," he said, "is responsible for my health. No one but me."

What he had felt in her, earlier, was not anger but mistrust and a vague stirring of discomfort that verged on regret. She said irritably, "Even if I were a healer, I could not rebuild a knee. It's only the autonomic nervous system that they—"

He pushed his hand through the air in a cutting-off gesture of impatience. "I know what they can do." He was aching and very tired and he did not care that her face flared with annoyance. "If I want my knee repaired, I'll have a surgeon do it. If I'm in pain, I can take a drug. There's nothing I want from you but obedience to the law. If you have a healing gift, register it. Make yourself available in emergencies. I don't want anything else."

There was only sullenness in her face. She went on past him then, silently. But he had felt for a moment a surprising needle-pointed sliver of her anguish. And found, with another kind of surprise, that there was no pleasure, no triumph in it, only uneasiness.

Jin had stood silently beside him with his hands in his pocket and his eyes fixed on his feet. Now, with Lisel gone, he looked diffidently at Neye. "Did you ever know anyone who was a healer?"

Neye shook his head. But he had seen, once, a healing. A man had touched a woman who was bleeding from an artery. He had put both his hands on her, on the hole in her neck, and in a moment she had stopped spurting blood. By the time the ambulance came, there was a thin brown scab on the wound.

He was still thinking of that, seeing it, when Jin said, "Her father's mother was a healer. I told you that. Well, she died of old age, essentially, when Lisel was ten or eleven. At fifty-three. Which is how old Lisel is now."

Neye looked at the boy. His chest began to feel heavy, as if from fatigue.

"She was a metallurgist," Jin said. "Three or four times in

the lab she used her gifts—burns, probably, but Lisel didn't say. And a couple of times, other places, when she just happened to be there. Once I guess a bus hit a downdraft and crashed on the footway right in front of her house. Maybe there were a dozen times, altogether, that she . . . was useful. But. Every day. There were these people who came. Amputees wanting her to regenerate tissue. Quadriplegics. Every terminal and incurable and hypochondriac on the continent. They'd stand around her door when she'd come out or go in and they'd touch her, grab at her sleeve or her wrist, like they thought that would do the healing, like she was a holy font and all they had to do was put their hands in the water. Because it isn't medicine, after all, is it? It smells supernatural or something, and that's what would draw them. Still draws them. She'd explain it to them, or sometimes I guess she'd have to try first, and afterward she'd explain. They were hardly ever angry. They'd just thank her and go away, all quiet, with their shoulders pulled in, and the next day another one or two or three of them would be there waiting by her door. They just . . . wore her out. One by one. By the time she was fifty-three."

Neye stood hunched as if he was protecting himself from blows. He was able to see, still, the woman with the hole in her throat, the man's small blunt hands touching her. So he was able to wait, steadily and stubbornly, until he was sure the boy had finished. Then he looked up.

"It's a great gift," he said, as though that needed no proving. "If I had it, I would maybe have felt it worth the trade-offs. And I think Lisel never asked her that, her father's mother. Whether she thought it was worth it." Behind his eyes, irresistibly, he saw the others: the thin, solemn face of Cirant, his son, who would surely have died anyway, like the ones who waited before the door of Lisel's grandmother. And the face, too, of that grandmother, graven with unendurable, endless griefs.

Now that they had done with the fence, Lisel and the boy began to work the reefs, culling out the old exhausted banguii and replanting with freezer-fresh "seed."

The cove held at least a million and half cubic meters of cropland, artificial reefs, all planted to banguii. The cobb growing on those racks in the shallows would be a high-yield investment if they made it to harvest, but they were notoriously difficult to raise—vulnerable to disease and several kinds of predators and, sitting up high that way in shallow water, prey to storm damage and drought. The banguii was the money crop.

Twice a year their legs could be harvested, all six legs behind the forward clapperclaws, and they'd simply grow new ones, and continue to do so over a useful life-span of four or five years, while the legs diminished in size a little with every cutting. It was necessary only to feed them keefish, and the kee were easy to grow, generally needing only a bubblefence to keep them in and a pelleted food that could be pressed from banguii by-products and seaweed. The kee's other predators, larger and quicker and able to wipe out a school at one meal, seldom hazarded the small pores of reefs or the aggressive pincers of banguii. It was a neat, self-sustaining microecology, so wherever the offshore was suited, it was a prevalent companion cropping.

Lisel had planted successively, with all the oldest crop bunched just shoreward of the fence line along the north margin of the cove. Neye could follow the stream of bubbles from the submersible reaper, crosshatching back and forth there between the rocks of the northern headland and the anchored bylander, but Jin and Lisel didn't ride in the reaper; they followed behind it, seeding by hand, working as ever from the raft, while the submersible found its own way up and down the furrows between the reefs.

Neye did not climb out on the rocks to watch them. His knee was hurting him. And he thought Lisel's fear might be old and stiffened. He wanted to let her alone a little, back away, let her come in on her own if she would. So for quite a while he sat as he had the first day, watching them benignly from the salt grass of the dunes above the buildings.

The storm stood just off the coast. There was a light wind at sea level, lifting spray so the air was chill and damp, but there was little rain and no gale. He thought maybe the front would after all slide north and past them. Still, it was cold sitting high and idle there, and he could see little of Lisel from this distance. So finally, in the afternoon, he went down to where he had left his duffel by Jin's shed and he heated coffee and sat with his back against the building and his hands wrapped around the warmth of the cup.

He had assumed they would work until the light failed. But as he sat bored and faintly glum with a gelid pack on his knee, the boy came alone up the slope from the beach. Neye had thought both of them indifferent to the cold, but now he was near enough to see the cracks in Jin's lips and the roughened skin of his arms.

The boy gestured toward Neye's outstretched leg. "Okay?"

Neye tore off the cold-pack, flexed his knee and pushed to stand, as though there was no pain. "Yes. All right now."

Jin made a stiff smile. "Sure." And went on past him to one

of the dobes, came out again with a couple of amphibious drone carts set up to haul something—many somethings—tall and thin and vertical.

"I thought you were replanting."

Jin had already started the carts down toward the cobb beach, and Neye, following, pushed his leg long-strided to keep up. The boy flapped one hand vaguely toward the overcast. "We thought this would roll by us. It was supposed to. But now Lisel thinks it's coming in, and she's usually right. So we'll move the cobb. As many as we can before the weather turns, or the tide, whichever is first. They drift, you know. When there's a heavy sea, they just let go and drift until things calm down, and then the ones that don't end up high and dry set up housekeeping in the new neighborhood. You can lose a whole crop that way."

He seemed not much worried, at least not yet, just in a hurry. He and the carts, with Neye trailing, went quickly down through the dunes to the beach where Lisel was already wading out among the rows of cobbs. The racks came apart from the piers in their original settling tank configuration, big open frames gridded with crosspieces, all the surfaces spangled dark with the knobby, algae-slick shellbacks of mollusks. The tide was out, or nearly so, and Lisel worked the outermost row first, standing to her chest in the water, then climbing the piers, uncoupling the latches there and lifting the frames out and down, one by one, pushing them through the water to Jin, who stacked them upright between the struts of the cart.

For a while Neye stood on the dry sand above the mud flats, watching them. He couldn't see that the weather had worsened at all, maybe had even lightened. And his knee was aching, not greatly but steadily. And Lisel seemed not to see him there. So for a while he only stood and watched.

When they filled a cart, Jin followed it up out of the water and along the trough of dunes to the tide pond. And while he was there, off-loading, Lisel worked the other end alone, lifting a frame out and then balancing it with one hand, climbing down laboriously herself to put it on the other cart. Neye watched her do that three or four times. Then he went across the low rise to the tide pond, going all the way out on the mud to where the boy was hanging racks on the low piers.

"Go on," he said. "I'll send the cart back when I get it unloaded."

Jin looked at him once, not very surprised, not speaking, and went off at a trot. After that, Neye saw only the drones as they purred up the sand from the beach, one and then the other, freighted with slick, wet racks of mollusks.

The pond was meant to hold only the young spat, the graduating class from a settling tank; there were four or five times as many racks of cobb out in the cove as there were piers here in the pond. So when the hanging space was gone, he began to set the racks between rows, leaning them to rest on the others. The racks were plastic. Naked, they'd have been light, but they were crusted heavy with shellfish, and his shoulders and arms began gradually to ache from the monotonous, relentless lifting.

He was just beginning the third rank, and the incoming tide stood to his thighs, when Lisel came walking in to him not from the mud flats but from the low rise that sheltered her buildings. She toted an insulated bag, holding it against her body as if it were too heavy to hang by the handle.

"You can eat with us," she said, without quite looking toward him. She walked on past the pond and along the beaten-down track of the drones.

Neye leaned a rack against the others and wiped his hands on his shirt and followed her, splashing up out of the water and through the last rise down to the beach. Jin was lying on the grass there, on his belly, with his head on one arm. Lisel squatted by him and began to haul food out of her bag, a couple of tall bottles, hunks of smoked fish, round stones of bread. She brought out a knife, too, sliced a tewit in half, put part of it in the hand Jin outstretched to her. And then, with a stiff gesture, she offered the other half of the tewit to Neye.

He took it and sat on the damp grass a little way from her, with his legs drawn up in front of him. He would have liked to rub the ache from his knee, but he kneaded, instead, his stiffened shoulders, first one and then the other, with the fingertips of his free hand while he ate the tewit and looked out at the cobb racks. Not quite half of them were skeletal piers.

Jin was propped up on his elbows now, his mouth and chin stained with the green juice of the fruit. He took a mug of coffee from Lisel and held it between his two hands.

"I'll bring the lights down here," he said to her, "after we eat." She nodded. She was cutting slices from a block of white cheese.

Neye had not been much aware of the failure of daylight, only now saw that before the tide pushed over the last of the racks it would be dead dark. And there was a little wind, seeming sleety cold against his wet clothes. The leading edge of Lisel's storm.

She handed him coffee, pushed some of the food in his direction, and then herself began to eat, sitting cross-legged more or less between Jin and Neye.

"I think she was worried about hypothermia," Jin said, with his voice low as if he spoke a confidence, but leaning out past her to say it to Neye. "Otherwise, we'd never have been fed."

She did not bother to look at him. "You could eat shit," she said, so it had almost the sound of well-meant advice.

Jin was still looking past her to Neye as he said, "The first symptom is unprovoked hostility." Still privately, as if she did not sit there between them.

Around the food, she made some grumping sounds, perhaps an obscenity, but also clearly a private message, a cutting off. Enough.

Jin obliged her by falling silent, but in a while they exchanged a look of gentle amusement, of affection, and Neye, watching them both obliquely while he ate, surprised himself by feeling only faintly excluded.

Jin brought sodium lamps on high telescoping stands, and they worked a while longer in that insufficient, long-shadowed glare. But the wind was rising, and a dark, cold rain rode in on it. The tide pushed in too, until it slopped over the tops of the piers in the pond. Neye waded in it to his armpits. The water was dark, and sometimes he had to feel with his hands even to find the drone cart standing waiting in the water beside him.

He did not hear Jin coming, only heard him say, "We're quitting," and when he turned he could see the boy in the wind-shaky light standing at the edge of the pond, leaning on a cart burdened down with lamp heads and collapsed uprights. Behind him, Lisel came slowly up the path from the darkened beach, carrying a sheaf of poles in her arms. She kept her eyes on her feet as if she needed to remind them to move.

Neye sent the cart up out of the pond and waded up after it. Jin was already dismantling the two lamps there, and Neye found he could only stand lumpishly and watch, could not quite summon the energy to help. Now that he was out of the water, he was acutely aware of his hands, swollen thick and numb.

In darkness, finally, and windy silence, they crossed the little rise of grass and went down among the farm buildings. Neye fumbled with his stiffened hands, attempting to help the two of them stow away the carts and the lamp pieces in one of the sheds, but when Lisel looked at him with a sort of disgusted embarrassment, he was not surprised. He knew his clumsiness was slowing them down.

She said, "You can take a shower and sleep inside, I guess." It was only a little grudging. He was too tired to be other than relieved.

"We left the raft out where we were planting," Jin said. "Maybe we should bring it in."

She made a hissing sound through her teeth. "Shit. I forgot about that." Her shoulders seemed to drop a little, and it was that, more than the words she'd spoken or the spurt of disappointment he could feel from her, that reminded him: while he had drunk coffee and rested his knee all morning, they'd been diving in the cove.

With some care, so it was a straightforward question, he said, "Is it worth going out again?"

Lisel gave him a perfunctory glance, then said, "It's a cybernetic," and looked back at Jin. "I want to put on a dry shirt, at least. I'll see you down at the skiff." She went past Neye into the windy darkness.

To Jin, when it occurred to him, he said, "Is it anchored?

Maybe it would just ride out the swells, like a boat would, as long as it's out on the open water."

Jin shook his head. "It's so damned underpowered. The anchor mode won't hold it in a gale, and then it would end up on the rocks."

Neye followed him through the rain to his building, stood self-consciously beside the shipping crates while the boy peeled off his sodden shirt and looked for a dry one. His own arms felt clammy and cold. He could hear the wind-pushed rain sheeting off the roof of the dobe, could feel the heat in the room and its dry comfort. He did not want to go out again.

Finally, Jin looked toward him. He had put on the bright yellow tunic. His forearms below the edge of the sleeves seemed thin, knob-wristed, pale. The fine hair stood out with the cold. "Stay put," he said. "Get a hot bath. You look like your body heat is really down. We don't need you."

Neye had seen the raft at fairly close range. It was heavy enough, he thought it would take at least the three of them to horse it up out of the water. But they were used to handling things themselves, without his help; they must have worked out a method. And the boy spoke matter-of-factly, as if what he said should be indisputable. So hell. Maybe he would just stay inside.

Jin went out, and for a while Neye stood leaning against the crates. He could hear rain running down through the cistern pipes to the underground, the wind whumping against the outer wall of dobe. After a while he went out too.

He put his head down and pushed a way along the slick, wet path toward the tide pond. It was very dark and the rain beat almost horizontally against his lowered head. He placed his feet carefully in the puddles between the dank tufts of grass.

If he fell now, there would be no one to see it. From the top of the rise, he could see the ocean leaking into the pond along the low notch between the dunes, running thin and fast as snow-melt there where the drone carts had earlier worn marks in the grass. So he turned and went up the steep pathless slope of the seaward dune, stepping carefully in the darkness heel first, sliding a little on the wet grass. From the crest he peered against the wind-driven rain out at the sweep of cove. The sea was breaking just above the tidemark in narrow fluorescent lines of surf.

It was Jin's yellow shirt and Lisel's sand-colored one that he saw, finally, against the darkness. They were not very far below him, bailing rainwater out of the skiff. He thought of waiting, watching them from here. Or going back. They had surely pulled out the raft before, just the two of them. And Lisel might see it only as an extravagant and insincere gesture. But he started over the hill and down to where they were dragging the skiff seaward. As he helped them push the prow out into the swells, he saw Lisel's face turn, a pale glance of surprise, no more than that. But it was Jin's hand he felt boosting him up when he had trouble getting his leg over the gunwale into the boat.

They did not speak to one another. He crouched in the sloppy water between the thwarts, with his hands gripping the ribs of the bottom and the thrum of the little engine coming up through his fingers.

In the darkness on the choppy water, he could not see the raft, but he thought he knew where it lay, just off the fence line at the point of the north cape. He watched the headland rise like an edge of sky, high and black above the black water. In its shadow, in a wet crosswind, they plied back and forth looking for the raft, saw it finally, low and awash, west of them and just off the rocks.

Jin turned the stern to the wind so they could come alongside, and when their port side scraped the fiberglass timbers, Lisel went over the edge, crawling out on the heaving deck to secure the line and then as quickly back again. As she crabbed over into the boat, the sea swelled under them both and for a moment she teetered above the water. Neye grabbed for her, caught his hand in her shirt, but she was already in the boat, had never lost her balance. In the darkness he saw her looking back at him gently, felt her kindly amusement.

The raft was heavy and cumbrous, three or four times as big as the skiff. They towed it endlessly through the darkness. The wind out of the southeast pushed them always north, so Jin finally turned them that way, toward any part of the beach where they could safely push the raft up out of the water. Neye sat hunched behind Lisel, peering against the rain. His eyes had begun to burn a little, but he sought the black line of the shore. Finally, above the sea there was a bumpy dark rise, the dunes.

Neye crouched on his heels in the bottom of the boat. He put one hand on a gunwale. In front of him he could see the faint rise of Lisel's spine stiffening under her tunic.

When the skiff rose on the first comber of surf, Neye went over the side with her. He thought he would be able to stand; instead he sank, and the tide sucked him sideways and down. He was not much aware of the cold, only the utter blackness. His hand touched the skiff, felt it sliding by him, borne in on the water.

The sea swelled again, pushed him hard against the side of the boat, and he grabbed with both hands, hugged it to him.

When his head and shoulders broke above the water, he could see, through the smear of wet, Jin, belatedly clambering over the port side into the water. Lisel was right in front of him, bobbing with one arm clasped over the starboard gunwale. She turned her head, looking back at Neye to be sure he was there. They did not speak.

The bottom of Neye's feet rubbed the sand. Ahead of him Lisel tried to run, chest-deep in the water, pulling the boat up with her or the reverse. Neye set his heels down hard, but there was no running, only a sluggish torpid sort of striving against the sea.

Maybe Jin yelled, but there were no words. Neye only felt the sudden bright burn of the boy's alarm.

Across the gunwale he could see the tight cap of the boy's hair plastered so the scalp seemed bare and burnished. And behind him the raft, skewed on its towline, coming up on a white line of surf. Gently its rear end lifted high on the water and it began to come in, quick and light as a chip of wood.

He did not feel the raft ride down on top of them all. He felt only a sudden unbearable heaviness in his chest. Afterward he was cold, and he thought someone was twisting his leg, or jumping on it.

He said, "Don't," yelled it, and the sea filled his mouth. It was very dark and there was sand in his eyes and his teeth. Sometimes the water was not deep and then he tried to crawl up out of it. He did that several times. After a while, someone—it was Lisel—came and put her shoulder under him and hoisted him up. He wanted to help her, but she staggered up out of the water carrying his whole weight across her back. He could hear the sobbing gasp of her breath, could hear it even over the boom of the ocean. Okay, he wanted to say. I'm okay, put me down. But he did not know what sound would come out if he opened his mouth.

She let him down or dropped him on gravelly sand, on his back, so the rain falling out of the darkness struck his face and ran in his ears. He lay partly across one of her arms or a leg, and she tugged it out with a fierce whistly sound like a wail, a sound he felt in his bones. He heard her feet go away again, running across the sand, and after that he lay alone in the cold, loud darkness. His head hurt, and hurt more when he vomited thin dribbles of salt water.

He was alone quite a while before he remembered Jin. He sat up and then, a little later, stood. There was something broken, or rent, this time in his knee. And sticky blood in his eyebrows. But he went down deliberately toward the water.

She had brought the boy most of the way out of the breakers but then probably she had dropped him and not been able to get him up again. She was hunched over on her knees with his head in her lap so his face was off the sand and out of the shallow low foam of spent surf.

Neye braced his leg and bent for one of the boy's arms.

"Here," he said.

Lisel looked up at him abstractedly. There were bluish arcs like bruises beneath the bones of her cheeks. She stood and took Jin's other arm and they dragged him up, all the way up, out of the water. The boy's heels scuffed a pale furrow in the sand. At the edge of the hill, Lisel sat again and put Jin's head again in her lap, and Neye lowered himself to the grass beside her. He did not look at Jin. He peered out at the dark ink line of the horizon. A bead of blood ran down from his eyebrow alongside his nose.

"He was already dead," Lisel said after a while. "I went out to him first, but he was already dead. So I left him while I went to look for you." A little later, as if she thought it would comfort him, she repeated, "He was already dead." And then, as if she thought to comfort herself, "I couldn't have helped him."

The boy's head was in her lap, she was holding him by the shoulders, but she didn't look at him. She looked sideways, away from Neye, up the dark curve of beach. He could see only part of her face, a corner of mouth pulled in like a little drawstring purse.

Before too long, she put one hand under Jin's head and lifted it and slid out from under him. When she stood up, Neye could see the dark shine of blood on her hand. She didn't wipe it off. She said, "It'll take a while. I'll have to go clear around on foot to tele for the ambulance."

He thought she was asking him something, so he said, "I can wait," and in a little bit, solemnly, she nodded and started off along the beach. He didn't want to watch her going away, so he closed his eyes. And then, carefully, he lay beside Jin, on his side, curled a little. The wind blew wet against his spine.

He didn't hear Lisel come back to him, but when he opened his eyes she was there, squatting beside him. He felt she had been waiting several minutes. He was the only one of them who was crying, but the tightness, the pain in Neye's skull now was hers.

"There isn't much I can do for the knee," she said. As if she had come back to him just to say this one thing, something she'd forgotten to say before setting off for the tele. "I could make it quit hurting but you'd have to be careful. If you walked on it, or turned it the wrong way, you could injure yourself more."

He did not answer right away. When he did, he just said, "No."

She looked at him as Jin sometimes had, sideways, as if she was turning away. There was a quality of reticence about it, or of shyness, that he had not seen in her before. Abruptly, he knew what she would do. When her hand came out, reaching for the bleeding place above his eye, he reached too, clasping her lightly by the wrist.

"Don't," he said. "It's nothing. It doesn't hurt." There was a hardness at the back of his throat so the words came out squeezed and small.

There were beads of rain or of the sea in her eyelashes. She let him hold her that way, briefly, and then with only a small change in her face she pulled her hand free of him.

"Yes," she said. "It does." And she touched his eye, denying gently several things at once.

A Story

CINDY IS BACK IN HOSPITAL—she's got COPD, is that the right term? Respiratory something—so last night I went down the dock to their place to take care of the cat, and then I had the weirdest experience. I always sit down for a few minutes to talk to the lonesome thing, and I'm sitting at the table and the cat is rubbing against me and purring while I commiserate with him about the absence of the people in his life, and the phone rings. Naturally, I don't answer it, but I'm within earshot of the message. It's Mike—or I guess I'd better say it sounds like Mike, exactly like Mike, his rumbly low mutter. The cat when he hears that voice really perks up—he was always more Mike's cat than Cindy's—and he stares at the machine. I do too. Mike, or whoever it was, said he was sorry he hadn't heard from the two of them in a while but he hoped they were doing all right, hoped they were having a good Christmas. He was lonesome, he said, really lonesome, and he loved them both and missed them. Goodbye, and the message clicks off.

The cat held still for quite a while, like he was waiting for Mike to say something more, and then he went over to the table where they keep the phone, jumped up there, and tried to get inside it. Well, not inside, but he was nosing around the phone base and batting at it with a paw like he thought Mike was hiding behind it or under it. And he launched into a long, forsaken-sounding yowl.

For a couple of minutes I was knocked off kilter too. Trying to make sense of it, frankly. And then picturing Mike, from wherever he is, saying, *Here you go, friend. A ghost story for you.*

So now I'm just trying to figure out how to tell it. Should I say up front, Mike has been dead at this point about four months? And I'm wondering how much I should tell you about Cindy and Mike—kind of an odd couple for sure, but does their backstory have much to do with that weird phone message? Should I tell you how the two of us, me and Mike, used to talk about the speculative stuff I write, how it's good for asking the big questions, *is reality even knowable*, that sort of thing? Which would make the story kind of meta if I'm using that term right. Then there's Mike's "inklings," and that weird moment at the hospice right before he died. The cat really did go crazy when he heard the voice on the phone, like he absolutely knew it was Mike calling from wherever he was in the afterlife. And the truth is, for just a minute, when the voice said "I hope you're both doing well," I thought so too. I guess I could speculate about whose voice it was if it wasn't Mike's, but I don't think I will, and I'll leave it up to you, where to land on the ambiguity spectrum.

So okay, Cindy and Mike. When I moved onto this moorage twenty years ago they had already been here a good ten years, so something like thirty years for them. They were together all that time without ever being married, which I think was Cindy's choice—they were always up and down, those two.

She had put herself through law school, and when they met she was working for a big firm downtown, and Mike was tending bar at the Teardrop, the lounge she went to after work. Then he had four or five different jobs over the years but spent a fair amount of time unemployed, which meant money was always a source of tension between them. Maybe that's why she never put him on her insurance? Medicare kicked in a couple of months before he died; that was all he had. No idea if insurance would have made a difference in finding the cancer before they did, but I've wondered about it. And Cindy had walked out of a marriage when she was young, so maybe that was part of the reason she never wanted to marry again?

The other thing, maybe related, maybe not, is that she had a daughter from an unplanned pregnancy in high school, and gave up the baby, which nobody knew until a couple of years ago. The whole thing came out when the daughter traced her biological parents, and one day Cindy just brought the girl and the adoptive mother around and introduced them to everybody on the moorage. That girl—well, I guess she's a grown woman at this point—looks exactly like Cindy, and now they talk on the phone every week.

None of this is probably relevant to a story about Mike calling from beyond the grave, but I keep thinking it's history, circumstance, something, and maybe I should tell it?

I guess if I was looking for a metaphor, the moorage would be the thing—all of us afloat on the dark depths, floorboards rocking under our feet. But you'll need to know about living in a "floating home," as the real estate people like to call it. How it makes for close neighbors, all the houseboats lined up along the riverbank with a floating dock like a long front porch and everybody's backyard being the river. This is a small moorage, sixteen houses, so we're always running into each other coming and going along the dock, hoofing it up the ramp to the parking lot and the mail boxes, hauling trash up to the bins, bringing groceries down in a cart, that sort of thing, which is how Mike and I first got acquainted, passing each other on the dock, each of us holding the same book, *Golden Days*, I think it was. That's the kind of coincidence you can't get away with in fiction these days.

I've never met anybody who loved to read more than Mike. He was into the cerebral stuff—he had made it through *Ulysses*, so help me—but he wasn't snobby about it. He'd ask me what I was reading and whether it was any good, and then if he hadn't already read it he'd have read it by the next time we talked. And he'd have an opinion. I got him hooked on the Swedish who-done-its and *Stranger Things Happen*. He got me started on Whitehead, who I wouldn't have tried except Mike knew my fondness for the weird stuff, and he told me *Zone One* had a zombie apocalypse hiding in Whitehead's fancy literary language. We argued about Murakami. He thought *Kafka on the Shore* would be right up my alley, but I couldn't get through it, couldn't take all that winding around into cul-de-sacs and asides, with no clear path though the plot.

He was always sort of a mystery man, Mike was. I knew him for twenty years, but I can't say I really knew him. If you were chatting with him by the mail boxes or down on the dock, talking about anything other than books, you'd see his bartender personality coming out—you'd end up learning little or nothing about him, while spilling private stuff from your own life. Which is how he came to know about my writing back when I was just getting started, still keeping it a secret from everybody else on the moorage. Back then, if I said I was a writer the next thing people wanted to know was whether I was published, and when I said *no* or *not yet* they'd start looking around for somebody else to talk to. But not Mike. He asked questions about my "writing process," and he wanted to read what I'd written, and when I finally showed him a story, he had things to say about it, as if my work was worth the same serious attention he would have given Whitehead or Murakami. He got me through some early rejections, for sure, and he was a good first reader, a good sounding board for me. It's not like I've got a lot of other people I can talk to about books and about my work, so I miss that. Miss talking with Mike about what I've been reading, what I've been writing.

He wasn't a total mystery. Over the years I picked up a few things about him. I know his mother died early of Alzheimer's, and his dad died just a few years ago after lapsing into some kind of dementia himself. And Mike had a brother who was basically blind from birth, which Cindy said the mother denied for years—but how do you deny a child being blind, I wonder?— and he had an older sister who was, as Cindy said, a big mucky-muck down in California, something to do with the insurance business. She was the only one in the family who had done well for herself, and I've wondered if this bothered Mike—whether it made him conscious of not getting his life going in a constructive direction. I don't know if it did, but I know he wasn't close to his sister. Or for that matter, his dad and his blind brother.

Those two lived together at the coast somewhere around Waldport. Mike used to go down and see them a couple of times a year, but after the dad died he quit going because by then he was sick himself, and the long drive would have taken it out of him. Cindy could have driven him—I think she had met the brother and the dad a few times—but after Mike's first surgery she had enough on her plate, taking care of him. Or anyway, that's what Mike told everybody—that Cindy had too much on her plate. Also he must have thought, since the brother had gotten along without his help all the time their father was losing his faculties, he could go on managing without him. I don't know what reason he gave his brother for not visiting, but I know he never told him about the surgeries or his cancer. I guess that's just the way their family dealt with things.

Before Mike got sick, he and Cindy used to go antiquing, and Cindy has boxes and boxes of Christmas decorations, old collectibles she always would put out right after Thanksgiving and take down the day after Christmas. This year she didn't decorate at all, which I can understand. The other change I've noticed since Mike died is that she's given up reading the newspaper or following politics on television. They were big lefties, both of them, and they watched all the news shows, watched Maddow every night. Now she watches only one channel, the Golf Channel, even though she never played golf. My mother-in-law did that too, in her last years. She was ninety-six and having trouble tracking, and golf was such a quiet, slow-moving story she could follow it without losing the thread. I don't know if that's Cindy's reason, or if she just can't bring herself to watch the news without Mike there to kibitz. She used to be a reader, too, not as much as Mike, but still, a reader, and she gave up books almost entirely after Mike's last surgery.

The big thing about Mike, in terms of this story, is what he called his "inklings." When I showed him a story I'd written about a woman who called herself an intuitionist, we got talking about whether we believed in that sort of thing ourselves, intuition, ESP, all the slightly woo-woo stuff, and when I said I did, or anyway that I leaned that way, he let slip that he had always had what he called inklings, where he would know something before it happened, like if somebody was about to get bad news, or if somebody was having an illicit affair, things like that. He said he'd had an inkling about Cindy's daughter getting in touch, right before her call came out of the blue. And this—the inklings—had led to him working as a fortune-teller for a while in a second-rate casino off the strip in Reno. This was before the bartending, before he met Cindy. I tried to get him to tell me more about it—I said I wanted to use a fortune-telling character in one of my stories—but he would only say it hadn't worked out, and he'd left Reno after just a couple of months.

As to fortune-telling, Mike predicted that Trump would be President clear back before the primary stuff started. I poked fun at him but he swore he knew this was coming. I wish he'd lived to see it. Or no, I guess I don't wish that, but I wish he could have known he was right, after I gave him a hard time about it.

So back to the cat. The whole point about the cat.

Mike had wanted a dog but Cindy wouldn't let him have one. He was slightly lame on one foot from some sort of misadventure in his twenties—you couldn't get him to talk about it—and Cindy didn't feel he could walk enough to keep a dog happy. But that cat followed him everywhere just like a dog. Up and down the moorage ramp, over to the mail boxes, wherever Mike went. He would whistle for it to come instead of calling kitty, kitty or anything like that. When we stood on the dock talking about what we'd been reading, or a story I'd been working on, the cat would nuzzle Mike's foot, trying to get his attention, and then start mewling, complaining about the delay, but after a while he'd sit down, gazing off at the river, waiting, the way a wife waits when her husband runs into a colleague from work and they're talking about people she doesn't know. Polite but bored. When Mike would finally start back down the dock the cat would keep sitting, staring off into distance, until Mike whistled for him. Then he'd make a point of getting up slowly, stretching slowly, before he ambled after Mike. That's a cat for you.

So just at the end of Mike's life, after he'd been in a coma for two or three days, he just suddenly opened his eyes, looked around at all of us in the room—it hadn't been a vigil, exactly, but four of us had come up from the moorage to keep Cindy company at the hospice for a couple of hours—and he said, "What are you all doing here? Is somebody dying?" And he winked, which was totally Mike, totally himself, as he hadn't been for weeks. Then he looked at Cindy, smiling slightly but dead serious. "I've been worrying about the cat, honey. You know I'm counting on you to take care of him after I'm gone." Maybe he had had an inkling about it? Or maybe not, maybe he just knew he had reasons to worry. Cindy hadn't ever seemed to care all that much about the cat, and to be frank she hasn't been herself the last year or so. I don't know if it's her COPD or the beginning of some sort of dementia or what, but I've noticed it, and Mike had watched both his parents go down that road so I know he had seen it too. He was worried Cindy would forget, or just not care enough, to bring the cat inside at night, to feed him, to clean his litter box.

Then he said, still smiling, "I'll be checking up on the two of you after I'm dead. You know I'm not kidding about that, Cindy."

She flushed a bit, but then she nodded, like she knew what he meant and she was just taking him at his word, *you know I'll be checking up on you after I'm dead*, which I thought at the time was a little bit strange. And now I'm thinking, geez, maybe she knew something weird about the guy, something beyond just the fortune-telling and the inklings, and when I tell her about that phone call she won't be a bit surprised about Mike calling her from beyond the grave.

Okay, last night after I fed the cat I came back here and wrote down these notes in case I might want to turn this into a story— what Mike would call my "process"—and then this morning things kind of got derailed. I went up to the hospital to visit with Cindy and I told her about the message I had overheard on the phone. I didn't say it was Mike—I wasn't ready to go that far—but I told her the voice had given me a shock, and the cat too, both of us thinking it sounded exactly like Mike. I said whoever-it-was had asked how she was doing, or not her, but "both of you." Then with a laugh I said, "So I guess it must have been Mike checking up on you and the cat, like he said he would."

She was taken aback for a minute—gave me such a startled look—but then I could see her working through it, and she said, "Oh, I'm pretty sure that was Mike's brother." Turns out, when Mike died Cindy had phoned the sister in California to let her know her brother had passed away, and she had asked the sister to break the news to the blind brother—"Two birds with one call," she said, which is classic Cindy.

They hadn't been in touch since that one call, but on Thursday when Cindy went in the hospital she had phoned the sister to ask a question about insurance, some problem she was having with her coverage, and it had come out that the sister hadn't ever told the blind brother about Mike's passing. He'd been sick, the sister said, and she just hadn't known how to tell him. Anyway, now he was dying himself—the hospital in Waldport had phoned her with this news. He was at death's door, really, in a coma for days, and not expected to live more than another day.

So Cindy figured *both of you* meant Cindy and Mike, inasmuch as the brother didn't know Mike was dead. And of course I knew, we both did, that sometimes a person at the end of their life can have a lucid day, can wake up and carry on a normal conversation. Cindy thought the brother must have done that, must have woken from his coma yesterday, just as Mike had, and then picked up the phone to call his brother and wish him Merry Christmas. She said she was sorry to hear about the call—sorry she hadn't told him about Mike—but maybe it was for the best, and anyway now it was too late. Likely by this time he was dead.

Now I'm wrestling with the whole thing. Wondering how I can ever turn this into a story, one of my weird stories. I thought I had something, which was me listening to Mike's voice message, thinking it must be Mike calling to check on Cindy and the cat, just as he'd said he would on that last lucid day of his life, and the cat perking up, happy to hear from him after so long. I thought I could write it the way it happened, hardly anything magic about it, just *goodbye* and then the cat jumping up to nuzzle the machine, meowing the way cats do when they're complaining or asking for something.

But I went back over there tonight to feed the cat and I listened again. It was a pretty sad message—I guess I haven't said that yet. To tell the truth I wish I could stop hearing it, stop hearing that mournful, rumbly voice, *haven't heard from you in a while, miss you, love you*, and just before *goodbye* something about *dying of lonesome*, or maybe *dying is lonesome*, something to that effect. I keep thinking of the story Cindy told me, the blind brother in a coma, dying alone in a hospital room, waking up alone with nobody standing around his bed, just him in that permanent darkness, waking up and wondering why his brother hasn't called him in months, hasn't checked up on him, hasn't wished him well at Christmas. Picking up the phone but not able to reach anybody at the other end.

But then I come back to the other story, to what it would mean if it really was Mike on the phone, what it would mean if you went on being lonesome even after you've died, what sort of story that would be. *Dying is lonesome.* Thinking if it really was Mike, well, that might be too real for me.

So I've been wrestling with it, trying to find a story that makes some sort of sense. Or not sense, but meaning. I keep coming back to the cat. How he was so sure it was Mike, and so happy to hear from him again. How tonight, the second time we listened, he jumped off my lap after the message ended, went and sat by the patio door and was still sitting there when I left, staring out at the river, his eyes out of focus, faintly bored, just like he was waiting for Mike's whistle.

Little Hills

IN THE NIGHT, AND IN the snow, they gradually lost the road. The humped ground went away in all directions, without landmark, featureless white in the darkness, and by the time they were sure of being lost, surer of being stuck, there was no way to know how far they had come from the pavement. They were both, or had been, Montana people, and this was no blizzard, only a snow that fell straight and thick through the cones of the headlights. They were perhaps a little more annoyed than frightened.

Lyle pulled up the collar of his coat and stepped outside briefly, tramping behind to the trunk, to the old pieced quilt folded up there beside the jack and the jumper cables, and then back to sit beside Claire, close together under the quilt in the front seat of the car. They had brought a suitcase for what would have been the overnight at the house of the eldest child. In a while they opened it, put on cardigans beneath coats, doubled stockings inside shoes.

They spoke, at times, of other snows, other landscapes, and only once of the children, who were no longer children, who would begin to worry soon, waiting, looking out through the living room windows into the darkness. Claire remembered, with sudden and unaccustomed clarity, that they had begun to carry a quilt in the car when the children had been still babies, for the going-home-late times with all three sleep-sweaty, legs tangled, in the back seat of the Ford. She thought of saying that to Lyle. But of the two of them, he was the more sentimental, the more prone to long, nostalgic remembrance, and she had a dim, unreasoned dread of that tonight. She said finally, "It's good we had this old blanket," and he made a small sound of agreement, not remembering the reason they'd begun to keep it in the trunk.

Eventually, in the darkness, and without discussion, they climbed over onto the back seat to lie down together under the quilt. "Oh for Pete's sake," Claire said, and lifted one elbow to fend his hand from her small old breast. She used a tone of exasperation that had been worn down over years to ritual only. He said, with innocent surprise, a ritual voice also, "Oop. Sorry dear, didn't know I had my hand there."

He shifted his weight in the darkness, turning sideways on the narrow bench seat and drawing up his knees. She nested behind him, pressed against the back of the seat with her knees tucked behind his.

"Spoons," he said, reaching around to pat the rise of her hip. "We haven't laid like spoons since you bought that damned big bed." In the little pause afterward, she could feel him trailing out to the end of the thought. "Can't catch you . . . hell, can't even find you in that damned bed."

"That's not the bed's fault, you dotty old goat."

"Too much pepper," he said, grumbling. "I read that once. I'm cutting back on my pepper."

She had one arm around his soft middle. Her other arm, pressed under her own body, her bony hip, already had begun to numb with the loss of circulation. She wriggled it out, tried to find a place for it parallel between them without contorting her shoulder. Her neck ached a little too, without a pillow. Finally she bent the arm up, put it under her head. In a moment the hand slept, needling. She pulled it down again.

"What . . . ," Lyle said. By the furred edge of his voice she thought he probably, irksomely, already had dozed off. He slept anywhere, like a child, she not at all without a good firm mattress and a pillow, sheets, a blanket.

"I'm seventy-two years old. This is not a comfortable way for me to sleep. That's what."

He edged away from her wordlessly, making room, until she was driven to clasp him tighter—he would have fallen or lain down on the floorboards.

"Damned little foreign car," he said, without annoyance.

"That one was your idea," she said.

They slept little or not at all. Lyle occasionally looked at the digital display of his watch, and Claire occasionally asked for a report of the time. Frequently they found new positions, sitting, lying, sitting again. When finally there seemed a little thinning of the darkness inside the car, Lyle rolled the driver's window down and pushed against the vertical pane of snow with a flat plastic folder of car papers from the glove box. The little white wall fell out and away, and a colorless daylight came inside with them.

"Roll up the window, Lyle, for heaven's sake." The light—or the opened window—had made the space inside the car seem suddenly much colder.

She sat on the back seat holding on to the quilt while Lyle went out to clear the exhaust pipe, and when he had the engine going and the heater, she climbed stiffly over the seat and put her hands and feet in the tepid gush of air. She looked past Lyle, out the cleared side window.

"I don't think it snowed too much more after we stopped," she said, making a cautious choice of words, deciding not to give shape to their situation by naming it "lost."

Lyle may have been engaged in something like that himself. He made a low, grumping sound. "They wouldn't know snow in this part of the country if it fell on them." He put his thick, big-knuckled hands under the heater vent, rubbed them briskly together. "I'll lay odds the plow's already come by on that road back there."

In pale daylight they trudged along the car's obliterated back trail, lifting feet high, setting them down carefully in knee-deep powder. Lyle held her hand: he was disposed to think of her as frail, though not as a result of old age, simply old fictions. They went back along a flattish track, the way they must have come in the car, to another flat place that seemed to wind between rises and may have been the road. Lyle kicked down through the snow seeking the asphalt, while Claire stood with her hands in her coat pockets, staring out against the gray. The land seemed only vaguely like the one they had traveled in other weather, low smooth rises and sometimes in the gullies clumps of box elder, or along the slopes the wide-crowned canyon oaks, looking hunched now under shawls of snow.

"Lyle, isn't that a house?"

He left off his kicking and followed where she was pointing, south and east, a small chip of darkness beside the larger, rounder form of a single big tree. He put one hand flat above his eyes, peering. He was the long-sighted one, without eyeglasses even now, on the day when his children would have celebrated his seventy-third birthday. "Might be," he said finally.

They left the place that might have been a road and went toward the place that might have been a house, striking out for it in a straight line, high-stepping in the snow. The slopes that had seemed trivial became now unexpectedly formidable. In a little while Lyle left off holding her hand, and they each climbed alone, swinging arms to balance, gusting clouds of their breath in the chill air.

They often were out of sight of the house—if that was what it was—and the distance gradually seemed to dilate. In the clear, chalk-gray light, without curbs or neighbors lawns to measure against, they remained always a mile from it. The snow began to warm and weaken, and their shoes made loose plopping sounds when they set them in the slush. Claire, under the coat, the wool sweater, the doubled stockings, began to sweat.

Once, Lyle stood bent with his hands resting on his knees and called to her. "Maybe we ought to go back to the car."

There had been a moment, as the first cold light had come in the opened window, when she had seen suddenly, clearly, a little headline: "Elderly Couple Found Dead in Stranded Auto." But now, in the wet flat daylight, she was only miserable and sodden and tired, and there was no melodrama in any of this, or even the possibility of it. And she was more stubborn then he, liked it less when they must turn back from anything they'd started for. She stood wide-legged, resting her fists on her hips, considering Lyle's pink, unpressed face. "We're more than halfway there now, don't you think?"

So they went on over the little hills.

It was, in fact, a house. Claire was able to see it, finally, from the next to last hillock, standing higher there where stones had been piled up or had fallen down in a sort of cairn.

"Someone's little summer cabin," Claire said, and looked back to Lyle for confirmation. He toiled up to the rocks without lifting his head. His mouth was open, puckered, sucking in the air with a wheeze like an asthmatic.

Old man, she thought suddenly. She was, despite his little masculine fantasies, the harder and stronger one, ever had been. She would outlive him. She had chided him with that occasionally, but the conceit, the mischief went out of it now all at once, and it lay deflated and heavy and cold against her chest.

When he had come up to where she was, she put one hand on his arched back, patting through the bulk of his clothes.

"Poor old baby," she said, teasing a little, irresistibly.

"Out of shape," he said, all on one panting exhale of air. She waited with one hand still on his back while he gained his breath. "I'm gonna start walking more," he said. "Read that, more than once. Walking is better for you than that jogging business." He straightened stiffly, squinting out toward the small house. "Well, hell," he said. "Won't be anybody there. No phone either. Should've stayed with the car or followed up the road."

Claire looked behind them. From where they stood, there was no seeing the car, just the broken track of their feet going away across the snow, and she had a sudden, not clear, premonition, one of several now in this strange long day. As she looked around again at Lyle, he sat down without warning in the watery snow.

She made a quick small sound of surprise, of embarrassed amusement, standing there above him. It was rather a long moment later before she was able to make a truer sound, looking down on the face he turned up to her, white against the whitened stones.

"Lyle. Oh Lyle. Oh."

It had been a great, childish fear of his that he might be buried or burned mistakenly when he was not yet truly dead. There were occasional small pieces in the newspaper, some person who sat up suddenly or blinked an eye as the mortician readied his tools, and Lyle would always fold the page there and tap it with his finger and hand it over to her to read. "Now don't you bury me until I'm stone cold."

She sat beside him through the rest of the morning, with her sweater folded up under his head, and she held his hand until the hand she held was utterly cold and stiff and sooty gray, like the snow that lay in little icy doilies on the rocks around them.

At one point early on, she wept a little. But, as had been the case now for several years, she found tears less satisfying and less necessary than they once had been. Afterward she only sat beside him, holding his hand, with her chill wet feet tucked under her buttocks.

Finally she went on the rest of the way to the little cabin, found it silent, locked, the windows shuttered. She'd had in mind that she might find something there, a blanket or a sheet, something, to cover Lyle's body. But she was unwilling to break in, even if it were possible. So she went back to him again, and as she came back from that distance, his body lying on the snow seemed quite small, unprotected. She had thought she might strike out for the car, but found she couldn't go off again and leave Lyle lying so alone.

She began to think of covering his body with stones, with the stones that were piled up or had fallen down all around them. But in the afternoon a little snow began to fall, fine and brittle, the flakes gathering individually in Lyle's eyelashes, the sparse hair along his brow, the seams beside his nose. And in the snowfall, in her dry grief and fatigue, she waited and watched as he was slowly settled beneath this more gentle white comforter.

And she slept briefly, resting against the stones, dreaming she was a child, lifted and carried sleep-heavy against her daddy's chest, her long thin legs dangling cold beneath the carriage robe.

Unforeseen

IT WAS ONE OF THOSE stucco bungalows over in the hilly part of Los Feliz, on a narrow street with a high bank on one side and houses built down the slope on the other side so their roofs were not very much above road level. This house was on the high side, perched above the street with a long reach of stone steps climbing up from the sidewalk to the porch. Steep yard overgrown with flowers. Italian cypresses along the edge of the porch trimmed short and chunky to make a hedgerow. A fence along the sidewalk with a gate and a coded lock to keep out rapists and burglars but the fence no more than six feet high and charmingly made of wood; any serious burglar or rapist would have been over that fence quicker than sin, it wouldn't have stopped anybody except maybe slacker pot-heads cruising around looking for an open door and a helpful note tacked to the jamb, *jewelry in the bottom drawer under the T-shirts.*

I pushed the admit button, which made a squawking sound inside the house loud enough I could hear it clear down at the sidewalk—loud enough to wake the dead, which, yeah, is a professional joke so old it ought to be retired but I still like it, it still gets a smirk out of some people. In the right crowd. After a minute a woman said something through the speaker box, a few unintelligible words, and I said, "RDI, I'm here about your mother," which was a leap, since I didn't actually know if the garbled voice belonged to the claimant, whose name was Madison Truesdale and who had checked the box Daughter of Deceased and who was black, which I mention only because twelve or fifteen Madisons had cluttered up the rolls of every school I'd gone to since first grade, and every one of them had been white. Anyway, she clicked the lock open and I went up the steps to the porch and she swung the door wide open for me. She was maybe forty, impressively tall, her mouth more than a little bit too wide. She wore pale yellow slacks that didn't look good on her.

I said, smiling slightly, "You should have asked to see my ID before you let me through the gate." I was serious. You get a little paranoid about security when you do this kind of work. A fair number of the claims showing up on my desktop are violent deaths: a woman opening the door to a neatly dressed guy she doesn't know; somebody putting up a six-foot wooden fence and calling it good. Not that better security would have kept Madison Truesdale's mother from being dead, but people should at least try to load the dice.

She gave me a puzzled look. "Well, I was expecting you," she said, in an aristocratic tone of you-be-damnedness.

I let it go. Really, it was her choice whether to play it safe, and anyway her house was just off that tricky Hollywood Boulevard/Sunset Boulevard intersection, which meant statistically she was way more likely to die in a car wreck than murdered by a guy jumping her fence.

I said—the standard patter, so I could later say I'd warned her up front—"The forensics report and the accident reconstruction report have both come in and been approved, but this is, I want to emphasize, still an investigation. A lot of people don't understand the somewhat narrow criteria for coverage, and the purpose of an on-site interview is to close the door on any disqualifying factors. You should know: a significant number of claims are eventually denied." I tipped up the last word of the sentence so she'd know I was asking a question.

"Of course." Her face, her tone of voice, said: *You are not talking to a thickwit.* Which probably meant that Madison Truesdale had read the claims form, and especially the FAQ page. Unfortunately for her, the phrase "snowball's chance" was nowhere on that page.

There was a metal porch chair and a tile-top table just to one side of the door; I figured the stain on the back of the chair was blood. "Was your mother sitting here?" I asked her.

Her mother had been dead all of twenty-four hours, I wouldn't have been surprised if this question provoked some tears. But she only flattened her wide mouth, nodded, said, "Yes. In that chair."

I sat down in the chair and looked out over the tops of the pruned cypresses. I'd been wondering if there was a view from the porch, which there was, the classic L.A. view of hills thickly dotted with houses in a greenscape of palm trees, pepper trees, unpruned cypresses. Smutty sky over it all, of course, this was July, high smog season, and brushfires as usual over in Griffith Park.

"I thought you'd want to come inside and go over the claim," the woman said after a moment, frowning, but not seeming particularly unhappy with me sitting there, making myself comfortable in the chair where her mother had died. I sometimes tried to chafe them like that, just to get an early sounding of their feelings.

"Yes, sure," I said.

When I stood up, she didn't move out of the doorway to let me pass through. "I think I'd better see your ID first," she said, which I guess comes under the heading Better Late Than Never, but if I was a serial murderer I'd have pushed my way inside the house and had her on the floor several minutes ago, and by now might have been quietly disarticulating her corpse.

"Forbes Kipfer," I said, and showed her the ID and waited while she studied the virtual me and then lifted her eyes and studied the biologic me.

"You don't look very happy in this photograph, Mr. Kipfer," she said when she handed it back.

I hardly knew what to say to that, but what popped out was, "It's not a happy job," which was true but not something I'd ever said to a claimant. She nodded, as if this answer didn't surprise her at all. So: maybe not a thickwit, Madison Truesdale.

Every morning there's at least a hundred claims waiting on my desktop, twice that on Monday because they pile up over the weekend. But fuck. Fuck Monday. The first skim is easy, it's always easy. Every goddamn morning I'm denying claims for old folks who died in bed. You have to wonder what in hell people are thinking when they file a claim for their eighty-nine-year-old grandpa with a history of emphysema or congestive heart failure, you wonder whether anybody reads the Policy Summary in the first place, or pays any attention to the bold print on the Declarations, Exclusions, and Special Provisions page.

Then you toss out the cancer cases—most of the deaths by illness, period, regardless of age. There are the obvious issues: if what killed you was something that couldn't be cured while you were alive, it won't suddenly become remediable when you're dead. If it was systemic, or triggered by a gene that hasn't been parsed yet, you're out of luck until the science catches up. But sometimes it's a question of Specifically Excepted Perils. "We do not insure against loss directly or indirectly caused by, resulting from, contributed to, aggravated by, or which would not have occurred but for any of the following, blah blah blah." You're responsible for your own health, is the bottom line. Or we're all responsible in a general way, the whole country, on account of fucking up the air and water. Claims involving death from illness rarely make it past Investigation, and usually come to nothing in Dispute Resolution. Little kids, and young mothers who leave three orphans, okay, those are the hard ones. But if you're dealing for the house, it's your job to deal out hands that go bust. Live with it or quit the game.

Then you weed through the accidentals and the homicides. Some of those are easy too: the gang-bangers and drug dealers making it their life's work to shoot and knife each other. The working girls who get in the line of fire, and the cops and firefighters. You throw out the idiots piloting private planes, mountain climbers, kite surfers. Everybody bites the dust sometime but if you hurry toward it dangling from a belay or rushing into a burning building, don't expect an RD policy to come to your rescue.

After that it gets imprecise, and this is where research and experience comes into play. A standard RD policy has thirty-five pages of print so small you need a magnifier to read it, and it's full of trapdoors—densely worded sub-paragraphs or clauses a sharp investigator can cite to deny a claim. Death by homicide, you learn early on, can often be pinned to Uninsured Location—they picked the wrong neighborhood to live in, or they were driving down the wrong street—and you back it up with statistics. I hardly ever send in car crashes any more, not even the outrageously bizarre ones. A pickup truck traveling the interstate skids on a patch of oil, climbs up and over the lane abutment, T-bones a school bus traveling in the other direction, knocks the bus flying; it lands wheels-down on a two-lane county road at the only point where the road comes close to the highway and the bus then rolls into a guy out for a Sunday drive in his cherry 1963 Ford Fairlane: I sent in a claim for the Sunday driver, and Accident Reconstruction sent it back with a note saying they'd seen almost that same scenario half a dozen times. Anybody who gets into a moving vehicle is just asking to be killed, is what they said. Car, motorcycle—Christ! motorcycle!—plane, train, bicycle, there's almost always a way to deny those claims under the heading Personal Liability or in some cases Acts, Errors and Omissions.

We don't throw out everything sports related, but we try. The first time I got a claim for a minor league third base umpire hit in the neck—a foul ball crushed his artery against his spinal column and he was dead before he could think *Safe!*—I checked the box for Unforeseeable and the box for Nonhazardous Activity, and wrote what I thought was a pretty persuasive argument that umpiring minor league baseball was essentially riskless in terms of life-ending events, and this poor sap had just been standing in the wrong place at the wrong time. Half an inch in one direction or the other and the ball would have left a bruise. Couple of inches, it would have missed him entirely. Well, a message came down from a statistician in the home office: Baseballs in the neck kill two or three people every year in the minor leagues alone, not to mention college, high school, pro ball. Mr. Third Base Umpire hereinafter referred to as Claimant could reasonably be expected to know bodily injury could arise from said activity, blah blah.

So by the time you throw out most of the deaths by illness, most of the accidents, and all the obvious "natural causes," you've winnowed the pile down to a small handful of deaths, mostly freakish things that maybe nobody could have foreseen or avoided. Statistical anomalies. What you're left with is people minding their own business and the sky falls on their head.

We went inside. It was the kind of poorly thought-out space you see in these old unrenovated houses, the front door dividing the room neatly into living and dining, hallway piercing the middle of the far wall, glimpse of kitchen through a doorway on the right side of the hall, glimpse of a tiny bathroom at the far end, couple of closed doors on the left side that must have been bedrooms. Los Feliz was a real estate hotbed, people bought these places, remodeled them with track lights, raised ceilings, bamboo floors, but this one looked pretty much the way it must have looked when it was built, with dusty plate-shaped light fixtures in the low ceilings, oak hardwoods with the finish worn down to dull bare wood in all the high traffic pathways. My guess: Madison Truesdale's mother had put her spare change into paying the premiums on her RD policy. If she had asked, I'd have told her to put the money into bamboo floors.

Another guess: in the day or so since her mother's death, Madison Truesdale hadn't been using the dining room for dining, if she ever had. The table was cluttered with arrangements of flowers no doubt carrying sincere expressions of sympathy, loose stacks of papers that no doubt included her mother's insurance policies, and an assortment of unrelated things that I had fun trying to fit into her story of recent grief: a new Angels baseball cap, a screwdriver and box of screws, a pump jar of skin cream for cracked heels and hands, and a cheap plastic sculpture of a horse tipped over on top of one of the piles of papers. Now that she was alone in the house maybe she was using the dining room for living and the living room for dining: there were a couple of plates with dried-on food, and glasses holding the ripe dregs of tomato juice on the coffee table in front of the sofa.

Madison didn't apologize for the clutter or make any move to pick up the dirty dishes. She gestured that I should sit down in the overstuffed chair that took up a corner of the living room, so I perched myself on the edge of the seat and took out my notepad and stylus and a recorder; she sat down on the end of the sofa that was farthest from me.

I clicked on the recorder and smiled slightly without looking up and started with, "Madison is a very popular name," just to see where that took us.

She knew what I was getting at; I was not the first person to mention it. "It's a family name," she said drily. "My grandmother's maiden name. I was born before they started giving it to all those little white girls." She made a small dismissive sound. "If she'd known what was coming maybe my mother would have called me D'Shawna."

I smiled again. "Your mother lived here with you?" I always went over everything, including everything I already knew the answer to, because sometimes small details emerged from an interview. You were always looking for what would tip the balance.

Madison Truesdale shook her head. She was having none of it. "I'm the one who lives with her."

"Is that right? So did you grow up in this house?"

"Yes I did."

"How long ago did you move back home?"

"I left my husband at the end of April. I'm waiting for my divorce to settle so I'll have money for a down payment on my own place."

I was thinking you might say you'd been here four or five years. That would almost be the cliché, wouldn't it?" I laughed. "Anyway, I guess my parents were worried about it; afraid I'd move back home after my divorce and expect my mother to have dinner ready every night and start doing my laundry; afraid I'd never move back out."

She crossed her legs carelessly, looked away. "I do my own laundry and bring home take-out." I waited a bit, which is sometimes a useful tactic. Sometimes it nudges them; they don't like the silence, and then something shows up. "My mother has her own life and so do I," she said after a moment and turned her head to look at me again. She was deliberately choosing the present tense.

I waited, but so did she. Finally I said, "Can you tell me where you were when your mother died?"

"I was here. At the computer." She gestured toward a little drop-front desk in a corner of the dining room.

I said, "Would you tell me about it?"

She looked out the front window to that smudged view of the Hollywood Hills. "I heard a loud bang. Before I was married I lived in Oakland in a neighborhood where we'd hear gunshots sometimes so I knew it wasn't a gun. Or backfire, this wasn't like a backfire. I thought it was a car accident, two cars crashing into each other. That's what it sounded like. Right in front of the house. So I got up and looked out the window and saw just the one car coasting to a stop. And that's all. So I went out on the porch to ask Mother if she'd seen anything." She crossed her arms and looked right at me. "There was a piece of metal sticking out of her chest, something shaped like the handle of an umbrella, with a curve on the end."

"Was your mother conscious?"

She uncrossed her arms and made a brushing-away gesture. "Oh no, no, she was already dead. I wonder if she even heard the bang."

"Did you realize this metal was from the car in the street?"

She looked at me in some surprise. "I'm fairly sure that wasn't my first thought."

"And did the people in the car realize what had happened?"

"No. Of course not. I could hear them down there in the street, upset about their car, that it had made this terrible noise and then quit running. Who would think? No, of course not."

A car throws a piece of metal off the undercarriage and it strikes a woman sitting on her porch thirty feet above the road, strikes her in her healthy heart and kills her before she has time to turn toward the sound of the bang. Who would think?

. . .

I wasn't kidding about the sky falling on your head. Here's the ad that launched our NewLife Youth Protector Policy: A man and a woman in their thirties step onto a porch very early in the morning, barely dawn, sky heartbreakingly clear, air filled with birdsong. Camera pulls back to show a big, handsomely weathered cedar shingle house, oceanfront. They step off the porch, walk down through the low dunes and saw grass onto the hard sand, and set out on their morning walk. Camera follows them as they clasp hands and begin to swing their arms like kids. Back inside the house two kids are asleep upstairs in separate bedrooms. Close-up of a boy's bare foot sticking out from the edge of the covers. Yellow moons and stars on a little girl's pink pajamas. In the kitchen, a couple in their sixties stirs around making coffee, oatmeal, murmuring to each other just enough so we get the message: they're the grandparents of the children upstairs; this is a family vacation. Then, jarringly, a series of edits from newsreel footage and YouTube clips: the demolished house gouting a thin column of black smoke; the stabilizer fin from the tail of an airplane rising incongruously above the wrecked roof and shattered bricks of the chimney; clumps of neighbors, some of them still in their night clothes, standing on the sidewalk staring at the house openmouthed or taking pictures with their cell phones; plastic sheet–covered bodies lined up on the lawn, two of them very small. Then a long shot of the young couple walking back from the far end of the beach, you see them begin to notice the smoke, see their hesitation, see them begin to hurry. Then cut to the hard pitch, the couple in close-up with the sea at their backs, the woman's hoarse plea: Don't make the mistake of thinking, as we did, that because your children are young,

Remediable Death Insurance is unnecessary or an extravagance. We'd give anything to bring back our children. And if they'd been insured, they'd be with us right now. In our arms, both of them. Her voice breaks. The man, bleak and worn down, pulls her to his chest, looks away from the camera toward the headland at the far end of the beach. Cut to black screen, then the NewLife logo, the sound of the surf in the background.

That advert was fucking perfect.

The plane had an industry-best reliability record, had been recently inspected and serviced, the pilot had a thousand hours incident-free in single engine fixed gear aircraft. It was a clear day. The house was not under any regularly scheduled flight path or near any small airports; the pilot had simply decided to take his wife out that morning on a pleasure flight. The plane struck a pelican along a part of the coast where pelicans hadn't been seen in a decade, and it went down so fast there wasn't time for the pilot to finish saying Mayday. And the kids had died of trauma to the head and chest, their bodies not badly burned or dismembered. It was exactly the sort of thing we can't wriggle out of paying, the sort of thing I don't see more than half a dozen times in a year. Thank god they didn't have insurance.

Of course the parents wanted us to revivify their children in exchange for appearing in the ad, but that would have destroyed the point of the ad; they finally settled for an endowed foundation in the kids' names, something to do with art therapy for impoverished youth I think.

If your mother or your uncle or your brother was suddenly struck dead and you stood to inherit their nice little estate, would you file the paperwork to bring them back to life? Or would you quietly ignore the insurance policy they'd been paying on for years, let them stay dead, and collect your inheritance? It used to surprise me, how often family members would go ahead and file an RD claim, even against their own financial self-interest. I used to think, in cases like that, love for the dead person must trump avarice. Heartwarming, if that was always true. But sometimes it would turn out the dead person had thought ahead and tried to cut off the family's options. Here's what I knew about Madison Truesdale: Her divorce settlement wouldn't buy a studio apartment in Anaheim, but she stood to inherit her mother's house free and clear. Los Feliz, with that view. Plus a little nest egg in CDs and bonds. She and her mother had no other relatives, there had been nobody holding Madison's feet to the fire, nobody to know or care if she had failed to pursue her mother's Remediable Death claim. And Madison hadn't exactly been effusive in her grief. So it was possible she and her mother weren't on the best of terms and her mother had put a coercive clause in her will, something like: In the event of my untimely death, and in the event my daughter fails to make the RD claim, I revoke the previously stated terms of my will and give the entirety of my estate and assets to charity. I hoped for this, actually, because there were ways for the Legal Department to work that angle; ways to make Madison Truesdale a happy heir by making the RD claim go away quietly; and in that case I wouldn't have to keep looking for something to cite—a particular word or phrase in a sub-paragraph of Exclusions or Personal Responsibilities—denying Madison Truesdale's mother an expensive new life.

"Did your mother leave a will?" I asked her.

Madison gave me a dry look. "Yes she did have a will. Were you thinking that's why I filed this claim?"

Her look should have warned me off but I missed the signal; I went ahead with the script, rolling out the words in tones of grave concern. "If there is a clause in your mother's will regarding her RD policy, you may want to get in touch with our Legal Department to discuss your options."

She fixed me with a cool and very hostile stare. "My mother was sitting on her porch reading a magazine and was killed by a piece of shrapnel from a car half a block away. She was insured for this. I insured her. I've been paying her premiums for fifteen years. There was no clause in her will. She left me her house and everything in it, without restrictions. You and your legal department can go to hell."

Okay, sometimes you have to roll over on your back and put all four feet in the air. I fixed my eyes on my hands, twisted the stylus a few times, and then tipped my chin up just enough so I could glance at her from beneath my eyebrows. "I admit, I asked the question in case you were looking for a way to withdraw the claim. I'm uncomfortable with it, but this comes up with some clients, questions of inheritance and probate. We try to let every insured know what their rights and alternatives are." I made a slight gesture with my shoulders, not quite a shrug, more a motion of embarrassed apology. "Not everyone I deal with has loving motives."

She inhaled sharply through her nose, which I thought at first was disgust, disbelief; but then she said with sudden fierce emotion, "I just want my mother back!" and she glanced away, tearing up for the first time. After a moment more she said, choked and passionate, "I love my mother! I just want your company to give me what I've paid for."

I think I let a little silence go by before saying, boilerplate double entendre, "That's why I'm here."

You hear rumors about billionaires a hundred and fifty years old who've had their life restored three or four times, but I happen to know that's crap. People get old, their ability to regenerate tissue slows down and finally stops, even if said tissue is carefully nurtured in a green-tank and then a forcing bed. Plus, most people die of something irremediable anyway, and this is especially true after you hit seventy or so. It's what insurance companies count on. But we love those billionaire rumors; we're happy to foster them. Our advertising is all about fairness, equity, rightness. We play the class card. The resurrected people we showcase in our ads—people who had NewLife policies when they died from an unforeseen event—are welders and bus drivers and schoolteachers. Look, we say, it's not just the wealthy who should be able to come back from the dead. Our premiums are modest; we want to make it possible for the average man or woman on the street to afford the prohibitively expensive cost of revivification—when possible, of course. To the old question, "Who deserves to be repaired, and restored to life, when they've died before their time?" our answer is, "You!"

What we don't say is that the wealthy aren't bound by the limits of an insurance policy. They foot that astronomical bill themselves, which means they don't have to fear Perils and Exclusions even if they died skiing into a tree at Chamonix Mont-Blanc or trying to set a round-the-world record for high-altitude hot air balloons. If somebody in the family is willing to write a check, and there's sufficient healthy tissue on a fairly intact body, they're good to go. Again.

None of this is a secret, or not much of one, and you'd think by now the hoi polloi would be wise to it. You'd think they would know that most people die of something quite irremediable; that "sufficient healthy tissue on a fairly intact body" is the exception, not the rule, in cases of early death. But I guess people are still looking for a hole card, a winning lottery ticket. Or they think a Remediable Death policy somehow takes randomness, meaninglessness, out of the equation. They haven't realized yet: in this game the cards are marked. I don't know anybody in the insurance business who owns an RD policy, and really, why would we? There's a nasty little saying in the industry: only the rich die twice.

Madison Truesdale had surprised me with that sudden display of feeling. I'm unimpressed by the weepers and wailers, which is what I mostly run into. Or the ones who don't give a rat's ass and don't try to hide it. The dignified and private grievers, people like Madison, people holding it in, holding it together, they're like snow in August, and I'm always surprised when one turns up. Plus, I thought I had this woman pegged and now she'd thrown me off my stride.

I clicked off the recorder, which people often take as the end of the official interview. Then I settled back in the chair and started again, dealing out just a few more questions like face cards between runs of aimless impersonal chitchat—making up for that rude business about wills and legal loopholes. There was a chance this tactic would dull her into an unexpected or careless revelation; or maybe not, and this would turn out to be a claim I could forward to the home office for payment. I asked how long her mother had lived in this house, and when she said thirty years I shook my head and smiled and told her I hadn't ever lived anywhere longer than a couple of years. Told her I used to live in Los Feliz myself, used to go to the old Liberty Theater just up the block from here, too bad they didn't still run it as an art house, nothing playing there now but Hollywood buzz bombs. She didn't seem to think any of this required a response. I said I lived over in the Valley now, the cheap edge of Thousand Oaks, brushfires pretty much all summer, which, if I stayed there—little sad smirk—probably improved my chances of dying from pulmonary issues. This time she looked away and pursed her mouth, impatient or offended. I asked, did her mother often sit out on the porch? Yes, she said, just the one word. Great view from that porch, I told her, too bad about the smoke from Griffith Park obscuring the hillside but in the winter the view must clear up, was I right about that? Which got a small acknowledgment. Finally when I said I recognized the horse on her dining room table, Da Vinci's very famous clay model horse, she looked over at it and said dismissively, "That's a cheap plastic copy Mother picked up in a gift shop in Florence on her one and only trip to Europe."

I smiled. "I was in Florence two years ago. I saw a full-scale model of that horse. When was your mother there?"

She said, "I don't remember," but then turned back to me and seemed to think over the question. After a bit she said, "Eight or nine years ago. She went with her sister Drewsy. Drewsy died the next summer, an aneurism, so I guess that makes it seven years ago." After another moment, she gestured toward the front windows. "Drewsy used to help Mother keep the garden up. I had forgotten that. It's overgrown now. Mother hasn't been able to keep up with it on her own."

"I like the look of it, the wildness," I said, which was true. Then I smiled and said I wasn't in favor of the cypresses pruned along the porch—too formal for the lovely disorder of those flowers. I thought this might provoke a friendly argument, but she may have known I was playing her. Or she meant it when she said she didn't know anything about flowers, that the yard was her mother's thing. I rattled off the names of the flowers I recognized—fleabane, Catalina lilies, coreopsis—and that I had learned the names of flowers from my mother, which was also true.

After a silence, she said, "Is your mother still living?"

"Yes she is." I considered whether to play the next card and then I said, "I had a younger brother who died of lymphoma"—this was another true thing—"and my mother has never really recovered from it."

She looked over at me. "How old was he when he died?"

"He was twenty-eight."

She went on looking at me and then nodded as if this was information that did not surprise her in any way.

Here is the complicated thing about staring too hard at death, at the causes of death. You start to think every death has a cause; or rather, you start to think every death would not have occurred but for one small thing. That every death was caused by, resulted from, was contributed to or aggravated by—something. And on the one hand this is comforting. You think, if you could just control all the factors, you'd live forever. When you can dig down and find the little misstep, the oversight, the omission, the thing that gave just enough push to start the bones rolling, you feel reassured, and you put that little thing onto your mental list of things you will never, ever do.

And on the other hand you think, fuck it, the sky could fall on my head.

I had not asked her for details about the minutes right after her mother's death. But at some point as we went on talking she simply began to tell me, how she had called down to the couple in the street, the ones with the broken-down car, because they were the only people around. She told me how they had come up to help her, and how all three of them had suddenly and at the same time and with horror realized what must have happened. She told me these were neighbors she knew, neighbors her mother knew, a young couple who smoked too much dope and stood outside late at night with their loud friends swearing and arguing. Madison's mother had come out once in the middle of the night and called down to them that she was trying to sleep, and someone among them—she didn't know if it was one of her neighbors or one of their friends—had yelled, "Fuck you, you old nigger bitch," and laughed. After that, Madison's mother usually got up from the porch and came inside the house when she heard their loud, jacked-up car pulling into the street—she was a little afraid of them, Madison thought, or she may have believed the act of getting up, going inside, was sending them a mute little message of disdain.

Madison Truesdale said, "I don't know why she didn't come in, this time. She wouldn't be dead if she'd come inside." Her eyes were so dark I couldn't see the irises, and bright with unshed tears.

I told her that she would receive a report within forty-eight hours. She asked me if I saw any reason why the claim might be denied and I said I wasn't able to comment. She offered me a lemonade and I accepted it and we talked a little bit longer about things unrelated to her mother. We talked about Oakland where she had lived for a short time and where my ex-wife now lived. It turned out we had both been to Greece, to the islands off the coast, and we talked about that, the houses so white against the bright blue of the sea and the sky.

On the way downtown I stopped at a bar and had a couple of drinks, Grey Goose and tonic, doubles. They didn't do me any good. It occurred to me I was killing a few brain cells, but alcohol, besides having a long time horizon, just fucked up your life too much; it wasn't how I'd want to go out. On the other hand, sitting there, I began to think of taking up smoking. Smoking plus living in Thousand Oaks under that cloud of dirty air might take some of the randomness out of the equation. Anyway, that's what I was thinking.

Lambing Season

FROM MAY TO SEPTEMBER DELIA took the Churro sheep and two dogs and went up on Joe-Johns Mountain to live. She had that country pretty much to herself all summer. Ken Owen sent one of his Mexican hands up every other week with a load of groceries but otherwise she was alone, alone with the sheep and the dogs. She liked the solitude. Liked the silence. Some sheepherders she knew talked a blue streak to the dogs, the rocks, the porcupines, they sang songs and played the radio, read their magazines out loud, but Delia let the silence settle into her and by early summer she had begun to hear the ticking of the dry grasses as a language she could almost translate. The dogs were named Jesus and Alice. "Away to me, Hey-sus," she said when they were moving the sheep. "Go bye, Alice." From May to September these words spoken in command of the dogs were almost the only times she heard her own voice; that, and when the Mexican brought the groceries, a polite exchange in Spanish about the weather, the health of the dogs, the fecundity of the ewes.

The Churros were a very old breed. The O-Bar Ranch had a federal allotment up on the mountain, which was all rimrock and sparse grasses well suited to the Churros, who were fiercely protective of their lambs and had a long-stapled top coat that could take the weather. They did well on the thin grass of the mountain where other sheep would lose flesh and give up their lambs to the coyotes. The Mexican was an old man. He said he remembered Churros from his childhood in the Oaxaca highlands, the rams with their four horns, two curving up, two down. "Buen' carne," he told Delia. Uncommonly fine meat.

The wind blew out of the southwest in the early part of the season, a wind that smelled of juniper and sage and pollen; in the later months it blew straight from the east, a dry wind smelling of dust and smoke, bringing down showers of parched leaves and seedheads of yarrow and bittercress. Thunderstorms came frequently out of the east, enormous cloudscapes with hearts of livid magenta and glaucous green. At those times, if she was camped on a ridge she'd get out of her bed and walk downhill to find a draw where she could feel safer, but if she was camped in a low place she would stay with the sheep while a war passed over their heads, spectacular jagged flares of lightning, skull-rumbling cannonades of thunder. It was maybe bred into the bones of Churros, a knowledge and a tolerance of mountain weather, for they shifted together and waited out the thunder with surprising composure; they stood forbearingly while rain beat down in hard blinding bursts.

Sheepherding was simple work, although Delia knew some herders who made it hard, dogging the sheep every minute, keeping them in a tight group, moving all the time. She let the sheep herd themselves, do what they wanted, make their own decisions. If the band began to separate she would whistle or yell, and often the strays would turn around and rejoin the main group. Only if they were badly scattered did she send out the dogs. Mostly she just kept an eye on the sheep, made sure they got good feed, that the band didn't split, that they stayed in the boundaries of the O-Bar allotment. She studied the sheep for the language of their bodies, and tried to handle them just as close to their nature as possible. When she put out salt for them, she scattered it on rocks and stumps as if she was hiding Easter eggs, because she saw how they enjoyed the search.

The spring grass made their manure wet, so she kept the wool cut away from the ewes' tail area with a pair of sharp, short-bladed shears. She dosed the sheep with wormer, trimmed their feet, inspected their teeth, treated ewes for mastitis. She combed the burrs from the dogs' coats and inspected them for ticks. *You're such good dogs*, she told them with her hands. *I'm very very proud of you.*

She had some old binoculars, 7 × 32s, and in the long quiet days she watched bands of wild horses miles off in the distance, ragged looking mares with dorsal stripes and black legs. She read the back issues of the local newspapers, looking in the obits for names she recognized. She read spine-broken paperback novels and played solitaire and scoured the ground for arrowheads and rocks she would later sell to rockhounds. She studied the parched brown grass, which was full of grasshoppers and beetles and crickets and ants. But most of her day was spent just walking. The sheep sometimes bedded quite a ways from her trailer and she had to get out to them before sunrise when the coyotes would make their kills. She was usually up by three or four and walking out to the sheep in darkness. Sometimes she returned to the camp for lunch, but always she was out with the sheep again until sundown when the coyotes were likely to return, and then she walked home after dark to water and feed the dogs, eat supper, climb into bed.

In her first years on Joe-Johns she had often walked three or four miles away from the band just to see what was over a hill, or to study the intricate architecture of a sheepherder's monument. Stacking up flat stones in the form of an obelisk was a common herders pastime, their monuments all over that sheep country, and though Delia had never felt an impulse to start one herself, she admired the ones other people had built. She sometimes walked miles out of her way just to look at a rockpile up close.

She had a mental map of the allotment, divided into ten pastures. Every few days, when the sheep had moved on to a new pasture, she moved her camp. She towed the trailer with an old Dodge pickup, over the rocks and creekbeds, the sloughs and dry meadows to the new place. For a while afterward, after the engine was shut off and while the heavy old body of the truck was settling onto its tires, she would be deaf, her head filled with a dull roaring white noise.

She had about eight hundred ewes, as well as their lambs, many of them twins or triplets. The ferocity of the Churro ewes in defending their offspring was sometimes a problem for the dogs, but in the balance of things she knew it kept her losses small. Many coyotes lived on Joe-Johns, and sometimes a cougar or bear would come up from the salt pan desert on the north side of the mountain, looking for better country to own. These animals considered the sheep to be fair game, which Delia understood to be their right; and also her right, hers and the dogs, to take the side of the sheep. Sheep were smarter than people commonly believed and the Churros smarter than other sheep she had tended, but by midsummer the coyotes had passed the word among themselves, buen' carne, and Delia and the dogs then had a job of work, keeping the sheep out of harm's way.

She carried a .32 caliber Colt pistol in an old-fashioned holster worn on her belt. If you're a coyot' you'd better be careful of this woman, she said with her body, with the way she stood and the way she walked when she was wearing the pistol. That gun and holster had once belonged to her mother's mother, a woman who had come West on her own and homesteaded for a while, down in the Sprague River Canyon. Delia's grandmother had liked to tell the story: how a concerned neighbor, a bachelor with an interest in marriageable females, had pressed the gun upon her, back when the Klamaths were at war with the army of General Joel Palmer; and how she never had used it for anything but shooting rabbits.

In July a coyote killed a lamb while Delia was camped no more than two hundred feet away from the bedded sheep. It was dusk and she was sitting on the steps of the trailer reading a two-gun western, leaning close over the pages in the failing light, and the dogs were dozing at her feet. She heard the small sound, a strange high faint squeal she did not recognize and then did recognize, and she jumped up and fumbled for the gun, yelling at the coyote, at the dogs, her yell startling the entire band to its feet but the ewes making their charge too late, Delia firing too late, and none of it doing any good beyond a release of fear and anger.

A lion might well have taken the lamb entire; she had known of lion kills where the only evidence was blood on the grass and a dribble of entrails in the beam of a flashlight. But a coyote is small and will kill with a bite to the throat and then perhaps eat just the liver and heart, though a mother coyote will take all she can carry in her stomach, bolt it down and carry it home to her pups. Delia's grandmother's pistol had scared this one off before it could even take a bite, and the lamb was twitching and whole on the grass, bleeding only from its neck. The mother ewe stood over it, crying in a distraught and pitiful way, but there was nothing to be done, and in a few minutes the lamb was dead.

There wasn't much point in chasing after the coyote, and anyway the whole band was now a skittish jumble of anxiety and confusion; it was hours before the mother ewe gave up her grieving, before Delia and the dogs had the band calm and bedded down again, almost midnight. By then the dead lamb had stiffened on the ground and she dragged it over by the truck and skinned it and let the dogs have the meat, which went against her nature but was about the only way to keep the coyote from coming back for the carcass.

While the dogs worked on the lamb, she stood with both hands pressed to her tired back looking out at the sheep, the mottled pattern of their whiteness almost opalescent across the black landscape, and the stars thick and bright above the faint outline of the rock ridges, stood there a moment before turning toward the trailer, toward bed, and afterward she would think how the coyote and the sorrowing ewe and the dark of the July moon and the kink in her back, how all of that came together and was the reason she was standing there watching the sky, was the reason she saw the brief, brilliantly green flash in the southwest and then the sulfur yellow streak breaking across the night, southwest to due west on a descending arc onto Lame

Man Bench. It was a broad bright ribbon, rainbow-wide, a cya-
notic contrail. It was not a meteor, she had seen hundreds of
meteors. She stood and looked at it.

Things to do with the sky, with distance, you could lose perspective, it was hard to judge even a lightning strike, whether it
had touched down on a particular hill or the next hill or the valley between. So she knew this thing falling out of the sky might
have come down miles to the west of Lame Man, not onto Lame
Man at all, which was two miles away, at least two miles, and
getting there would be all ridges and rocks, no way to cover the
ground in the truck. She thought about it. She had moved camp
earlier in the day, which was always troublesome work, and it
had been a blistering hot day, and now the excitement with the
coyote. She was very tired, the tiredness like a weight against
her breastbone. She didn't know what this thing was, falling out
of the sky. Maybe if she walked over there she would find just a
dead satellite or a broken weather balloon and not dead or broken people. The contrail thinned slowly while she stood there
looking at it, became a wide streak of yellowy cloud against the
blackness, with the field of stars glimmering dimly behind it.

After a while she went into the truck and got a water bottle
and filled it and also took the first aid kit out of the trailer and a
couple of spare batteries for the flashlight and a handful of extra
cartridges for the pistol and stuffed these things into a backpack and looped her arms into the straps and started up the
rise away from the dark camp, the bedded sheep. The dogs left
off their gnawing of the dead lamb and trailed her anxiously,
wanting to follow, or not wanting her to leave the sheep. "Stay
by," she said to them sharply, and they went back and stood
with the band and watched her go. *That coyot', he's done with us*

tonight: this was what she told the dogs with her body, walking away, and she believed it was probably true.

Now that she'd decided to go, she walked fast. This was her sixth year on the mountain and by this time she knew the country pretty well. She didn't use the flashlight. Without it, she became accustomed to the starlit darkness, able to see the stones and pick out a path. The air was cool but full of the smell of heat rising off the rocks and the parched earth. She heard nothing but her own breathing and the gritting of her boots on the pebbly dirt. A little owl circled once in silence and then went off toward a line of cottonwood trees standing in black silhouette to the northeast.

Lame Man Bench was a great upthrust block of basalt grown over with scraggly juniper forest. As she climbed among the trees the smell of something like ozone or sulfur grew very strong, and the air became thick, burdened with dust. Threads of the yellow contrail hung in the limbs of the trees. She went on across the top of the bench and onto slabs of shelving rock that gave a view to the west. Down in the steep-sided draw below her there was a big wing-shaped piece of metal resting on the ground which she at first thought had been torn from an airplane, but then realized was a whole thing, not broken, and she quit looking for the rest of the wreckage. She squatted down and looked at it. Yellow dust settled slowly out of the sky, pollinating her hair, her shoulders, the toes of her boots, faintly dulling the oily black shine of the wing, the thing shaped like a wing.

While she was squatting there looking down at it, something came out from the sloped underside of it, a coyote she thought at first, and then it wasn't a coyote but a dog built like a greyhound or a whippet, deep-chested, long legged, very light-boned and frail looking. She waited for somebody else, a man, to crawl out after his dog, but nobody did. The dog squatted to pee and then moved off a short distance and sat on its haunches and considered things. Delia considered too. She considered that the dog might have been sent up alone. The Russians had sent up a dog in their little Sputnik, she remembered. She considered that a skinny almost hairless dog with frail bones would be dead in short order if left alone in this country. And she considered that there might be a man inside the wing, dead or too hurt to climb out. She thought how much trouble it would be, getting down this steep rock bluff in the darkness to rescue a useless dog and a dead man.

After a while she stood and started picking her way into the draw. The dog by this time was smelling the ground, making a slow and careful circuit around the black wing. Delia kept expecting the dog to look up and bark, but it went on with its intent inspection of the ground as if it was stone deaf, as if Delia's boots making a racket on the loose gravel was not an announcement that someone was coming down. She thought of the old Dodge truck, how it always left her ears ringing, and wondered if maybe it was the same with this dog and its wing-shaped Sputnik, although the wing had fallen soundless across the sky.

When she had come about halfway down the hill she lost footing and slid down six or eight feet before she got her heels dug in and found a handful of willow scrub to hang on to. A glimpse of this movement—rocks sliding to the bottom, or the dust she raised—must have startled the dog, for it leaped backward suddenly and then reared up. They looked at each other in silence, Delia and the dog, Delia standing leaning into the

steep slope a dozen yards above the bottom of the draw, and
the dog standing next to the Sputnik, standing all the way up
on its hind legs like a bear or a man and no longer seeming to
be a dog but a person with a long narrow muzzle and a narrow chest, turned-out knees, delicate dog-like feet. Its genitals
were more cat-like than dog, a male set but very small and neat
and contained. Dog's eyes, though, dark and small and shining
below an anxious brow, so that she was reminded of Jesus and
Alice, the way they had looked at her when she had left them
alone with the sheep. She had years of acquaintance with dogs
and she knew enough to look away, break off her stare. Also,
after a moment, she remembered the old pistol and holster at
her belt. In cowboy pictures, a man would unbuckle his gunbelt
and let it down on the ground as a gesture of peaceful intent,
but it seemed to her this might only bring attention to the gun,
to the true intent of a gun, which is always killing. *This woman
is nobody at all to be scared of,* she told the dog with her body,
standing very still along the steep hillside, holding on to the
scrub willow with her hands, looking vaguely to the left of him
where the smooth curve of the wing rose up and gathered a
veneer of yellow dust.

The dog, the dog person, opened his jaws and yawned the
way a dog will do to relieve nervousness, and then they were
both silent and still for a minute. When finally he turned and
stepped toward the wing, it was an unexpected, delicate movement, exactly the way a ballet dancer steps along on his toes,
knees turned out, lifting his long thin legs; and then he dropped
down on all fours and seemed to become almost a dog again.
He went back to his business of smelling the ground intently,
though every little while he looked up to see if Delia was still

standing along the rock slope. It was a steep place to stand. When her knees finally gave out, she sat down very carefully where she was, which didn't spook him. He had become used to her by then, and his brief, sliding glance just said, That woman up there is nobody at all to be scared of.

What he was after, or wanting to know, was a mystery to her. She kept expecting him to gather up rocks, like all those men who'd gone to the moon, but he only smelled the ground, making a wide slow circuit around the wing the way Alice and Jesus always circled round the trailer every morning, noses down, reading the dirt like a book. And when he seemed satisfied with what he'd learned, he stood up again and looked back at Delia, a last look delivered across his shoulder before he dropped down and disappeared under the edge of the wing, a grave and inquiring look, the kind of look a dog or a man will give you before going off on his own business, a look that says, You be okay if I go? If he had been a dog, and if Delia had been close enough to do it, she'd have scratched the smooth head, felt the hard bone beneath, moved her hands around the soft ears. *Sure, okay, you go on now, Mr. Dog:* This is what she would have said with her hands. Then he crawled into the darkness under the slope of the wing, where she figured there must be a door, a hatch letting into the body of the machine, and after a while he flew off into the dark of the July moon.

In the weeks afterward, on nights when the moon had set or hadn't yet risen, she looked for the flash and streak of something breaking across the darkness out of the southwest. She saw him come and go to that draw on the west side of Lame Man Bench twice more in the first month. Both times, she left her grandmother's gun in the trailer and walked over there and sat in the dark on the rock slab above the draw and watched him for a couple of hours. He may have been waiting for her, or he knew her smell, because both times he reared up and looked at her just about as soon as she sat down. But then he went on with his business. *That woman is nobody to be scared of,* he said with his body, with the way he went on smelling the ground, widening his circle and widening it, sometimes taking a clod or a sprig into his mouth and tasting it, the way a mild-mannered dog will do when he's investigating something and not paying any attention to the person he's with.

Delia had about decided that the draw behind Lame Man Bench was one of his regular stops, like the ten campsites she used over and over again when she was herding on Joe-Johns Mountain; but after those three times in the first month she didn't see him again.

At the end of September she brought the sheep down to the O-Bar. After the lambs had been shipped out she took her band of dry ewes over onto the Nelson prairie for the fall, and in mid-November when the snow had settled in, she brought them to the feed lots. That was all the work the ranch had for her until lambing season. Jesus and Alice belonged to the O-Bar. They stood in the yard and watched her go.

In town she rented the same room as the year before, and, as before, spent most of a year's wages on getting drunk and standing other herders to rounds of drink. She gave up looking into the sky.

In March she went back out to the ranch. In bitter weather they built jugs and mothering-up pens, and trucked the pregnant ewes from Green, where they'd been feeding on wheat stubble. Some ewes lambed in the trailer on the way in, and after every haul there was a surge of lambs born. Delia had the night shift, where she was paired with Roy Joyce, a fellow who raised sugar beets over in the valley and came out for the lambing season every year. In the black, freezing cold middle of the night, eight and ten ewes would be lambing at a time. Triplets, twins, big singles, a few quads, ewes with lambs born dead, ewes too sick or confused to mother. She and Roy would skin a dead lamb and feed the carcass to the ranch dogs and wrap the fleece around a bummer lamb, which was intended to fool the bereaved ewe into taking the orphan as her own, and sometimes it worked that way. All the mothering-up pens swiftly filled, and the jugs filled, and still some ewes with new lambs stood out in the cold field waiting for a room to open up.

You couldn't pull the stuck lambs with gloves on, you had to reach into the womb with your fingers to turn the lamb, or tie cord around the feet, or grasp the feet barehanded, so Delia's hands were always cold and wet, then cracked and bleeding. The ranch had brought in some old converted school buses to house the lambing crew, and she would fall into a bunk at daybreak and then not be able to sleep, shivering in the unheated bus with the gray daylight pouring in the windows and the endless daytime clamor out at the lambing sheds. All the lambers had sore throats, colds, nagging coughs. Roy Joyce looked like hell, deep bags as blue as bruises under his eyes, and Delia figured she looked about the same, though she hadn't seen a mirror, not even to draw a brush through her hair, since the start of the season.

By the end of the second week, only a handful of ewes hadn't lambed. The nights became quieter. The weather cleared, and the thin skiff of snow melted off the grass. On the dark of the moon, Delia was standing outside the mothering-up pens drinking coffee from a thermos. She put her head back and held the warmth of the coffee in her mouth a moment, and as she was swallowing it down, lowering her chin, she caught the tail end of a green flash and a thin yellow line breaking across the sky, so far off anybody else would have thought it was a meteor, but it was bright, and dropping from southwest to due west, maybe right onto Lame Man Bench. She stood and looked at it. She was so very goddamned tired and had a sore throat that wouldn't clear and she could barely get her fingers to fold around the thermos, they were so split and tender.

She told Roy she felt sick as a horse, and did he think he could handle things if she drove herself into town to the Urgent Care clinic, and she took one of the ranch trucks and drove up the road a short way and then turned onto the rutted track that went up to Joe-Johns.

The night was utterly clear and you could see things a long way off. She was still an hour's drive from the Churros' summer range when she began to see a yellow-orange glimmer behind the black ridgeline, a faint nimbus like the ones that marked distant range fires on summer nights.

She had to leave the truck at the bottom of the bench and climb up the last mile or so on foot, had to get a flashlight out of the glove box and try to find an uphill path with it because the fluttery reddish lightshow was finished by then, and a thick pall of smoke overcast the sky and blotted out the stars. Her eyes itched and burned, and tears ran from them, but the smoke calmed her sore throat. She went up slowly, breathing through her mouth.

The wing had burned a skid path through the scraggly junipers along the top of the bench and had come apart into about a hundred pieces. She wandered through the burnt trees and the scattered wreckage, shining her flashlight into the smoky darkness, not expecting to find what she was looking for, but there he was, lying apart from the scattered pieces of metal, out on the smooth slab rock at the edge of the draw. He was panting shallowly and his close coat of short brown hair was matted with blood. He lay in such a way that she immediately knew his back was broken. When he saw Delia coming up, his brow furrowed with worry. A sick or a wounded dog will bite, she knew that, but she squatted next to him. It's just me, she told him, by shining the light not in his face but in hers. Then she spoke to him. "Okay," she said. "I'm here now," without thinking too much about what the words meant, or whether they meant anything at all, and she didn't remember until afterward that he was very likely deaf anyway. He sighed and shifted his look from her to the middle distance, where she supposed he was focused on approaching death.

Near at hand, he didn't resemble a dog all that much, only in the long shape of his head, the folded-over ears, the round darkness of his eyes. He lay on the ground flat on his side like a dog that's been run over and is dying by the side of the road, but a man will lay like that too when he's dying. He had small-fingered nail-less hands where a dog would have had toes and front feet. Delia offered him a sip from her water bottle but he didn't seem to want it, so she just sat with him quietly, holding one of his hands, which was smooth as lambskin against the cracked and roughened flesh of her palm. The batteries in the flashlight gave out, and sitting there in the cold darkness she found his head and stroked it, moving her sore fingers lightly over the bone of his skull, and around the soft ears, the loose jowls. Maybe it wasn't any particular comfort to him but she was comforted by doing it. *Sure, okay, you can go on.*

She heard him sigh, and then sigh again, and each time wondered if it would turn out to be his death. She had used to wonder what a coyote, or especially a dog would make of this doggish man, and now while she was listening, waiting to hear if he would breathe again, she began to wish she'd brought Alice or Jesus with her, though not out of that old curiosity. When her husband had died years before, at the very moment he took his last breath, the dog she'd had then had barked wildly and raced back and forth from the front to the rear door of the house as if he'd heard or seen something invisible to her. People said it was her husband's soul going out the door or his angel coming in. She didn't know what it was the dog had seen or heard or smelled, but she wished she knew. And now she wished she had a dog with her to bear witness.

She went on petting him even after he had died, after she was sure he was dead, went on petting him until his body was cool, and then she got up stiffly from the bloody ground and gathered rocks and piled them onto him, a couple of feet high so he wouldn't be found or dug up. She didn't know what to do about the wreckage, so she didn't do anything with it at all.

In May, when she brought the Churro sheep back to Joe-Johns Mountain, the pieces of the wrecked wing had already eroded, were small and smooth-edged like the bits of sea glass you find on a beach, and she figured this must be what it was meant to do: to break apart into pieces too small for anybody to notice, and then to quickly wear away. But the stones she'd piled over his body seemed like the start of something, so she began the slow work of raising them higher into a sheepherders monument. She gathered up all the smooth eroded bits of wing, too, and laid them in a series of widening circles around the base of the monument. She went on piling up stones through the summer and into September until it reached fifteen feet. Mornings, standing with the sheep miles away, she would look for it through the binoculars and think about ways to raise it higher, and she would wonder what was buried under all the other monuments sheepherders had raised in that country. At night she studied the sky, but nobody came for him.

In November when she finished with the sheep and went into town, she asked around and found a guy who knew about stargazing and telescopes. He loaned her some books and sent her to a certain pawnshop, and she gave most of a year's wages for a 14 × 75 telescope with a reflective lens. On clear, moonless nights she met the astronomy guy out at the Little League baseball field and she sat on a fold-up canvas stool with her eye against the telescope's finder while he told her what she was seeing: Jupiter's moons, the Pelican Nebula, the Andromeda Galaxy. The telescope had a tripod mount, and he showed her how to make a little jerry-built device so she could mount her old 7 × 32 binoculars on the tripod too. She used the binoculars for their wider view of star clusters and small constellations. She was indifferent to most discomforts, could sit quietly in one position for hours at a time, teeth rattling with the cold, staring into the immense vault of the sky until she became numb and stiff, barely able to stand and walk back home. Astronomy, she discovered, was a work of patience, but the sheep had taught her patience, or it was already in her nature before she ever took up with them.

The Visited Man

IN APRIL, AFTER THE DEATH of his son followed hard on the heels the death of his wife, Marie-Lucien stopped going out of his apartment. It had been his habit to go out every morning to buy a newspaper, five bronze centimes for *Le Petit Journal*; but as he stopped caring to read about assassinations and political scandals, or anything else occurring in the world, so he stopped going out to buy the paper. Then he stopped going to the butcher, the tea shop, the fish market, the bakery. Every Wednesday and Saturday his landlord M. Queval brought a few groceries and sundries to him from lists he scribbled on scraps of old newsprint. He and M. Queval exchanged perhaps a dozen words while standing on the landing, words about frostbit spinach or the freshness of the fish, but otherwise Marie-Lucien saw no one, spoke to no one. Friends who came to the house went away without sight of him, or after a curt word passed through the cracked-open door; and after the first weeks they stopped bothering to inquire of his well-being.

He had taken his pension from the service more than a year earlier, a pension barely sufficient to pay the rent and the groceries, and had been working mornings for a trinket vendor in order to eke out a decent living for himself. Now he stopped going out to work, which meant the matter of money would eventually become acute; but he ate very little, spent nothing on clothes, and the weather in April was warm enough to put off the question of coal. He slept in his clothes. In the morning he warmed up yesterday's bad coffee and drank it while looking out at the traffic in the street. Then he undressed slowly and performed the necessary morning ablutions, before dressing again in shabby clothes. Most of the hours of his days were spent turning over a deck of cards in slow games of Patience.

Late in May, after Marie-Lucien had spent the better part of two months alone with no expectation or wish for this to change, someone knocked on his door. He would not have bothered to answer, but the knocking became continuous and insistent and finally he felt forced to open to whoever it was. The apartment directly below his, and just above the landlord M. Queval's metal foundry, was occupied by an artist, a painter of poor reputation who people in the neighborhood said was either a clever joker or slightly mad, a precocious senile. It was this painter who now stood on the landing, wearing a tranquil expression as though he had not for the past many minutes been pounding vigorously on the door in a demand to be let in. He held in one arm a skeletal brown tabby, and announced matter-of-factly that the cat had followed him back from his morning walk through Montsouris Park, and that he could not take it into his own apartment because "as you know, there are the other cats." He spoke as if Marie-Lucien was privy to information he in fact was not privy to. The two men had seldom met, seldom exchanged more than a remark about the weather as they passed each other going in or out of their apartments; and in the past two months they had not met or spoken at all. Now, as if they had already discussed the matter and reached some sort of agreement, he delivered the little tabby into Marie-Lucien's hands. "She is starving, you realize, and her stomach must first be calmed with tiny portions of oatmeal before she will be able to keep down cream and fish and begin to put on weight."

Marie-Lucien, who was startled out of words, managed only, "I cannot . . . ," and the painter, who had already begun to descend the stairs, replied cheerfully without turning, "Oh my dear, none of us can."

Marie-Lucien put the cat on the floor of the landing and shut the door, but her continuous piteous crying was difficult to listen to. He finally opened the door again, but only to put out scraps of a lunch he had not eaten, which she ate and then immediately vomited. He was forced to boil up some oatmeal and feed it to her slowly until her starving stomach became calm. And of course by the time she began to put on weight from being fed little tidbits of fish and sips of cream, she had made herself at home in his apartment.

The arrival of the cat did little to change Marie-Lucien's habits. He continued to sleep in his clothes and to spend his days playing solitary card games. But now that his attention had been drawn to it, he frequently heard the voice of the painter rising up from the apartment below him, particularly at night, muttering to himself or perhaps speaking to his paintings; sometimes declaiming lines of poetry; sometimes singing badly or playing a few fragile notes on a violin, the refrains of humorous and nostalgic songs Marie-Lucien remembered from his own childhood and from the nursery days of his son. When Rousseau thumped heavily against the walls or the floor and woke him in the night, he complained aloud to the cat: "Do you hear him? The damn painter? He is stumbling drunk again." Presumably these sounds had been coming up through the floor during the entire year the painter had lived in the apartment; Marie-Lucien had simply been oblivious of them until now—preoccupied with watching over the illness and death of his wife, and then his son.

In June, after a string of unreasonably cold and rainy days, there was again a banging on the door and the painter held out a squat black dog whose wiry coat was muddy and matted. "Abused and abandoned," he said, with a brief, commiserating smile.

"I cannot," Marie-Lucien said, and shut the door.

The painter began beating on the jamb, calling and repeating, "M. Pichon, M. Pichon."

Finally Marie-Lucien opened the door again. "I am not M. Pichon," he said unhappily. "Please go and find this man Pichon, give him the dog and leave me alone."

The painter shook his head, still smiling. "Ha ha, I am famous, among other things, for getting wrong the names even of my friends." He bowed slightly. "M. Guyard, I apologize." This was not Marie-Lucien's name any more than Pichon, but it seemed pointless to say so. "He likes tomatoes," the painter said, "and chicken," and for a confused moment Marie-Lucien thought he was speaking of Pichon, or Guyard; but then the painter placed the dog in his arms and turned for the stairs.

Hurriedly Marie-Lucien started after him, holding out the animal, which smelled of mud and oak leaves and the sewer.

"This is impossible!" he protested. "M. Rousseau, take him back." He intended to sound strict and authoritative but he had been speechless for so long that his voice came out hoarse and thin: even to his own ears, his urgent insistence that he could not keep the dog seemed as querulous as an old woman's whining; and as he trailed the painter down the stairs, he ridiculously called out that he could not afford chicken even for himself. Nevertheless, he went on repeating his refusal as he followed the painter right into his apartment, where he was startled to find himself suddenly in a jungle—huge umbrellates, fans, rockets, cascades of intense greens, spangled with the enormous cups and corollas of unimaginably bright magenta and yellow flowers.

"Oh!" he said, and staggered back.

They were paintings, of course, many of them quite large paintings, standing along all the walls of the rooms, and Marie-Lucien blushed and straightened up when he realized it. In fact, they were not even very good paintings, having no more than a child's sense of perspective, and drawn entirely without shadow or relief. The tiger, which had seemed so ready to spring at Marie-Lucien from among the leaves, he now saw was flat and simple and unconvincing as a picture postcard. He frowned, and said the first thing that came into his mouth, which was, "The flowers are too large. I have never seen flowers in life this large."

"Haven't you?" the painter said, and gazed about at his own work, entirely unpersuaded.

Many of these jungle scenes were of death and dismemberment—jaguars and tigers and lions variously attacking Negroes, a white horse, a hunch-shouldered Indian buffalo. Yet there was something oddly innocent in all the expressions, as if the creatures were only playing at a game, and in a moment would scramble to their feet laughing, their wounds nothing more than circus greasepaint. Now that Marie-Lucien had regained his composure, the feeling this summoned in him was odd as well: odd, that paintings of such violence and bloodshed conjured for him an ingenuous child's world, a world in which the lion lies down with the lamb.

After several moments the little black dog in his arms squirmed to be released, and woke him from the brief dream state he must have slipped into.

"M. Rousseau, I cannot keep this dog," he said unequivocally, and let the dog down onto the floor. The little thing immediately ran out the door and up the stairs, where his claws could be heard scrabbling across the floor of Marie-Lucien's apartment. This was followed shortly by the cat's yowl and then the dog's tortured yelp.

The painter laughed: "A dog is the emblem of fidelity," he said, as if pronouncing from a pulpit. Then he began rustling through cupboards, apparently in search of glasses or a bottle, for he said brightly, "We should first have a glass of wine," though he did not say what he meant by "first."

"I must . . . ," Marie-Lucien tried to say, but Rousseau waved a hand and said, "All the more reason not to." He poured a few drops of vin blanc, the last from a dusty green bottle, into two paint-smeared cups and held out one of the cups to Marie-Lucien. "Santé!" he said, and downed the bit of wine in a single swallow. Marie-Lucien, because he could not readily think of a reason not to, drank his also. The wine was vinegary and tasted of the dust of the bottle; or perhaps there had been dust in the cups.

The painter then clapped him on the shoulder and began steering him from room to room, declaiming before every painting as if he were a docent in a museum. Not all of his work was of the jungle. There were a few commissioned portraits of children whose parents, Rousseau cheerfully admitted, had refused payment on grounds the painting did not resemble their child. Two were small portraits of the artist, painted not from mirrors but from "the image of my handsome self I carry in my own mind, ha ha!" One was a very strange painting of a man resembling Rousseau standing over an infant apparently abandoned beside a country road, though neither the child nor the man appeared the least frightened or disturbed by their circumstances. There were, as well, scenes from the Parisian countryside and the suburbs, and of Laval, where the artist had spent his childhood. In them, cows grazed in stiff profile, completely without perspective; roads ran between hedges and fences without any sense at all of a third dimension. It was evident to Marie-Lucien that Rousseau was a second-rate amateur; but at the same time he felt himself helplessly drawn into the world of the paintings, a world beyond everyday life, beyond time, a strange and dreamlike world in which childhood's careless days had deepened without abandoning their purity.

"The colors . . . ," he said at one point, without any notion of how to finish the thought.

"Yes, yes. But it's my blacks that Gauguin admires: the perfection of my blacks."

Marie-Lucien did not for a moment consider the painter's boast to be true—Gauguin, after all, being a somewhat notorious artist—but he was more alert than most people to the color of hearse cloth, having watched undertakers' mutes carry off, one after the other, an infant child, then his wife, and lastly his only grown son. Now that his attention had been brought to it, he became aware of the depth, the rich inkiness of the blacks in all the paintings; and he realized what it was he should have said about the colors: that their bold frankness must come from offsetting them with so much black.

When they finished their tour of the "Imaginary Museum," as Rousseau laughingly called it, Marie-Lucien went back up to his apartment where the black dog and striped cat had come to terms of uneasy détente; and he resumed his sequestered life, though the conditions were somewhat moderated from the need to bring a dog down to the street twice a day to relieve himself. He and the painter did not speak to each other again for more than a fortnight, or only on the handful of occasions when they passed on the front stoop as Marie-Lucien carried the dog out to the gutter. But one evening late in June Rousseau came to his door well after dark, banging on the jamb and calling out, "M. Bernier, M. Bernier." Then, as if they were old comrades, he took Marie-Lucien's arm and said, "*Jardin des Plantes*! Best seen at night, you know, leaning through the fence," and pulled him toward the stairs.

"I am not Bernier," Marie-Lucien said, but without expecting to accomplish anything by it.

"No, no, of course not, I have known Bernier for years and he is a vast pig of a man, lacking completely in charm, you are much superior in every way to Bernier." The painter spoke consolingly, as if Marie-Lucien had confided a terrible dissatisfaction with himself.

They walked along the streets in silence, Rousseau's arm looped through Marie-Lucien's. He was not an old man, the painter, not even as old as Marie-Lucien who was not yet seventy, but he strolled along at an old man's pace, limping slightly and facing straight ahead when he walked, turning his entire body on the frequent occasions when he paused to peer into shop windows with a concentrated frown. Marie-Lucien waited while he carried out these examinations, waited without interest but also without impatience. It had been three months since he had traveled farther than the sidewalk directly in front of M. Queval's foundry; he was astonished to find himself out and about so late at night, astonished to find he was not afraid of the streets largely emptied of all but the unsavory and the wretched.

At the gates of the Botanical Gardens the painter clasped the iron bars with both hands and thrust his head as far into the closed park as his shoulders would permit. "Such a strange and mysterious world," he said very quietly. Marie-Lucien, standing behind him, peered into the darkness without seeing anything he considered strange or mysterious. But he became gradually aware that, away from streetlamps as they were here, the trees and bushes were wrapped in fantastic black shadows. He pushed his own head between the iron bars and leaned into the fence; and after several moments he began to make out amongst the shrubbery the vivid yellow blossoms of a rose, magnified hugely against the blackness.

In the nights that followed, Marie-Lucien and the painter, after sharing a bowl of soup at one apartment or the other, shut the aggrieved cat and dog in the upstairs apartment and strolled through the Luxembourg Garden and Montsouris Park and leaned into the fences of various private gardens. They explored not only the parks and woodlands and brushy clearings but traversed the bridges and aqueducts and watched the late-night goings-on at the quais and along the banks of the rivers and canals. They spoke little, which suited Marie-Lucien: he found Rousseau to be a strange sort, just as people had said, possibly a confidence trickster or a candid idiot. Once, while they were studying the statue of a lion in the darkness of the Luxembourg Garden, the painter said matter-of-factly that the "other cats" he had spoken of, the ones that occupied his apartment, were in fact lions and jaguars and tigers that wandered in from the jungles to visit him at night and sit for their portraits. It was impossible to know if he was speaking figuratively, or if he was genuinely hallucinatory, or if he merely enjoyed playing the part of an eccentric artist. But Marie-Lucien, walking with him at night, looking into the dark corners of the city—coming suddenly upon the black silhouette of a lion in the midst of clipped hedges and graveled paths—felt as he had when he had walked into the painter's apartment and gazed on his strange canvases: a vivid awareness of how beautiful and dangerous the world was, how tender and cruel, consoling and heart-rending. And this was the closest he had come, since the deaths of his wife and his son, to discovering any sort of meaning in the world.

One night while they were standing on a viaduct watching the body of some sad unfortunate being fished out of the water, the painter said thoughtfully, "I have run into ghosts everywhere. One of them tormented me for more than a year when I was a customs inspector."

Marie-Lucien did not believe in ghosts. Belief in ghosts would have required him to believe in something beyond death, a world of the spirit. He had been, as a young man, at the Battle of Sedan where thousands had died; and he had watched his wife and his son on their deathbeds; and he had never had the least inkling that any scrap or glimpse of the people he loved remained anywhere in the universe. He had come to the unshakable conclusion that death was unremitting and permanent; death, he believed, was death. He said to the painter, to turn him aside from his ghosts, "You were a *douanier*?"

Rousseau smiled modestly. "Nothing so grand. A mere inspector." But he was not put off the track. He said, "Whenever I was on duty this ghost would stand ten paces away, annoying me, poking fun." He turned to Marie-Lucien with a sour grimace. "Letting out smelly farts just to nauseate me."

Marie-Lucien smiled slightly.

"I shot at him, but a phantom apparently cannot die again. Whenever I tried to grab him, he vanished into the ground and reappeared somewhere else."

Marie-Lucien asked him uninterestedly—mere politeness—"Was he someone you knew? An old acquaintance?"

"Not at all. He was not haunting me, but the post, which was at the Gate of Arcueil. When I left that post, I never saw him again. I suppose something must have happened there, perhaps something in the way he was killed, that caused his soul to attach itself to the gate, or to the person guarding the gate." At the muddy edge of the canal several men were now standing around the naked body of a young woman, a woman only recently dead, her body still lovely, unblemished, not sufflated, her long brown hair from this distance seeming to hang in a neat braid across one shoulder and breast. The painter's expression, looking down at the scene, slowly softened into satisfaction. "I don't like to read the big tabloids that talk a lot of politics, what I read is the *Magasin Pittoresque*." He laughed. "The more drowned bodies in the river the greater my reading pleasure."

Marie-Lucien was taken aback. "That's a terrible thing to say."

"Is it?" Rousseau said, in a tone of complete sincerity, and might have been about to turn to Marie-Lucien to collect his answer, but suddenly swept his hand and his glance skyward. "There goes that poor woman's soul," he said, with surprised delight.

Marie-Lucien looked quickly where Rousseau had pointed but saw only the full moon hanging low and white on the night sky, as perfectly round as if it had been drawn with a compass. "What?" he said in frustration. He did not at all believe the painter had seen a drowned soul flying up to heaven but couldn't help his question, or its meaning: Not, *What did you say?* but *What did you see?*

"Ah, such joy!" the painter said quietly, which he may have meant as an answer.

In the early part of August, Rousseau came to Marie-Lucien's door unexpectedly—it was morning, and Marie-Lucien was still drinking his terrible coffee, still wearing the rumpled clothes he had slept in. The painter took hold of his arm and said, "*La Ménagerie*! Best seen at night when the animals are at their most alert, but sadly open only in the daylight, ten centimes and you're in." Marie-Lucien attempted to refuse. It was one thing, their nightly strolls, the two not-quite-old men leaning into fences, peering at trees and flowering shrubs in dark public parks and private gardens; but the daylight hours he intended still to keep for his own use, which was not grieving, as his friends had supposed, but a prolonged, expectant waiting for his own death.

Rousseau, of course, would not be put off. He had a

long-established morning practice of strolling through one or another of his favorite amusement parks, and he had made up his mind to share that pleasure with Marie-Lucien. Shortly, they were out on the lively daytime streets, and Rousseau, brisk with morning energy, led the way to the Zoological Gardens, where he spent a good long while studying a mangy lion rocking restlessly in a space too small to accommodate pacing; serpents stretched out under covers handed down from hospitals; kinkajous and gibbon apes quietly pining in their cages. None of this was of much interest to Marie-Lucien, or only insofar as to strengthen his old opinion that he lived in a brutal, godless universe. He stood back from the animal pens, shifting his weight in anxious boredom.

When finally they left the zoo, Rousseau insisted they must visit the Palmarium, and the Orangerie; and once inside the hothouses, Marie-Lucien felt as if he had slipped into a dream. Confronted with a spectacle of perpetual novelty—huge Paulownia trees, tropical palms, mango and pineapple trees, thick-stalked grasses taller than any man—he seemed to recognize everything, to rediscover it all in his memories. It struck him suddenly that the foliage under the translucent glass vault was the most exalted green he had ever seen outside Rousseau's jungle canvases, and when he said this to the painter—a bit of mild praise coming rather late in their acquaintance—Rousseau replied offhandedly, "I don't seek and invent, my dear, I only find and discover."

"Well then, it seems to me, you find and discover strangeness above all," Marie-Lucien said, which the painter took as true praise and which provoked in him a pleased laugh.

In the weeks that followed, because Marie-Lucien had little

interest in visiting the Zoo or the Monkey Palace again, they confined their morning walks to the Orangerie, the Palmarium, and the Botanical Gardens, which Rousseau said was not an inconvenience. The animals in the menagerie were, after all, not suitable studies for his art—always either reclining or sitting in a torpor—and his genuine models (his expression guileless as a child's) were the wild ones who visited him at night.

One morning as the two men walked back through the streets from *le Jardin des Plantes* to the apartments, the painter wrapped an arm about Marie-Lucien's shoulders and said, "Come into the studio, M. Bernal, see what strangeness I've been about in recent days. The woman has been posing for me, the woman we met on the quai."

Marie-Lucien had no recollection of meeting a woman on the quai, but this did not surprise him, as the painter had a practice of striking up conversation with virtually anybody they passed, even prostitutes and obvious villains; and Marie-Lucien the practice of not joining in. "I am not Bernal," he said mildly, but only from habit.

The painting Rousseau wished him to see was of a nude reclining on a Bordeaux-red chaise inexplicably set down in the midst of a jungle lush with impossibly huge Egyptian lotus blossoms. The work was far from completed—the foliage flourishing before the woman—but Marie-Lucien could already see that she was no one he recognized; or, given the painter's awkward draftsmanship, perhaps he would not have recognized her even if she had been someone he knew well. It was a very strange painting, of course, very much in line with the greater part of his work, and the sort of thing that caused Marie-Lucien to lose his foothold in the world: in the trees were exotic birds and monkeys, in the sky a perfectly round bone-white moon, in the foliage a glimpse of an elephant, as well as lurking lions and serpents; and oddest of all, a Negro snake charmer holding a musette to his lips. Even half-finished as it was, the painting gave an impression of stiff, stark peace, of Dantesque silence.

Marie-Lucien's wife had died slowly of consumption; for years before her death she had been unable to engage him in sexual congress, and it had been years since he had bothered to abuse himself. At the intersection of circumstance and advancing age, he had become celibate without taking a decision, and was somewhat interested in the fact that paintings and photographs of naked women no longer aroused him. In any case, this particular painting of a nude was not, to his eye, erotic. Her ankles were chastely crossed, her pubis neatly hidden behind the flesh of her thighs. One thick arm outstretched on the back of the chaise seemed in gesture toward the snake charmer or the lions, but whether this was to beckon or fend off, was difficult to know. She was dark-haired, dark-eyed, two twisted strands of her hair falling across one of her perfectly globular breasts. It seemed to Marie-Lucien that this was a woman not ashamed to be naked—not living in the world he knew, but in some universe absent the Biblical tale of sin.

"She is a Pole," the painter said, standing back in admiration of his own work. "A pious Polish girl, though I've drawn her as she is now, not pious at all but an innocent, an angel, restored to Genesis."

This was not quite what Marie-Lucien had been thinking, but near enough that he murmured, "Eve in Paradise."

The painter corrected him, in a tone of surprise, "Yadwigha, after death. Do you not recall how we watched her soul float up to the clouds?"

Marie-Lucien grappled through memory until he remembered the young woman lying dead on the bank of the canal, naked under the stares of half a dozen men. "It was only you who saw . . . ," he began to say, but the painter was already going on, gesturing toward a Louis Philippe sofa that was evidently the model for the chaise in his painting. "She has been posing for me here, every night. Her spirit has attached itself to me, which I suppose is due to my catching sight of her as she departed her body. Poor girl drowned herself out of grief."

Marie-Lucien said, smiling very faintly, "So not as pious as all that, if she killed herself. God condemns the suicide."

The painter brushed this away with a gesture. "God condemns no one, it's the priests who are always in a mood to condemn." He gazed at his painting in silence. "The girl had suffered greatly, her husband and child dead in an overturned taxi. How can we condemn her for finding this world unbearable? I should have found it unbearable myself, years ago, and ten times over, if I weren't a bit of a spiritist." He turned to Marie-Lucien with a smile. "Art is the confession of its maker. You shall have to look at my art, to know why sadness has not grabbed hold of me in its teeth."

It was Rousseau's nonchalance that offended Marie-Lucien, and caused him to remember suddenly a remark the painter had made, a remark about the pleasure he took from reading about drowned bodies hauled from the river. At the time, he had been distracted from it; but now, recalling the tone and the words, Marie-Lucien said bitterly, "What do you know of unbearable? of grief? of great suffering? When you have lost your wife and your son, as I have, then speak to me of unbearable."

The painter gave him a startled look. "Oh my dear M. Derain, I am sorry to hear of it. Sorry to hear of it. Your poor heart." He draped his arm across Marie-Lucien Derain's shoulders and drew him close.

But this was the beginning of the end of their friendship. Marie-Lucien took work soon afterward with a neighborhood pork butcher, and seldom found time to join Rousseau on his morning visits to the pleasure gardens. They carried on their evening explorations for a short while, but ended them after an argument: when Marie-Lucien objected to hearing another tale of ghosts, the painter said to him that people who had never dreamed when fully awake were loath to admit the realness of dream; and Marie-Lucien took this badly. Afterward he merely nodded when he passed Rousseau going in or out of the apartments, and if the painter spoke to him, he replied in as few words as possible.

In January during a spell of cold, bright weather, Marie-Lucien began working very late helping the butcher render fat, and one night climbing the stairs after midnight carrying scraps of meat for the cat and the dog, he passed the painter's open door and saw a naked woman posing on the Louis Philippe sofa, her arm outstretched and beckoning, her pallid body clothed in moonlight. The woman, who may have heard his steps on the landing, turned to him a face not beautiful at all but transparent and luminous, lit from within; and then she resumed her pose, fixing her gaze perhaps on the moon that he could not see but which he imagined must be visible through the apartment window. Her expression in profile was difficult to interpret, her mouth seeming at the verge of amusement but her thick brows intent and straight. The painter, too, turned and stood very poised and erect, one thumb pushed through the hold of his palette, his brush held down in the other hand. The look he gave Marie-Lucien was a questioning frown of expectancy and joy; but they did not speak, and Marie-Lucien continued up the stairs, his heart thudding. When he sat down inside his own apartment the animals came immediately into his lap, and he rested his trembling hands in their fur.

In March, Marie-Lucien heard from M. Queval that the painter had hung a new canvas at the *Société des Peintres Indépendants*, a painting of a naked woman dreaming on a Louis Philippe couch. Word later went around the neighborhood that this new painting had brought Rousseau a flurry of minor attention, and the admiration even of other artists. When the pork butcher took his wife to the salon to view it, Marie-Lucien stayed behind and kept the shop open.

Often, during that winter, he heard the painter's voice in conversation with himself or with his paintings, and from time to time the voice of this or that visitor. Twice, Rousseau gave parties to which Marie-Lucien was invited, but which he did not attend, parties at which the host played his violin very badly, and Marie-Lucien heard rising up through the floor the sounds of people applauding and laughing at the same time.

After the second party, the painter knocked on Marie-Lucien's door to plead poverty and beg twenty-five francs. "I imagine if you had saved all the money spent on parties, you would not need to beg from your friends and acquaintances," Marie-Lucien said to him, after he had given over the twenty-five francs. He had not wished to be the man's friend or to be invited to his entertainments, so could not quite account for the sound of bitterness in these words. The painter was not at all taken aback. He kissed Marie-Lucien on both cheeks and said fondly, "My dear, you are like a brother to me," which Marie-Lucien felt to be a grandiose figure of speech.

In the months afterward, he seldom saw the painter. Once, through his window, he watched Rousseau limping up the street to the apartments, appearing so sickly and pale that Marie-Lucien was struck with a moment of remorse; but then, to M. Queval who was standing on the front stoop, the painter complained in an aggrieved voice that he "suffered greatly" from a phlegmon in his leg. These were the same words he had used, speaking of the drowned woman, the very words that had begun their estrangement—that she had "suffered greatly"—and when he heard them, Marie-Lucien turned away from the window.

In September he opened his newspaper and was startled to read that the painter had died. *Le Petit Journal* was famous for the brevity of its reporting, and spent only a few lines to say that the minor artist H. Rousseau had died of a blood clot after surgery to remove a gangrenous leg; and that he had belonged to the Salon of the Independents, where he had paid twenty-five francs a year to hang his canvases.

It had been many months since Marie-Lucien had visited the Palmarium or the Orangerie. On the day of the painter's burial he walked through the hothouses slowly; and then went into the menagerie. A jaguar trudged in circles, dazed and ill, in a narrow box where he bumped into all the corners; the lion reclined in a stupor. As Marie-Lucien was going out again, he turned to see if it was Rousseau he had glimpsed going in one of the other gates, though of course it was only a man with a thick mustache, a sickly complexion, a slight limp.

He stopped at a newsstand to buy a copy of *Le Soleil* for the obituaries, and read as he was walking back to the apartments that Rousseau was "a painter without any of the notions required by art"; and that his friends had spoken of him as a man of generosity, credulity, and good humor. His living relations were a daughter Julia, and granddaughter Jeanne; he had been preceded in death by two wives and six of his seven children. In the painter's last days, *Le Soleil* reported, he had become delirious: had spoken of seeing angels, and of hearing their celestial music.

When Marie-Lucien, climbing the stairs, passed the open door of the painter's apartment he saw a woman standing inside, a woman he remembered having seen twice before. She was standing in front of an unfinished painting, standing unclad as the figure in the painting, which was a figure of Yadwigha herself, her dead body lying beside a stream, watched over by the wide eyes of lions and monkeys. The ghost of Yadwigha turned to Marie-Lucien with an expression innocent as a child's; a look of expectancy and of joy. And then she was a woman Marie-Lucien had never met nor heard the painter speak of, a woman in black crepe, the painter's daughter Julia. Behind her in the unfinished painting, death's bright angel ascended through the impossibly blue sky.

The Blue Roan

AS SOON AS THEY HAD the cast on my leg I loaded the mare in the trailer and drove down to Jim's place in the Indian Valley. I was overnight getting there, on account of my leg would swell up every little while, working that stiff clutch, and I'd have to pull the truck over to the shoulder of the road and prop the cast up on the windowsill or the dashboard and let the ache ease out of it for an hour or two. In the morning, in the town, I asked an old man standing in front of a store if he knew where the Longanecker farm was and I went where he said.

The house I took to be Jim's stood most of the way up a hill-side, above a flat, milky creek. There was a long slope of plowed ground between the creek and the house, and a woman working an old tractor across the field, towing a harrow. I don't think she could have heard the truck over the tractor noise, but maybe she saw the dust we raised going up her lane, because she looked around sudden from under the brim of her hat and then shut the tractor off and stood down from it and walked up across the plowed ground toward the house. It wasn't much of a house. The porch was rotted so it leaned downhill, and the roof had club moss along the eave edges. There was no barn, just a cowshed with manure piled up under it, and a lean-to at the end where she stood her tools. There was a post and wire fence that went around a couple of acres of grass and weed. An old pickup with a fender gone stood in the yard under the only tree.

There wasn't any bridge going over the creek. I had to ford the truck across. I took it slow on account of the trailer and the blue roan, but it was a shallow crossing and the rocks were cleared out of it so the trailer didn't buck too much getting over. The woman had beat me to the house and she was waiting for me when I got up the hill. She had her sleeves rolled up and was hugging herself so I could see she had rough red hands and rough red elbows, but her face under the hat-shadow looked smooth and fine-skinned, only a couple of pinch marks where the corners of her mouth tucked in. She had her hair drawn back in a knot but there was a thick bang of fuzz just under the edge of the hat and more of it leaking out at the neck. She maybe cussed that hair every day, too much of it and all frizzed like that, but it was a good color, gold-brown as wheat, and I can't say I minded the way it made a sort of halo around her face. She had on filthy jeans that fit poor, but I could see why Jim would have married her.

I stayed in the truck. "I'm after Jim Longanecker's place," I said across the windowsill. "I wonder if this is it." I was pretty sure it was, and as soon as I spoke his name those little tucks by her mouth squeezed in.

"Jim's gone rodeoing," she said, in a short way.

I had to ask her; I didn't want to tell it to the wrong woman. "Are you Mrs. Longanecker?"

She watched me, holding her head straight and keeping her arms folded up on her chest. "I'm Irene Longanecker," she said. "Who are you?"

"I'm a friend of Jim's. I've brought down some news."

Her mouth flattened out a little. It wasn't a frown, but as if she had got tired suddenly, and she spoke like that too, with a flatness. "Where's he at now? Lakeview?"

There was a big ark of cloud sculling across the sky above the ridge beam of the house and I looked at that while I took off my hat and sleeved the sweat-edge on my forehead. "The news I've got isn't good," I said. I had quit watching her, but I could see from the tail of my eye she had raised her head back a little out of the shadow of the hat and now she had one hand flat above her eyes to shade against the glare. "Jim's dead," I said. I had meant to say *Your husband Jim has been taken from you*—I had planned it, wooly and formal and old-fashioned like that. But I didn't remember until right afterward, so it came out straight and maybe sounding a little hard-boiled, though I wasn't feeling that way at all.

In the three years I'd known Jim he'd only come down to this place maybe a dozen different times, two or three weeks at a stretch during the off seasons. But he would get a letter now and then with his name spelled out in a spiky woman's hand, spelled all the way out, James Thomas Longanecker, like there might be more than one Jim Longanecker anywhere. And Jim used to speak of his wife like he spoke of his good bird gun or his handmade saddle, like she was something he had that he was proud of. So when I told her he was dead, I didn't know what I ought to expect.

She watched me a minute without moving, with the edge of

her hand against her bangs to shade out the sun, and then her mouth moved again, slipping down in that tired way, but there wasn't any sound out of her and the face she made wasn't grief. She began to shake her head like she couldn't believe it. She didn't say anything to me, she just shook her head half a dozen times and then turned around and went up onto the leaning porch and cracked the screen door back and went inside.

I sat quite a while after that, creasing the edge of my hat with my thumbs, and then I eased my cast out of the truck and set down on the dirt and stood up. I held on to the door of the truck and stood there looking across the plowed hill to where the tractor waited in front of the harrow.

The boy came from behind the hill, driving the cow and calf ahead of him. I could see him watching me while he switched the cow into her little shed, and for a while after that he stood by the buildings just looking down the hill at me. I thought the woman might come out to talk to him but she didn't. Finally he drifted down and stood at the edge of the field, watching me fight the tractor across those furrows, but he tired of that pretty quick and began to sidle up to the mare where I had let her out into the fenced pasture. She was soft-gaited, that horse, and light in the mouth, sweet-tempered and willing as any horse I'd seen. And she had that pretty roan color, that dark charcoal hide veined with while so it showed up blue, like the bluing on a new gun, and where the boy stroked her long stretched-down neck there was a shine I could see, bright as metal. Jim was killed on account of I loved that horse too much, I guess. So after a while I couldn't watch the boy with her anymore and I called to him, "She's testy. She's been known to bite," and heard it come out hard-boiled again. The sun was high up and hot and sweat was itching over my ribs and my leg was aching all the way up to the hip. I don't know if he heard me over the tractor, but he gave me a look and went back up to the cowshed. He was maybe seven or eight years old. There was a ditch in his chin, just like Jim had.

Before too long, the woman came out and she said something to the boy and then came downhill to where I was. She had her sleeves rolled down now and her hat was gone so the sun lit up her hair like it was burning along the scalp.

"Dinner," she said. "You'd better come in." She didn't come any closer than the edge of the furrows. She just shouted it out so I'd hear her.

The boy and I took turns at the outside faucet. I didn't know what his mother had said to him and I was afraid he might ask me something about Jim, but he just washed his hands real slow, looking at me sidelong, and then went ahead into the house. I stayed out a while, wetting my hair and combing it back smooth, and I left my hat in the truck when I went inside. The woman was already sitting, spooning food onto the boy's plate, and it felt like quite a while before she looked up and saw me standing in the door.

"Sit down," she said, and that was the last thing anybody said until the meal was done, though the boy kept sneaking looks in my direction. When the woman began to clear the plates, the boy pitched right in. That left me sitting there, so I made as if to help too. She said, "You can go on out and sit in the shade. I'll be out in a minute," and stuck her chin toward the door. So I went outside. I stood a while. Then I walked back down to the tractor and started in at the harrowing again.

After a while the woman came out. She walked down to the edge of the field and said something. I couldn't hear what it was so I shut off the tractor, and she walked across the plowed ground then, until she was standing right next to me.

"Thank you for the harrowing. Most cowboys don't like to do that work at all." Maybe she meant it as a complaint against Jim, but if she did I couldn't hear it.

I said, "My folks were farmers. I used to know my way around a tractor pretty well."

She nodded as if there was a meaning in this. "Well, I can finish it now. I appreciate you helping out."

There was a little speech I had readied while I was driving down here overnight. I said it now. "I'd help you out a while, if you want. I can finish up this field, get it put to seed. Or whatever else you need done. I can't rodeo much with this broken leg but I can do a little farming, I guess. I don't mind working for bed and board. I expect there's room for me to sleep in your toolshed, and I eat about anything."

She gave me a look, like she was hunting for something in my face. Maybe she was just making sure it was a true offer. Then she ducked her head and said, "I guess you're Glenn." That caught me short and I must have looked it. In a minute, watching me, she said, "Jim wrote that you were his friend." I'd seen Jim sweating out a few letters all right, but I'd never figured he would put me in one. I wondered what he had written. I don't know why it made me feel itchy.

"What killed him?" she said, so it came straight out without a warning, and I was caught short again.

I bent my broken leg up and rubbed the knee above the cast. I looked at my hand, my fingers working at the knee. "A horse kicked him," I said. "I guess he didn't feel it. At least that's what they said." She didn't say anything to that, so after a while I let out a little more. "I couldn't make it here right away but I came as soon as I was able. It happened Wednesday night. You don't have a telephone and I didn't think the news ought to be put in a letter if it could be otherwise." I thought it over and then I said, "I can drive you up there tomorrow if you want. Or tonight."

Finally she looked off, away from me, off toward her old house. "I appreciate you coming so far." I couldn't hear grief in it, just that same flat tone, like she was worn out, worn down.

I thought about it. "Jim would've done the same for me," I said.

She raised her head without looking around. "Yes, I guess that's so," she said. "Jim always set his friends high." She said it like she faulted him for it, and there was a look in her face, somewhat of bitterness. After a silence she said, "Were you with him?"

I had to think a minute what she was getting at, and then when it came clear I began to knead my leg again, working my knuckles at the knee. "Yes. I was there."

She nodded in that way she had, as if it meant something serious. Then finally she looked at me again, a straight look. "I want to hear about it."

I had thought I might get away with just telling her he had been kicked by a horse. But she stood there waiting for the rest, so I told her more or less what had happened, though I hadn't got myself ready to tell it.

I told her we had got drunk after the rodeo in Sprague and Jim had started in teasing me about that blue roan I loved so much. Actually, I never did tell her it was the roan. I just said it was a mare Jim had, which I had taken a liking to. She had lately come into heat and every stallion who stood within half a mile of her was probably rubbing himself against a post that night. Jim was kidding me about it, asking if I was man enough to service her myself, and so on. But after a while things took a turn and he started talking in a serious way, as if we weren't both drunk, sitting on our butts under the dark bleachers in the rain.

"Female needs offspring," he said solemnly. "She won't be happy until she throws a colt. I ought to put her in with that good-looking red stud belongs to Chip Lister. She'll get herself a little red roan baby to keep her happy."

"The hell," I believe I said and kept drinking my beer.

In a while he made a thoughtful sound and stood up. He walked off, dragging his boot heels in the mud in a lazy, strutting way. It was a while before I got up to follow him. I was pretty drunk. By the time I caught up to him, he had the mare in with Chip's stallion and was leaning on the rail watching them.

"Hey," I said. "Hey. What the hell are you doing?"

"If you weren't so blind-drunk you'd see what I'm doing."

I took off my hat and waved it. I don't know what good I thought that would do. "Jim, damn you, this ain't funny."

Jim clapped me on the shoulder. He was grinning. "The hell it ain't," he said.

The stud was driving the mare just ahead of him around the edge of the corral. In the rain and darkness the mare looked black, the stallion dark red, the color of old blood. I flapped my hat again. "Get away from her, you big bastard."

Jim laughed. "That old boy's going to make her a baby."

I stood holding my hat. Then I said, "The hell he is," and I went over the fence. Chip's horse had her pushed up against the rails by then and he was trying to work around behind her. I went up and just hit him in the muzzle with my fist. I was drunk. I should have got a stick of wood or something but I didn't. I just pushed in between them and starting hitting.

I don't know what happened. I guess I got bumped. I was sitting in the mud, all at once, and they were stepping on me. I heard Jim yelling, I still don't know if it was at me or at those horses, but a big drunk yell, and then he came wading in, beating at the stallion like I'd done, with his knuckles. The horse got up on his hind legs, squealing, I saw his big chest and his mane swinging loose, and then I heard the sound the iron shoe made against the solid bone of Jim's head. That was all there was, just that sound, because Jim never made any, just fell back straight as a tree and heavy.

I got up from under him and got hold of a two-by-four and beat the hell out of that stallion. I felt bad about it afterward, it wasn't the damn horse's fault. But I beat him off the mare and ran the mare outside, and then I went back and sat down next to Jim, with the rain falling on us in the dark. One of the horses had broken my shinbone and my boot was filled up with blood, but there was no pain there, just the sticky wetness, and I didn't know I was hurt until somebody told me afterward.

Jim's wife never said a word while I told her how Jim had got killed. When I was done she just stood there, looking out at the sky edge. Finally she said, "Well, I'll think about the work you offered," and she looked down at her feet and then walked back up the hill to the house. She had a deliberate way of walking, even across the soft field. I'd noticed it before. She walked like somebody who has a long way ahead and has set herself a pace to get there.

. . .

By the time I had got the harrowing done, the sun was low. I gave the mare what feed I had from the back of the truck and I was doling out the woman's hay to her cow when the boy walked out to me.

"I'm supposed to do that," he said, mumbling, pointing the words somewhere to the left of where I was.

"Okay," I said, and stood off and watched him do it.

"You're supposed to come in for supper," he said when he had finished with the cow. "We're both supposed to."

I followed him up to the faucet and we took turns again.

"Did you get bucked off?" he asked me, sideways, eyeing the dirty cast.

"Got stepped on," was all I said.

He nodded like his mother, in a solemn way. "Oh."

The woman had brought out a bit of a cold supper and we ate as before, silently, in the high-ceilinged kitchen. The daylight began to fail fast while we were sitting there, and when she stood to do up the dishes she pointed with her chin and the boy pulled the chain on the ceiling light without being told. I didn't wait for her to point her chin at the door. I went on outside.

I'd been hoarding the few cigarettes I had left, but I was needing one pretty bad tonight and, hell, that's what they were for, so I got one out. I went partway down the hill and sat down on the grass in the darkness with my cast stuck straight out in front of me while I smoked. I watched the mare grazing on the poor grass in that fenced field. I could hear her ripping the tough stalks with her teeth.

After a while I heard the screen door crack. I kept on sitting there, sucking up the last of my smoke, staring off at the mare like I didn't know, but I could feel the woman's eyes on me—I knew she was standing back there, watching me. I was about to get onto my feet again when she came down from the house and sat a couple of yards away, with her knees pulled up in front of her and her arms clasped around them.

In a bit she said, "Jim never could stay put. I guess you know that, you'd be like that yourself. So the boy and me, we've been alone half his life, and sometimes we get pretty hungry for a man's voice. Both of us do, I won't deny it; we get pretty lonesome." There was a silence. Then she said, "If I was looking for somebody to wear the edge off my lonesomeness, I guess you'd do; you have a kind face, as far as that goes."

I felt a heat start up from my neck. I took a long stem of grass and began to split it down the middle with my thumbnail. I guess I had known all along she might take my offer that way. Afterward, when I thought about it, I wondered if I might even have meant her to take it that way. I don't know. I sat there on the grass in the dark, looking at my hands.

"The truth is, I could use the help," she said. "There's more work than I can do, and no money to pay anybody." She waited again. "But the boy sees you with that good-looking horse, looking like you do, dressing like you do, just smelling of places a long way from here. And I can see his eyes going away from me." I didn't know what she meant, not then, but I figured it out later. She said, "Jim's eyes used to do that," and there was tenderness in it, or pain, the first I'd heard since telling her Jim was dead.

She didn't say anything else for a while. I wondered if she had started to cry. Then she said, "I guess I'm stupid, turning you away when you offer your help. I could use it, that's for sure. But it wasn't your fault, what happened; you don't owe Jim anything. And my saying no doesn't have anything much to do with you." She lifted her chin a little and gave me a straight look and then I saw her eyes were tearless. "It's just a lonesome woman isn't any mare in heat," she said in a level voice. I looked away. I looked down at my hands. "I'm just trying to hold on to my son," she said after a wait. Her voice dropped lower. "I appreciate you harrowing the field. And coming down here with the news. If you don't mind sleeping in the shed, I'll see you get a good breakfast in the morning before you leave."

She stood up without waiting for me to say anything else and walked back up the short hill to the house. I kept sitting where I was for a while. I watched the blue roan, the shadow of her, in that field.

She and the boy made a space for me under the eaves of the lean-to, amid the stack-up tools, and it was snug there; I'd slept in worse places. But after a while I just gave it up. There was a pretty good wind shaking the tree, and my leg was aching, and I blamed it on those things. In the dark I had to watch out not to kick over a rake or something, feeling careful with my boot and my cast until I was out in the open, where the moon gave some light to see what I was doing. I sat down and wrote on a scrap of paper the name of the mortuary where's Jim's body was in Sprague, and below that I wrote, *His horse and gear were sold, this is the sum of what it came to. The truck was his too.* Jim had had a little money and I put it with my own money, all I had, in a stack on the piece of paper, and I folded it so it was a flat packet. Then I went up and set it under a rock on the porch, where she would find it. I lugged the saddle out of the truck and put it on the mare. I had a hell of a time getting her saddled and a worse time getting myself up on her with that damn cast. I had to lead her up next to the house so I could stand on the porch and clamber up. I was afraid maybe the woman would hear me bumping around, but if she heard, she didn't come out to see what it was.

I left her the truck sitting there with the keys in it. It was a better one than she had, and the trailer was damn near new. Half of the rig was Jim's anyway, and I didn't have the money to buy him out, after giving her the money for the horse. Driving up here, I had thought I would give her the blue roan too, but I could see now, she wouldn't have wanted it there, around the boy. So that was the only thing of Jim's I held on to.

The Everlasting Humming
of the Earth

WHEN JOYCE WAS TEN YEARS old she woke in the night and went to the foot of the stairs and called up to her mother's bedroom that the earth was shaking. This was not the first time, nor even the hundredth. "Write it down in your journal," her mother said, in a voice rough with sleep. Her daughter's insomnia and nighttime anxieties had worried her at one time, but by now she was impatient with them. Writing her thoughts and worries in a journal had been the solution of a pediatric therapist they had seen when Joyce was eight.

Joyce pleaded. "I did, I wrote it down, but it didn't help. I can still feel it. Can't you feel it?"

"For Pete's sake, Joyce, no, I don't feel it. Nobody feels it. The earth is not shaking! Go back to bed and let me sleep. Please, please, I have to be up at six o'clock, I need my sleep, don't keep doing this. I mean it. Don't come to my door again."

This was not the first time, nor even the hundredth, Joyce was made to understand: No one, not her mother, her brother, none of her friends, no one else she had ever met, no one, only she could feel, could hear the low ceaseless droning of the earth under their feet. She alone could feel the juddering, tightening vibration that was the earth grinding its teeth in sleep. She alone in all the world could feel the great grinding of stone on stone, the sudden rumbling reverberation that was the earth rolling over, rearranging itself under the covers.

When she was seventeen she started a blog. She posted to it when she felt the earth making ready to shift its weight, and a day or three later she posted a link to the National Earthquake Information Center bulletin about the M 7+ quake that always followed. She didn't expect anyone to find the blog or read it, but shortly she had a few dozen followers. Some of them were disaster junkies, or had their own improbable theories of earthquake prediction. Someone from the NEIC wrote to ask that she delete her posts. "Fraudulent predictions of earthquakes," they said, was "fearmongering of the worst kind." Most of the comments that came in were salacious, or pornographic—an algorithm had picked up the sexual meaning of "I feel the earth move." She stopped blogging after a few months.

When she was twenty-five and married, Joyce woke in the night, went to her computer, and posted on a website called The Big One. It was a serious forum frequented by seismologists and geoscientists, focused on research and hypotheses aimed at predicting major quakes, the ones that ten or twelve or twenty times a year rang through Joyce's body like a struck bell. She wrote, "What if I have a way to know when, but not where? Would that be any help at all? I know there will be a quake tomorrow. Or the next day. I'm sorry but I don't know where. I don't know who I should tell or whether it would do any good at all. It probably wouldn't. I just feel like I have to tell someone." This was half past two in the morning, Arizona time, but someone, perhaps on the other side of the globe, commented immediately, "Are you nuts? What kind of a stupid-ass question is that? Prediction is when/where, that's what *prediction* f***ing MEANS!" There had been profane argument and flame wars on the site, around the question of whether accurate prediction would ever be possible.

Jimmy never wanted Joyce to make public predictions—he knew about all the fake psychics, the charlatans, he knew there'd been a lot of name-calling when she was a kid. He didn't want anybody thinking his wife was a nutjob or a quack. It was his job to remind her, over and over: If she couldn't say where it would happen, how would telling anybody do any good? How would it keep people from dying?

She only told Jimmy about the posting afterward—after the quake in Nepal that killed 9,000 people, and after her post drew a firestorm of argument and comment on The Big One. "I just felt like I needed to tell someone," she said to Jimmy. And she told him she had been banned from the website. "Good," he said, "that's good. You're well rid of it, Joyce, you know you are. When you need to tell somebody, you tell me."

When Joyce met Jimmy they were both living in Arizona, and they went on living there for the first years after they were married. But then Jimmy's job moved them over to the Bay Area, to San José, which was Joyce's idea of hell. She surrendered to it while Jimmy was still alive—he had been promoted, the move was good for him—but the summer after he died she sold the house and moved north to get away from all the tremors. She went up to Oregon, which was not exactly out of the earthquake zone but would be some relief, at least, from the 8,000, 9,000 minor quakes every year in San José, the shivers she could feel rising up from the bottoms of her feet into her bones.

Honestly, she would have preferred to move East—not Kansas or Oklahoma, where all the fracking and fracturing had been making the news for decades, but farther north, Wisconsin maybe, or Minnesota, where they hadn't had an earthquake in 10,000 years—but her son and his wife still lived in the Bay Area. She didn't want to be clear across the country from them when the worst happened, but she thought a few hundred miles might be a good thing. She and Michael weren't estranged; she still called him every couple of weeks, he called her at least every couple of months. But his mother was "an odd duck," he had said to Brenda when the two of them were first together. He had said it in Joyce's hearing and Jimmy had jumped on him for it. None of them had quite managed to forget it. She didn't know why it had been so easy for Jimmy to accept strangeness in his wife and so hard for Michael to accept it in his mother.

When they had first moved to San José, Jimmy had given Joyce a pillow embroidered with a famous quote of Richter's, "I don't know why people in California or anywhere worry so much about quakes. They are such a smaller hazard compared to things like traffic." Joyce had never been afraid of dying in a quake—she and Richter were of like minds—but she knew more than most people about earthquakes, enough to be cautious and to make plans. She couldn't live in Portland—there were crustal faults running up the West Hills and right under the downtown.

So she bought a small one-story stick-built house in Cornelius, a little farm town thirty miles west of the Portland fault line, and a hundred miles east of the Subduction zone off the coast. There were no buildings taller than the two-story Wilco Farm Store in Cornelius. In a big quake, bridges would go down, roads would buckle, the town might end up isolated for a few weeks, but she thought most people—at least people who planned ahead and stocked up their pantry—would be all right. Plus, there were a lot of Spanish-speaking farm workers in town and she was trying to learn Spanish in order to read Borges in his own language. This had been on Jimmy's list for his retirement, if he had lived long enough to retire. They used to read aloud to each other in the evenings, and she had the idea that if she could read Borges aloud it would be like Jimmy was still there.

Bienestar Dispensario Médico was a nonprofit alt-health storefront mostly serving the indigent, addicts and migrants. Joyce was not indigent, not a migrant, not an addict. She was fifty-five years old, she had her husband's pension to live on, she could pay for acupuncture, she told the woman on the phone. "I've just moved here. I'm not poor, but yours is the only acupuncture clinic in town. I can pay. Do you accept paying patients?"

In San José she had been used to hushed voices and noise-dampening carpet, dim lights, leather couches, vaguely Asian instrumental music played barely louder than a whisper. At *Bienestar*, she was led to a paper-covered exam table shoved into a corner of what appeared to be a storage closet, where she could hear the high cries of children and scolding parents continuing from the clamorous, crowded waiting room, and through the wall in the next treatment room a man speaking

Spanish, a fluent rush from which she gleaned a word here or there, his concern over missing work, and the terrible pain in his shoulder.

The acupuncturist was a big gray-haired woman named Raylene. Joyce told her that doctors in California had ruled out Parkinson's and Essential Tremor. She gave Raylene a slight, embarrassed smile. "They think these tremors are just nervousness. I suppose they are; I'm a worrier, I guess. It's not actual tremors, anyway, not that kind, it's more a vibrating kind, on my insides, it's like I'm ringing like a bell. Like I'm shaking, I guess, only nobody but me can feel it." She had honed this description over the years, and by now most of it was fairly accurate, or felt accurate, although not unabridged. "Acupuncture helps me. It calms me, or maybe just distracts me," she said, and this was a true statement. Over the years, after giving up on traditional medicine, and giving up on the numbing effects of wine and whiskey, she had tried every sort of homeopathic remedy and alternative treatment—reflexology, reiki, crystal light therapy, all of it. Acupuncture was the only thing that had done her any good, the only thing that helped her sleep through the "rumbles," as Jimmy used to call her night tremors.

In the Bay Area, most of the alt-health practitioners Joyce had visited had practiced a quasi-religious Meditative Silence. Raylene was not a disciple. She kept up a steady stream of chatter as she tapped the fine needles into Joyce's wrists and neck, her upper back, her ankles. How did she like the town, she must've been used to warm and dry down there in California, up here it would be nonstop rain October to June, but the price of houses must be a relief from California, which house had she bought, was it the blue one on Beech Street, small towns, honey, everybody knows what's for sale. She asked about Joyce's husband—Joyce was still wearing her wedding ring—and when she heard about Jimmy's death she said, "How long ago was it, honey? Oh, Jesus, not even a year? No wonder you got tremors. I lost two husbands. Well, I divorced the first one, but it's the same as. You lose them, either way. I always thought it was harder to lose a husband than anything else."

Raylene had married again after the death of her second husband. This new one, Benny, was a farrier. Joyce didn't know what that was. "He's a horse shoer, honey, that's what a farrier is. But Benny doesn't do much shoeing anymore, he mostly sticks with clients who like a barefoot trim." Joyce didn't ask what a barefoot trim was.

Raylene and Benny used to have several horses but now they were down to just one old gelding, a "pasture ornament" too stove up to be ridden, and when he was gone they didn't plan to have any more. Benny had the idea they might like to travel in their old age, which was coming up on both of them before long, and it would be hard to travel if they had animals to feed twice a day, and stalls to muck out.

Joyce had had a cat for a few years—well, it was her son's cat—but she hadn't wanted another animal after the cat died. She had always worried whether she'd be able to scoop up the jittery animal when a major quake hit, and she knew if he ran off she'd have to leave him behind to make her own escape through the collapse—an extra worry she didn't need. She thought of asking Raylene how you'd ever move an animal as big as a horse out of harm's way when an earthquake came, but Raylene went on talking, getting away from the topic of horses, and the moment passed.

Bienestar, it turned out, was a Portland-based outfit with satellites around the state. Raylene saw patients two days a week in Cornelius, three days a week over at the coast, in Tillamook. It was a long commute to Tillamook, more than an hour from where she and Benny lived, but Raylene didn't mind the drive "except for the idiots on the road." She didn't trust all the driverless cars—those were the idiots she meant.

In Cornelius she treated mostly farm workers who came to her with repetitive injuries, "but I get a lot of meth addicts in Tillamook. I've had some luck with addiction, I get referrals from the courts, but honey, sometimes I think I'm bailing out a sinking ship with a teacup. There's a reason people take up with meth, it's poverty, you know, and no hope of anything different."

In San José, Joyce had sometimes gone for acupuncture three or four times a week, but Raylene was the clinic's lone acupuncturist and she was only in the Cornelius storefront on Tuesdays and Thursdays, so that was the schedule they set up, twice a week appointments. Raylene wrote her phone number on the back of a *Bienestar* appointment card. "If twice doesn't keep those tremors dampened down," she said, "you just give me a call and I'll take care of you."

Tuesdays were always busy. Raylene would place all the needles but then leave Joyce alone in the treatment room—"your *chi* has got to have a little time to sort itself out, honey"—as she headed off to treat someone else. Joyce could often hear her big voice sounding through the wall, sometimes in Spanish, and she only paid attention when the conversation was in Spanish—a language lesson, not eavesdropping, was how she thought of it, although no one seemed to care very much about privacy here.

Thursdays were usually quieter. Raylene had time to sit in

the treatment room chatting with Joyce while her *chi* was finding its path. She never gossiped about her patients, which was a
relief to Joyce, but nothing in the woman's own life seemed too
private to bring up. None of her three children, she told Joyce,
were Benny's kids. "He was a prince to take us on, me with three
teenagers, and the middle one, I admit it, fairly screwed up at
the time, arrested already for DUI when he wasn't but sixteen."
It had done the kids a lot of good to be with Benny's horses,
and by now the children were grown up and mostly doing well.
But she always had a story about one of them, or one of the
five grandchildren, something funny or a new worry, and always
a story about a misbehaving horse or one of the "loony-tunes
horse people" her husband dealt with in his work.

Joyce was guarded about her own life but Raylene pulled a
few things out of her, neutral things, starting with the garden
she had planted in the big front yard of the Beech Street house.
She spoke softly, aware of the thin walls, listeners on the other
side, and said nothing about her plan to feed herself from that
garden in the event an earthquake cut off the town from the rest
of the world.

When she told Raylene she had been trying to read Borges
in his own language, Raylene slipped right into Spanish, a long
rush that Joyce only half-understood, something about the
weirdness, *extraño*, of Borges—or that's what people had told
her, she hadn't ever read him herself, was not much of a reader—
and then something about movies, she was a big *fanatica* of
extraño in the movies, she loved movies about time travel, alternate universes, extraterrestrials—these last three terms all ren-
dered in English.

Joyce, in truth, had a mild fear of being trapped in a dark

theater during an earthquake, but this was not something she could say to Raylene. She fumbled for the Spanish to say she wasn't much of a movie-goer. She said that she hadn't been to a movie hall in years. She said she and Jimmy had both been big readers, and the little she knew about time travel and alternate universes was not from movies but from reading—was it Coetzee? She had read a Heinlein novel when she was young, it could have been from that.

These were not names Raylene had ever heard of. The last book she had read was a Harry Potter novel, because her youngest son had been *fanatico* about Harry. And she had read *Fifty Shades of Grey*. She laughed when she saw Joyce's look. "Everybody was reading it, I had to see what all the *mania* was about." Then, laughing again, lapsing into English, "Honey, I guess we are just from different planets. But you've got me thinking maybe I'll give Borges a try. And I'm telling you, you ought to get yourself on Netflix or Hulu, one of those things, find a way to see *12 Monkeys*, then you'll see what *extraño* is. You'll be a movie *fanatica* like me."

Gradually, the clinic became Joyce's makeshift language school. Raylene made a habit of speaking Spanish, and Elena behind the reception desk took to greeting her in Spanish with a phrase that meant "one of our regulars." Sometimes, while Joyce waited to be called for her appointments, she forced herself to say a few words to someone else who was waiting, someone she had overheard speaking Spanish—an older woman, if there was one—polite comments about the weather, praise for a well-behaved grandchild, a question about cooking with chayote. The women she met week after week were a rotating group, but over time she became acquainted with several. Reading Borges was an excruciatingly slow struggle—she wondered if Jimmy would have kept with it—but she began to look forward to her conversations with the women in the waiting room. She smiled a lot to cover the gaps in her understanding, and then sometimes the women would laugh and slow down their chatter, to help her follow what they were saying. Other people in the room who were not Mexican, not Spanish speaking, sometimes watched these conversations sidelong, which had a surprising way of making Joyce feel part of a group, the group of women who spoke Spanish.

She signed up for Netflix, worked out how to order *12 Monkeys*, and afterward told Raylene that James Cole, going back in time over and over, failing over and over to change the future, but never giving up trying, made her think of something Raylene had said once about working with meth addicts, "bailing out a sinking ship with a teacup." Raylene laughed, but then said, "Honey, that's right. Me and Cole, just doing what we can. It's all we can do."

The weather was beautiful all through August and September, but by the middle of October had turned to rain and a leaden sky. Her friends in the waiting room, and Raylene too, told her this was only the beginning. "It will rain until the Fourth of July," they said, and they might not have been joking. It went on raining for days on end.

Joyce had read everything there was to read about earthquakes. She knew where they were most prolific, she knew their causes, and where they do the most damage (dense populations, shoddily built places, places difficult of access). She knew about the religious nuts who believed earthquakes were a sign of Jesus's return. She knew the several odd coincidences—Einstein leaving Pasadena one day before the quake that destroyed his hotel. And she knew that huge volumes of rain—rain dumped by tropical cyclones, for instance—were linked to earthquakes. There were theories that floodwaters lubricated the fault planes, or perhaps erosion from heavy rain reduced the weight on any fault below, and allowed it to move more easily.

If she had had the option, she'd have asked Elena to schedule a third weekly appointment with Raylene. Twice a week appointments were only barely keeping her insomnia at bay. She often woke at three or four in the morning, now, to the pounding of rain on the roof. Jimmy would have told her this wasn't rational. He would have told her this wasn't a tropical cyclone.

One Thursday in November Elena called just as Joyce was headed out the door. Raylene was sick, she said, all her appointments for the day were cancelled. Joyce undressed and went back to bed; she had had a sleepless night, the kind of night Jimmy always called her "rumbles."

When Elena called again to cancel Tuesday's appointments, Joyce wrapped herself in a blanket and turned on the television. She listened to a few minutes of mindless daytime programming and then looked up the Spanish phrase for "get well soon," picked up the phone, and called the number Raylene had written down for her.

Raylene's voice on the phone was hoarse and tired. She had come down with "a good and proper flu," she said, was feeling better by now but many of her patients were in fragile health, she didn't dare expose them to her virus. Joyce murmured a few sympathetic words and "*que te mejores*," but then couldn't stop herself from saying, "I could come out to you, I could bring some chicken soup, and if you feel up to it I wonder if I could please get a treatment, I'm not worried about flu, I just don't want to miss another treatment." Rushing the words like a crazy person. There had been an M 7.4 quake in Brazil that morning.

Raylene and Benny lived on twenty acres in the foot-hills of the Coast Range. Their long unpaved driveway after days of rain was a brown rushing stream. Joyce drove up the lane timidly, her old Honda lurching and sliding in the slip-pery mud. There was no yard at the front of the house, just a muddy expanse in front of the porch, no indication where she was meant to park, no place where she could walk to the house without splashing through a shallow lake. She imagined her car might just sink into the muck and be stuck there until the Fourth of July.

Raylene came onto the porch and called to her. "Sorry about the yard, sweetie. And the road. When it gets this muddy, we gotta just live with it. Cute boots!"

She had worn the ankle-high rain boots she'd bought at the Wilco Farm Store, red ladybugs printed on black rubber, which had seemed charming in the store but now seemed stupidly childish, insufficient for the muddy traverse from her car to the porch. She sheltered the cardboard carton of soup under her coat and hurried across. Raylene held the door wide for her. "Don't worry about tracking in mud. Benny and the dog already brought it in a bunch of times." She wore a frayed terrycloth bathrobe loosely cinched, and fleecy purple slippers. Her hair was an unwashed grey snarl.

In a wave of guilty distress, Joyce said, "I'm so sorry, Raylene, I shouldn't have bothered you. I should have gone to someone in Portland, I'm so sorry." She had never seen Raylene like this, bare-faced, her cheeks blotchy with rosacea, her eyelashes invisible without mascara.

Raylene flapped a hand. "It's all good. I'm good. We'll get you fixed up. You want some tea?" She headed off somewhere without waiting for an answer. Joyce didn't know if she was expected to follow. She stood in the front hall, holding the soup, her coat and her hair quietly dripping. It was true, plenty of mud had already been tracked across the floor, but there were jumbled shoes and boots on a throw rug at the door, and wet coats hanging along the wall, so finally she pushed out of her ladybugs and set the soup down on the floor to get out of her coat. She hung it with other coats on a wall peg, picked up the soup again, and found her way cautiously, sock-footed, to a long, high-ceilinged kitchen. Raylene was pulling boxes of tea from a cupboard.

Joyce held out the carton of soup. "Should I put this in the refrigerator?"

"Oh, sweetie, thanks. Just stick it in there wherever you can find room. Water's ready in a minute, pick out your tea. chamomile might be good for those shakes of yours." Joyce had brought a soup from Mama Leona's Mexican Deli, very spicy chicken tortilla soup. She always thought spicy food helped a bit with the flu or a bad cold. She had never found camomile or any other of the soothing herbals did anything at all for her "shakes."

They took their tea with them back to the living room. It was a big room with an odd jumble of furniture—heavy Mexican arm chairs, an old cracked-leather recliner, a low-slung Danish sofa with blond wooden arms. The room was blessedly warm—a big wood-burning stove took up half of one wall.

Raylene sat on the sofa and waved Joyce toward the recliner. "Let's take it easy for a minute, honey, just drink your tea, and then we'll get some needles into you."

Joyce wanted to say again, *I'm so sorry.* She wanted to put on her coat and boots and get back in the car and drive back down the muddy drive. But she held the mug in both hands, close to her face, and the surface of the tea shivered slightly with the shivering of the whole earth. Raylene, sipping her own tea, watched Joyce in uncharacteristic silence. Then she set her tea down. "Well, I can see you are a pretty mess, honey, so let's not wait, let's go ahead and get started."

She came over and cranked the recliner back with a sudden thunk so that Joyce was almost fully recumbent, took a box of new needles from a book shelf, pushed up the sleeves of Joyce's shirt and tapped the first needles into her wrists. For no reason she could name, Joyce began quietly, helplessly, to cry. Raylene went on working without comment, folding the cuffs of Joyce's pants to bare her ankles, opening the top buttons of her shirt to reach her collar bones, her neck, and then finding new placements as well, needles in Joyce's earlobes and behind the ears, folding down the top of her pants to place them at her waist. Joyce kept her eyes closed and focused on breathing slowly from her belly as she'd been coached by a massage therapist years ago.

Raylene, as soon as she had finished tapping in the needles, came around behind the recliner and reached down to massage Joyce's scalp with the tips of her fingers, which she had never done before. Her touch was light and warm, and Joyce's skin, tingling, rose to her touch. Emotion welled in her chest again and filled her throat.

"It's all right, sweetie, you cry if you need to," Raylene said quietly, and went on stroking Joyce's scalp, then moving her hands to Joyce's temples and her face, pressing thumbs lightly around the eye sockets and down the cheek bones and along the curve of the chin.

"Oh!" she said after a few minutes, in some surprise. "Your tremor, I think I just felt it. Is that what I felt?"

Joyce was startled. She didn't know what to answer.

Raylene began cupping her palms lightly around Joyce's neck, then her ears, feeling for the tremor. She was cradling Joyce's whole head between the palms of her hands when she said, "Oh! There! I do feel it, I can feel it. Oh, honey, not a tremor, kind of a humming, right? Like your whole body is a tuning fork. I feel it! What did you tell me, once, ringing like a bell? Jesus, ringing like a bell, you sure are!"

The quake in Brazil had rung through Joyce's body like the banging of a huge gong. *How could you* not *feel it?* she almost said. She whispered, "There was a big quake in Brazil this morning."

Raylene didn't hear this, or didn't note it. She made a slow, unfocused humming sound, *mmmm-hmmm*, and shifted her hands slightly. And then someone—Joyce thought it must be Benny—came suddenly stomping onto the porch and into the front hall. She couldn't turn her head without disturbing Raylene's hands, but she heard him noisily shucking his boots and rain clothes, heard a dog shaking water off its coat and the *tick-tick* of its toenails on the wood floor, and then Benny's solemn announcement, "Here I is, your man returned from the hunt." This may have been his customary joke—Raylene did not look up or trouble herself to respond. But she said, "Benny, come over here, see if you can feel this." She was holding Joyce's skull tenderly between her hands, fingers spread wide, as if she held a great, fragile egg.

In a moment he loomed over Joyce in the recliner. He was broad-faced, dark-skinned, there were crow's feet around his eyes and his mouth but his dark hair had not yet gone to gray. He might have been Indian. Mexican Indian? It occurred to Joyce that he was perhaps named Benecio or Benedicto, not Benjamin as she had always thought. Could Benjamin also be a Spanish name? *Ben-ha-meen.*

He said, "*Hola*, honey," to Raylene, and then, looking down on Joyce, "You gotta be Joyce? I gotta be Benny. Raylene don't care a thing about introductions so I gotta do it myself. And now we been introduced. *Perdón*, but I'm gonna put my hands on your head. I always do what my wife tells me." He cupped his cold hands around her skull as Raylene lifted hers away. His hands, or it might have been his clothes, smelled strongly of horses. His cold touch, after Raylene's warmth, was in some way soothing. "What am I feeling for?" he asked his wife. Joyce imagined him holding a horse's foot in his hands in the same way he now held her head, cradling it tenderly, appraisingly.

"Just see if you can feel it. I want to know what you can feel."

Joyce wondered again, as she had all of her life, how could anyone who touched her *not* feel it? Jimmy had felt it a few times; he was the only one. She didn't know what she hoped for.

A minute went by and then he said, "Nope. Nada. Sorry, Joyce." And she knew then what she had hoped for. He gently released her head and disappeared from her field of vision. She heard his sock-feet scuffing toward the kitchen.

"There's soup in the fridge," Raylene called after him. "It's Mama Leona's. Joyce brought it." Then, to Joyce, "We gotta give your *chi* some time to find its path, honey. I'll be back in a minute."

Joyce breathed slowly from her belly. She was finished with crying. A strong quake anywhere in the world would ring in her body for weeks, but her head, her mind, had by now begun to calm—this was the needles doing their work, redirecting her *chi*. Or a placebo effect, she didn't much care which it was. People had died in Brazil, but if she stayed off the internet as Jimmy always urged her, she would not learn how many. This, too, was a placebo effect.

She could hear Raylene and Benny talking softly in the kitchen, asking and answering in half-finished sentences the way they must always talk when it was just the two of them. Something about a woman whose lame horse had had to be put down, and something about a man named Josh, who must have been a patient of Raylene's. He had landed back in the Tilla-mook County jail, Raylene said, and Benny answered softly, "You did what you could, Ray. It's all you can do."

She imagined they must talk like this every night. It was what she missed most, now that she was alone, not being able to tell Jimmy every little thing, every big thing, that had happened in her day. It had always felt to her as if none of it was real until she had reported it to him.

Raylene returned and silently gathered in all the needles with the raining sound of pins landing on plastic, and swept the palm of her hand over Joyce's scalp and neck and collarbones to be sure she had found them all. When she stepped away, Joyce reached for the handle to straighten the recliner, and she would have stood up to make her escape—she was afraid of what Raylene might ask, or say; she didn't know what kind of answer she could make—but Raylene had already brought over one of the Mexican chairs and parked it right in front of the recliner. She sat in it, facing Joyce, leaning in with her elbows resting on her knees. The bathrobe fell open slightly, so that Joyce could see she was wearing a man's boxer shorts, bright yellow, printed all over with little brown horses.

"So here's what I think," Raylene said. She tapped her fingertips lightly on Joyce's knees. "What you've got going on is a kind of tinnitus. Anyway it's like tinnitus, like a ringing in your ears, but it's your whole body, not just your ears. Never seen it before, but if it's like tinnitus, I've had some luck with tinnitus. We'll try something different next time, I've got some ideas. But it's no wonder this thing drives you crazy. It would drive anybody crazy."

She didn't know what to say. She hadn't expected *tinnitus*.

She thought of saying something that Jimmy had once said, about the everlasting humming of the earth. But then Raylene slapped her own knees and got to her feet and put a hand down to help Joyce out of the recliner, and the moment for it passed.

Jimmy knew she suffered from insomnia, he knew she suffered from a tremor that kept her from sleeping. For a while this was all he knew. And she was a bit neurotic, he must have thought in those first weeks they were together, without thinking it was a reason to throw her over. He was her first long-term boyfriend, her first lover. They had been together four or five months when one night, lying in bed in the darkness with his arm resting across her belly, his fingertips touching the side of her breast, he said, "Huh. Is that the tremor you've been saying keeps you awake? I feel it. Like you're humming, kind of, or purring. Like this little vibration, only not. Weird."

He moved his hand, cupping her breast, then moved it again, down to her ribs. She held utterly still, willing him to feel it. There had been a big quake just yesterday in the Philippines, it was still ringing in her body.

"Wow, that's weird. What do you think that is? Did they ever check you for a heart murmur? Maybe you've got a leaky valve or something."

After a silence, she said into the darkness, "I should tell you something, Jimmy. This is a true thing, don't laugh"—Jimmy wasn't laughing—"this isn't woo-woo, well, it is a little bit woo-woo, but it's science. Like acupuncture, it's science." She told him about the sound the earth made, kind of a hum, a sound nobody could hear. "You know about that, right? That the earth is kind of singing all the time? They've made recordings. There's this droning, or purring, or swishing, it might be the oceans banging against the sea floor, always moving, or something else, maybe it's just the sound of the globe turning on its axis, they aren't sure, but it's a sound that's always going on under our feet, only nobody can hear it."

Jimmy waited for her to say more, and then he said, "But you can hear it," with a pleased-with-himself sort of flourish. "Is that what you're saying? You can hear it? Damn, Joyce, no wonder you can't sleep, who could sleep if they could hear the everlasting humming of the earth?" A laugh. "Like sleeping with the worst goddamn snorer in the history of the universe!"

Joyce was in the front hall putting on her coat and boots when Benny came back through the living room, trailed by a shepherd-looking dog with muddy legs and a muddy belly. "You heading out? Nope, nope, not before you meet the pony.

Nobody comes all the way out here without meeting the pony."

Raylene gave Joyce a small shrug. "He's serious, honey. You'll have to go out and meet the horse or he won't let you leave. Here, you better take one of my hats, I expect you'll be standing in the rain a while." It was a damp, wide-brimmed hat, a little too big for Joyce's head. A good rain hat and serious boots had already gone onto her mental shopping list for Wilco.

Benny shoved his feet into tall muddy boots, shrugged into a muddy coat, put on his own muddy hat. He and the dog led Joyce off the porch and around the side of the house to a fenced yard and a long, dark shed. Water ran off the slanted shed roof in a nearly solid sheet. The yard was deeply muddy, cratered with puddles and sloppy hoof prints. A dark shape moved in the open door of the shed and then an animal came out into the rain, crossing with slow, reaching strides through the mud to the fence. Not a pony, not anywhere near a pony, a huge black horse, its broad back and left side smeared with half-dried mud.

Benny opened a gate in the fence and stepped through, let the dog through, and lifted his eyebrows at Joyce. She was startled by the animal's size. When she shook her head slightly, he clanged the gate shut behind him. The dog trotted across the deep mud and disappeared into the shed. The horse ignored the dog but took another long step to Benny and bumped the man's shoulder with his enormous head. Benny knuckled the animal's muddy face and said, *"Anciano."* Not a description but a greeting, "Old man." The horse turned his head sidelong to move the knuckles around where he wanted them. Rain sluiced the dried mud in a brown stream off the horse's back.

Benny looked over at Joyce. "You afraid of horses? You ever

been around them? Come on in here, say hello. He won't bite."

There had been that little frisson of fear when the big horse first came into the yard, but it was gone now. "No. I mean, no I haven't been around them at all." She had never been this close to a horse in her life. Benny opened the gate for her and she stepped through. The horse was enormous. His huge head towered over her. He stretched out his neck and smelled her coat, nuzzled her pockets and then the brim of the hat Raylene had loaned her. Joyce reached up to keep the hat on, and he touched the back of her hand with his soft nose, a brief, warm, wet touch. She petted his massive wet neck, and when he brought his head around to her she scratched under his whiskery chin.

"*Bueno*, good on you, not scared no more," Benny said. "Now you oughta let him smell your breath, that's how horses get acquainted. That's how they figure who you are."

This made a kind of sense to her. She put her face close to his liquid brown eyes, leaned in, blew a breath into his big wet nostrils. The velvety muzzle twitched, and the horse breathed her in, then breathed out, a smell that was warm and grassy. Her hand was resting on his neck, and after a moment she became aware of the slight tremble, the purring in his body, not his heartbeat but his essential being, his aliveness. She took off Raylene's brimmed hat so she could rest the side of her head against his wet shoulder. The calm, steady hum against her scalp overrode the humming of the earth. His hide smelled of hay and mud and rain and his own sweet manure and something else, something she understood to be uniquely horse. He brought his head around to nuzzle her ear, her soaked hair. Breathed into her. She whispered against his muddy hide, "There was a big earthquake in Brazil this morning."

Benny came up on the horse's other side and draped his arm over the horse's withers. "Maybe you oughta get yourself a horse, eh, *chica*? Calm you right down. Better'n getting poked with needles, maybe, but don't tell Ray I said so."

There were certain animals, she remembered, who seemed to know, as she did, when the earth under their feet was making ready to shift its weight. Horses were among them. She laughed without lifting her head from the horse, and the sound reverberated through them both.

Joining

FROM WHERE I WAS LYING I could see the hole in Sevin's chest, the edges of his shirt still smoking, and I stared at that, I didn't look at his face. I focused on the hole. And the pain. There was a wide scald of it under my breastbone so I couldn't quite breathe, just these little sucks of air burning in and out. It felt like I'd lost a lung. I mean, it felt like Sevin had lost a lung. The robomed could come up with an artificial lung, I was pretty sure artificial lungs were in its programming. But the robomed was in the Osprey. And the Osprey was at the bottom of the hill.

I could see the farmer, too, crouching beside Sevin. There was a lot of buzz in my head, so I could just hear the peaks of her voice when she turned her face toward me—"can't . . . don't . . . won't . . ."—all the negative sounds bumping high and pointed through the static. But I could feel her brown tones of soundless anguish and I could see she was dropping some real tears over Sevin, as if she mourned him, as if she'd known him more than half a day—and I couldn't even think of her damn name.

I didn't see her come to me. I was so focused on the Joining that I lost track of her, and then she leaned over me, touching my chest, my arms, she was trying to find my wound, I guess, but it damn near killed Sevin. I broke thought a little when she startled me, so the pain slid away and down, slick as mercury, and I was so bone-tired and it was so good to be rid of it I almost let it go without thinking. Then Sevin—unresisting, sliding too—made this small sound that wasn't pain, only a sigh, but it cut me like a razor. I scrambled for him, and in about half a minute we were okay again, balanced again, teetering together.

"Si-Rad," I said, when I remembered the farmer's name, when the Joining grew smooth and seamless and there was room in my head to remember.

She said a word I didn't know, or maybe it wasn't a word, quite, just the sound you'd make if you stepped on your cat, surprise-grief-soothing-apology, and she touched my wrist. "Sevin's not dead," she said to me, or asked me. There were tears hanging fat and clear in her eyelashes.

"Not yet," I said. I had wanted to put it stronger than that, with more hopefulness, and I don't know why it came out straight and honest instead. I'd rather have lied a little and made myself feel better. He's not hurt too bad. I can fix it. Instead, like the farmer, I began to cry. I couldn't get enough air to do it right, but I lay on my back in the dry leaves with Si-Rad holding me by the wrist and I managed to squeeze out a few sticky tears that ran down through my beard into the corners of my open mouth.

"Give me a hand," I said to the farmer. I thought she might object, might make useless *you-shouldn't-be-moving* noises, so I quickly tacked on a little disclaimer—"I'm not hurt"—which wasn't strictly true and must've made me look a damn fool, since I was weeping, lying scrunched up and panting in the weeds. I don't know what she thought, whether she believed it, but she swiped at her wet face with the sleeve of her tunic and then took hold of me by the shoulders and helped me scrabble across the slope to where Sevin was. There was less pain than I was braced for, I just couldn't get enough air.

I touched him right away, took hold of his hand to feel he was still warm, which was a stupid, irrational thing, I guess, but I was better after I touched him, like after the crying. He looked at me sidelong. He didn't want to move his head. I could feel it, fragile as glass, knew like him that it would shatter if he was careless. So he looked at me sideways and tested out a smile, a stiff one showing a thin white rim of teeth, and then squeezed his eyes shut. Myles, he sent, as if my name were a string and he was drawing a bow across it, playing a dark chord, resonating inside my head. *Don't let me kill you.*

The hell with that, I thought, but I don't know if he heard me.

"Unsnap this," I said to Si-Rad. I couldn't get the damn storm belt undone, couldn't see the fastener or make my fingers work, and I had to wait for her to work it loose and snake it off my hips. I dumped everything out of it onto the ground and roamed through the emergency-med stuff.

"Get that open," I said, and then I scissored Sevin's shirt away from the hole while the farmer bit the nipple off my plastic tube of aseptic. It was gluey, the color of shit—tasted shitty, too, if you went by her face. I had her squeeze every last drop of it onto Sevin's chest. Then I ripped open the biggest seal I had and centered it over the hole and touched it in place. It made a small hissing sound when it pressurized. It was white and square with the corners rounded off, had a very sanitary look covering up that charred crater. It didn't do a whole hell of a lot of good, but as with the crying and the touching, I felt better seeing it done. Then she helped me spread the plastex sheet over him. He was breathing shallowly, carefully, this thin rheumy wheeze, but I could feel him hanging on to me a little, all the effort wasn't mine anymore, and the Joining felt smooth. Now that I wasn't working so hard, I was mainly tired because he was. I let myself down on my back beside him and closed my eyes. The lids scratched across the lenses as if there were sand between.

"Myles?" the farmer said, and managed with the one word to squeeze in a lot more, something along the lines of What the hell is going on with you? At least that's what I thought at the time.

"I need a minute. I'll be okay in a minute."

With my eyes closed, the ground moved a lot, as if I were in a boat and the sea was high. Rocking, awash, I didn't sleep but I dreamed a little, playing it over again against the back of my eyelids, the big shape of the cadmium miner standing out from the rocks along the escarpment, tangle-maned, thick-chested, giving off deep red ripples of enmity.

"That's the one," the farmer had said, and then wiped her palms on her trouser legs. I remember feeling the dim blue of her fearfulness.

Sevin spread his hands innocently. "My name is Sevin," he yelled to the rocks, to the big man standing among them. "This is Myles. We're with OS. You can see the ID from there?"

The man's chin lifted a little but he did not speak. There were streaks of black now, in the red that came from him.

Sevin kept his hands apart and open. "OS records show the land here registered for farming." He shaped the words so they were smooth and matter-of-fact and benign, and I stood behind him and painted a canvas of sympathy, patience, calmness, stroking those cooler colors over the man's reds, brushing out his clotted passion while Sevin spoke him down.

"Si-Rad here has filed a complaint with OS. She says you've cut off access to her summer graze, polluted a stream, butchered some of her goats. That's for the courts, we don't accuse you. But the fact is, this quadrant isn't designated for cadmium mining."

He would have said something more, something about filing with Ministry for a proper permit, a waiver to mine in this place. We had arbitrated these kinds of disputes a couple of hundred times before.

But then the miner's mouth opened slightly and the red went suddenly very dark. He never yelled a warning, the alarm I felt was someone else's, the farmer's maybe, or mine, a heartbeat late. The man's hand simply came out, pointing, and his gun sent its pale blue ribbon through the shadow under the trees. With an edge of eye or mind I could see Sevin arcing down, silent-falling, hands spread wide reaching, even while I killed the man who was killing him—soundless too, just the blue tracers spurting through the shade and the wide-eyed surprise above his mouth, above the place his mouth had been—and then I only saw, only felt Sevin, his heavy weight dangling from the edges of my mind. Sevin! And I sent him what I had, all I had, an umbilicus: *don't let go don't let go don't die damn you love you don't die don't . . .*

"Myles."

I opened my eyes. The farmer was sitting lotus-fashion

on the leaves next to Sevin. Her eyes were very brown under cramped-high brows.

"Just need a minute," I said again.

She watched me gravely without moving. There was nothing coming from her now except a faintly lavender anxiety. Behind her head, through the limbs of the trees, there were heavy clouds sliding toward the east ahead of the high-up winds. It would rain before too much longer, rain on Sevin's chest, on the white pressure seal and the smooth, closed half-circles of his eyelids.

"I don't suppose you know how to fly an Osprey," I said. What the hell, it was worth asking.

"I've flown Kites."

I looked toward her. I don't think I smiled. "Okay, well, an Osprey is not too much like a Kite."

"I have a talent for machines. I might be able to figure it out."

Then I guess I did smile a little, but it felt lopsided and faintly bitter. I said, "I don't think so. You stay with Sevin. There's a robomed in the Osprey. I'll walk down and fly it up here." Just like that.

I half-expected her to ask what a robomed was. Some of these outspace ruralists lead a pretty isolated life. But instead she said, "You left the ship there in the first place because there wasn't room to land in these trees."

"It's armed. I'll blast a clearing."

She studied me a while and then she said, "It's a couple of kilometers. I don't think you can walk that far."

I didn't want to lie outright if I could help it, and anyway there was no telling what she thought was wrong with me. So for now I only said, "It might be less than that," and I looked away. I needed to get up. To get to the Osprey. But it felt like I had five hundred kilos pressing on my breastbone. For a minute more I lay on my back and stared up into the crowns of the trees where the sky ran fast and dark. I could feel her watching me. She was working out the right words, I guess, or working up nerve.

Finally she said, "You're Joined," just as straight as that, so it wasn't a question. When I looked at her, she said, "I don't think anyone Joined to a wound like Sevin's could walk two kilometers." She didn't lower her eyes. She was sending a watery green now, so maybe she was a little embarrassed to know more than she should, but she never lowered her eyes from me.

"I thought you were a farmer," I said, after I'd thought it over.

"I am."

She damn well knew what I was getting at, so I just waited through the silence until finally she added, "My parents were both gifted. They freelanced for COM and DOC. Sometimes even for OS. I wasn't trained—I guess they thought that would lock me into government service and they wanted more choices for me—but I learned a few things at home. I don't eavesdrop. But a Joining—!" She lowered her eyes finally, lowered them to Sevin. Not to his patient closed-up face but to the place where the seal made a neat square on his breast, beneath the transparent plastex.

In a minute, she said, "I didn't think you could hold him. When he went down, I thought he was already dead, I thought you would die too. I could feel you make the Join, and I thought he would suck you down with him." Then she said, like it didn't matter, like an afterthought, "My mother died that way. Trying to lifeline a friend." There was an old, faintly violet grief in the air. I wanted to, but couldn't think of anything to say to that. Maybe she didn't need anything said. Anyway, in a while she offered again, "I can try to fly the Osprey. Maybe you can tell me enough so I could do it."

I had spent two years learning to fly an Osprey. But I just said, "Stay here with Sevin," and then I sat up. When I did that, Sevin opened his eyes. His face seemed very lean and colorless. I wasn't sure how much he'd heard until he thought, *You won't get a hundred yards*. With something like amusement. *The hell*, I thought. With something like irritation.

I drew my legs under me and pushed against the ground to get up. Tried to do it in one smooth motion. Didn't quite make it. The vertical lines of the trees tipped off sideways and then I felt the woman's hands holding me. She had wide hands, a good strong grip. Her face was right there, peering at me. She was giving off long streams of blues and browns. There were several narrow lines that runneled down alongside her mouth, and straighter ones, deeper, between her brows. Her skin was walnut-colored, walnut-seamed. With those great, clear brown eyes.

"Okay," I said, and then she dropped her hands from me and took a step back. I bent over and rested my palms on my knees and panted.

She said, "If you fall, Sevin will feel it." She must have been a good home study.

I didn't look at her, or at Sevin. "I won't fall."

"If you fall and strike your chest, the blow will probably kill him. Probably it will kill you too."

"I said I won't fall." I whittled my voice down thin that time.

I straightened out my back and looked down the slope where I would need to go. There were drifts of dry leaves between the trees. I would have liked it better if the ground had been clean. I wanted to see where I was putting my feet.

"Hold his hand," I told her, without looking at either of them, and then I started down the hill.

"Wait."

I kept going. I heard her boots, and then she put a hand on my arm. "Wait."

I expected more of her damn self-taught psy theory but she surprised me. "We're going at this backward," she said, like she was surprised too. "We can find a way to get Sevin down to the Osprey instead of the other way around."

I caught Sevin's dark blue alarm, had a vision of a glass skull spidering with cracks. "We can't move him," I said. I would have shaken my head to double the negative but my own skull felt thin-walled and distended.

She made a gesture with both hands, faintly impatient, dismissing me. "Yes we can, if we do it right. I told you, I'm good with mechanics. Maybe I can take parts off the Osprey and make some kind of powered litter. Air-cushioned. Will your comp talk to me? If I had the use of a good comp I might be able to make something that would work." Her voice had come up some, and she was running the words together like she was excited and maybe pleased with herself.

I looked sideways up the hill at Sevin, at the clean white seal and the trimmed back edges of burned shirt and him watching me under drawn-down brows. I could feel the woman's sureness. And by this time I was pretty sick. But I looked at Sevin and waited. He was the one with the glass head. And after a while he told me, *You wouldn't get a hundred yards*, but this time flat, resigned. And hell, he was right.

I walked back up to where he lay, then leaned against a tree and skidded down along the bark until I was sitting. She stood waiting, watching us.

"You'll need to a key to start the comp," I said. There were fourteen integers. I meant to drone them off but it must have seemed like too damn much effort because I wound up just sending her the whole thing in a tidy and soundless little package.

I thought about it afterward and I guess it had been quite a while since I'd bespoken anybody but Sevin. Quite a while. Anyway, there was a strong feel of awkwardness, of an ill-fit, with this stranger. She pulled a face—embarrassment, apology, bereavement, something. And I was sorry I'd done it.

I said, "You'd better get going," squeezing the words so they were small and hard.

But she didn't leave right away, just stood there watching me with that look around her eyes. Finally she ducked her chin and I saw her slide her eyes across Sevin, like he'd said something private to her. She took a couple of steps to go. Then she looked back. "I know a little about Peacers," she said. "My parents worked with a few. They said OS had a lot of trouble with the pairing, the bond getting too tight or something. They said if one of the pair died, the other would suicide."

My eyes began to ache. Or maybe it was Sevin's eyes. I pushed against mine with my knuckles. "Don't believe everything you hear," I said, from the darkness behind my closed eyes.

I felt her waiting a while and then she made a faint whistly sound, a sigh, and she went away, pushing her boots through the piles of dry leaves. I dropped my hands from my face and watched her walking long-strided at first and then breaking into a trot, with her arms pumping smoothly at her sides. I watched her until I couldn't see the brown of her tunic against the trees anymore and then I put one hand on Sevin's arm and closed my eyes and began to wait. As long as I didn't move, there was not too much pain.

I could hear Sevin breathing carefully. And after a while I could feel him thinking carefully too, thinking what he would say, how he would say it, how he'd get me to promise.

The hell with that, I thought.

After a while it rained. The first drops fell in big clear beads, stinging cold, few enough to count. Then they came finer, grayer, a tattered wet sheet. I crawled over to the pile of things I'd dumped on the leaves, all the stuff from my storm belt, and pawed through it for the khirtz tent. I didn't inflate it right away though; I looked at Sevin. He was watching me, blinking his lashes against the rain. He was pale and sooty-looking, the color of old snow.

"I'd have to move you a couple of meters," I said. "To get you inside it."

I guess not. Sounding easy inside my head, easy and familiar and undamaged.

I don't want you lying out in the wet.

You'd better not move me, Myles.

The rain was sliding sideways off his cheeks and running inside his ears and beading on the clear surface of the plastex sheet. I was cold. He had to be, too. But I didn't move him. I lay down next to him on the sodden leaves, got under the sheet and pulled it up over our heads, tented a little like we were kids reading under the blankets at night. I lay on my side and put my arm around him gingerly. It hurt me to lie like that, made it hard to get air in my lungs, but I could feel him shaking a little, and his cheek where it touched mine was chill and wet. So I held on to him. I lay on my side and took air in through my open mouth and I held him in the curve of my arm, the curve of my mind.

I could feel him worrying that old bone she'd dropped. And finally he spoke aloud, furry-voiced and phlegmy with only the one lung, the first time he'd spoken aloud since he'd been hit. "Tim made it," he said. "He lost An Ching and he made it back. He even paired up again. He and Solder are working somewhere out in the Badlands now."

"The hell with that. I don't want to hear about Tim. Shut up about him. I don't want to hear about it." I had begun to cry again so the last words were blurry wet. My chest was weighted down and hurting a lot, and this time weeping didn't help; I still had that ache behind my eyes.

Sevin gave me a couple of minutes and then he said, with a voice that was ragged-hoarse, that didn't sound like him, "I want you to wait, at least. Maybe they'll send Tim in to talk to you. They'll send somebody. And you can wait that long, until they get here. Whoever it is. There might be somebody able to see you through it." And then he said again, "I want you to wait," patient as hell, as though I was a little kid and needed drilling to get it to stick.

"Shut up," I said, or thought. Shut up. After a long pause I heard him sighing. And after that we didn't speak, or couldn't. We lay stiffly together trying to stay warm, and we listened to the rain touching the outside of the plastex sheet.

A long time later, a thousand hours later, it seemed to me, I felt the farmer coming back up the hill, sending ahead of her a bleakness, a defeat as gray as the rain, and as cold. Sevin must have felt her too. I started to speak, to tell him some utter lie or maybe just make some promise I couldn't keep, but he got there ahead of me. He put together the frayed strands one at a time until they wove a last dark line: *You know you can live without me.* And then he cast free.

I didn't know it right away because at first there was just the color, purple-black deepening, and we were together inside it in the dark purple under the sheet, and the ground melting under us, and there was no pain, finally, just the warm damp darkening. And then Sevin said, *Wait, Myles*, and he went down ahead of me. I was holding him, I thought I had a tight hold, and he just slid free of me and sank until the womb-dark closed over his head. I waited. He had told me to wait, so I waited inside the color that was like a bruise, and I patiently counted my heart-beats. I might have waited quite a while, but the color thinned, went violet and then lavender and finally gray; and in that new, cooler light I could see the walls that were rising slick-smooth, curving high around me; and inside them, in the silvered emp-ty-echoing space where I waited, I could see I was alone. And that was when I began to be afraid. I thought of what I would tell Sevin. I waited a while, I would say, but there was no one there and I was afraid of the aloneness.

Someone said, Myles. She pitched the name like a life-ring curving high over the wall and I watched it scribe its bright arc through my space, watched it sink in the darkness under me. I couldn't think of her name. I remembered there had been that chafing between us when we touched, that dissonance—she was the wrong, the unfamiliar one; I wanted Sevin.

She said *Myles* again, with more distress, so the name sang in my head, bow against strings, elegy for cello, grays and browns.

And there was something of Sevin in it, some of his voice, or his feeling. Sevin's dead, I thought then, with a sort of painless surprise. Sevin's dead. My eyes were very dry. Without tears. There was not much pain, it was just that I didn't want to be alone. So I let myself down in the darkness, at the place where Sevin had gone.

Then I felt something from the other one, a spurt of despair or terror, and unexpectedly she cast herself in where I was, a floundering clutch of mind in the blackness, ropes of purple and green and blue, no pale walls in the private place where she tried to tow me, only the vivid endless opaque colors of her anguish. She was clumsy and afraid—I should have been able to cut loose from her—but she clung stubbornly, had no muscle to check me but dragged heavily behind, setting heels in the soft darkness, terrorized, mulish, don't go don't die please wait don't, as though she did not remember or did not care that she might die with me. And in the darkness I could feel her-our excruciating pain, her-our loneliness and fear. And where we touched at those places, where we bled into one another, there was no strangeness. We just fit together. We made a whole.

So that, without ever deciding to, I decided to wait. And I began to weep. "Si-Rad," I said, remembering.

The Grinnell Method

IN THE LONG WINTER OF her absence, hunters and maybe soldiers had made use of the camp. They had left behind a scattered detritus of tin cans, broken fishing line and shotgun shells, had made of the fire pit a midden of kitchen garbage, burnt and sodden bones and feathers, clamshells, and the unburned ends of green and greasy sticks. She immediately sat down on the ground and examined the feathers and bones under a hand lens and found they were largely from pintail ducks and black brant.

The boy she had hired to transport her gear up the three miles of sand trail from Oysterville to Leadbetter Point had been warned of the woman's odd ways and refused to be amazed when she sat on the dirt like a Jap, peering nearsighted through her magnifier at feathers and shards of bone. He discharged his duty, which was to off-load her goods onto the dirt, and then he waited, drawing circles and figure eights on the ground with the toe of one gum boot, until she woke from her study and paid his wages in coin.

She had walked ahead of him, pausing only briefly to peer at something—a feather on the ground, a bird overhead—or to stand like a dog with her head cocked, and then pencil a note in the little book she carried in her hand, before immediately striding on. Hadn't offered a word of encouragement or a backward glance while he had struggled through the loose sand and mud pushing a wheelbarrow weighed down with her camp gear and strange paraphernalia. But she paid him a dollar more than the agreed upon price, which to his mind made up for many failings and eccentricities. He thanked her kindly and pushed his barrow off through the trees. There was something forlorn about the way the woman stood among her boxes and bags watching him go, and in consideration of that, he turned once and gave her a cheering wave of his hand.

In fact, she had lost heart a bit on first seeing the degraded camp, the men's stupid squalor, but when the boy had gone out of sight and left her alone she went directly to work burning the burnables in a smoky bonfire and burying the cans, the shells and bones, the garbage. She swept the disturbed ground with a branch and pitched her tent in exactly the same place as the year before, under the canopy of a massive cedar almost surely well-grown when Robert Gray first sailed the *Columbia Rediviva* into the Great River of the West. There was still a faint, weathered tracing of the ditch she had cut to carry rain away from the base of her tent, and she renewed this with a grub hoe; then, because she was holding the tool in her hands, she quickly dug a hole for her scat at a place chosen not for privacy but for proximity to a blown-down jack pine over which to hang her nether parts.

The day was already well-gone and she was anxious to get a

first look at the dunes and the salt marsh, so these things were all done rather perfunctorily—getting her ducks in a row, as Tom used to joke to her in his letters from the field. Then she put on her beach shoes, dug through her equipment until she had laid hands on field glasses and the .25 caliber Colt pistol, put them in the pocket of her jacket with the notebook and pencil, and set off through the trees toward the estuary.

The peninsula was not more than two or three miles wide at its widest point, a twenty-five-mile-long finger of land trapped between the Pacific Ocean and Willapa Bay, built of sand washed north from the mouth of the Columbia River and then overgrown with conifer rain forest which by now had become a patchwork of second- and third-growth woodland interrupted by small farms and cranberry bogs and half a dozen villages. Oysterville sat at the end of a tarred plank road, the last human settlement, and beyond it a woodland of western hemlock, jack pine, and spruce carried on for a little more than three miles before running out at the curved tip of the fingernail, which was Leadbetter Point. On the ocean side, the point was a world of shifting low dunes and tufted beach grass; on the bay side a rich estuarine marsh of pickleweed and arrowgrass, drowned and emptied twice each day by surging eight-foot tides. The whole of the point was a resting place for thousands of water-fowl and shorebirds during the spring and fall migrations, sum-mer nesting grounds for plovers and snipes, and winter home to black brants and canvasbacks.

It had rained much of the day, but by now the clouds had lifted somewhat and were massed offshore above a narrow understory of clear light. When she came out of the trees onto the bay shore, a great flock of wigeons and pintails flew up in unison against the dark sky, turning so the undersides of their wings caught the seam of sun at the horizon. The tide was out, and her shoes left a trail of shallow pug marks in the narrow strand of bayside beach. Crab molts were thick, and the mud was stitched with the lacy tracks of sanderlings and plovers as well as the spoor of deer, who liked to come down to graze the tidewater marshes at evening. She planned to make only a quick circuit to see what the winter tides had wrought and then get an early start in the morning, but she lifted the field glasses every little while and wrote a few words in her notebook.

At the hook-shaped tip of the peninsula where the dunes and salt meadows gave way entirely to marsh she stood a moment peering across the mouth of the bay to Tokeland, five miles distant, its wooded hills through the gauze of weather seeming to her like a long line of battlements. Ships traveling from British Columbia to San Francisco regularly came into the bay to pick up lumber at the South Bend docks—the entrance was wide and straight, they came in without pilots—and a ship was laboring through the swells a mile from shore. She watched it for several minutes, the white curl rolling off the rust-colored prow, and then turned and cut straight across toward the weather beach.

The earth barely rose above the sea along this coast, and the peninsula was everywhere pocked with little lakes and ponds and bogs. A maze of intersecting paths had been laid down through the woods and marsh by hunters and the hunted, which in her first year camping here she had tried to decipher and follow—countless lost hours scouting back and forth for the driest trail—but this was her third year, and she had long ago learned to slog straight through the standing water. Had learned, too, that it was useless to wade the marsh in gum boots. They were hot and clumsy when dry, heavy and clumsy when full of water or caked with mud, impossible to pull out of a sticky mire, desperately slow to dry out, even with the help of wind and a stove. She had taken to wearing old canvas shoes tied on with a piece of cord.

A Wilson's snipe broke from cover almost under her feet, making off to the west in a sharp and zigzagging panic flight. Grebes and pintails in small flocks rose in front of her and then settled again to the rear. Pelicans passed over her, keeping very high against the overcast. A peregrine falcon harassed a group of thirty or forty wigeons, trying to isolate a vulnerable bird from among the others. She stood still for several minutes watching him, and when he'd given up and flown eastward over the bay she held down the pages of her notebook against the gusty offshore wind and wrote a short note of his failure.

The weather beach had been dramatically rearranged since she had last seen it in September. The dunes were higher and steeper, the sand broader, stippled at low tide to form a field of shallow lakes. There were thousands of driftlogs piled along the dunes—this was usual—and thousands of board feet of milled lumber, shattered and waterlogged or coated with oil. There were pieces of twisted iron and wire cable, broken crates and baskets, drifts of gill-netting tangled with sea wrack.

Over the years, hundreds of ships had sunk or gone aground on this stretch of coast. Longtime peninsula folk told salvage stories as if they were proud family histories: sacks of flour still good in the center, protected by the glued-hard outer layer; rafts of coal floating ashore in calm weather two years after the wreck of a coal ship; a house built entirely from salvaged doors nailed together with salvaged stair rails. She was a habitual scavenger herself. When a spring storm and a high tide rolled in together she would be out scouring the wind-whipped beach for dead birds and feathers, while the dedicated locals were looking for cans of peas and wooden crab pot markers—or now, with the peninsula on a wartime footing, the shattered wreckage of warplanes floating in on the surf.

There were two lines of caved-in tracks going up and down the beach—the Coast Guard horse patrol, on the lookout for invasion by sea—but no footprints, none human at any rate, though a bear had come through the sand hills and laid down a trail that wandered northward along the high tide line. Looking for dead seals, fish or birds washed up on the sand—scavenging through storm wrack, exactly like every other peninsula native.

The sun was very low, the sky streaked with ragged orange clouds. She walked the wet sand south along the beach. There was little to make note of save the topography and the extravagantly painted sky, but when she turned inland and climbed over the foredune she disturbed several plovers who may have been feeding among the clumps of beach grass. When the migrating birds had passed through, it was the plovers, nesting and raising their young here, who would be the work of her summer, so she made a note about the birds (maybe/probably semipalmated) and then on the left-hand page of her notebook drew a crude map of the location, and paced off the distance to an oddly shaped driftlog that might serve as a reference point. Then she crouched down and waited through a long darkening hour until finally the birds returned to the area and she could get an accurate count and decide that, yes, they were semipalmated.

When she stood again, the plovers skittering away into the last of the light, it was already dark under the trees. Without a flashlight—she had not counted on the plovers keeping her out this late—she was half an hour scouting out the way back to camp.

Her things were in somewhat of a jumble but she was able to find tea leaves and a pot, as well as potatoes and a block of good white San Francisco cheddar. She lit her camp stove and while she waited for the potatoes to boil she drank tea and nibbled shavings from the block of cheese and read through her scratchy field notes by the light of a Coleman lantern.

She followed Grinnell's famous method of note-taking: Her notebook, small enough to slip in her pocket, was an abridged record of bird sightings, cryptic behavior notes in a shorthand of her own invention, quickly sketched drawings and maps, details of weather and vegetation, travel routes and mileage that would be difficult to remember with precision later in the day. It was scribbled in pencil, and none of it well organized—it all ran together.

The Journal, written in pen at the end of every day, would be considerably fuller and neater, her notes organized, sorted out, edited, expanded, with detailed observations of behavior recorded at the back, on separate pages for each individual species. For the Journal, and for Species Accounts, she created a narrative, free of sentiment or much personal reflection—a scientific document, not a diary, but with the skeleton of facts dressed in the clothes of complete sentences, so as to be readable by any stranger looking over her shoulder. All manner of facts might prove important to a student of the future, this was Grinnell's belief. Nothing in nature should be assumed insignificant.

It had been a long tiring day of travel, hauling half a year's worth of camp gear by ferry and motor coach and shank's mare, but Grinnell had always stressed the importance of transcribing field notes at the end of every day. "No Journal, no sleep," was his rather famous rule when he took students into the field—she had heard this directly from Tom. She dug the heavy binder out of her luggage, laid it flat across her lap, dipped the metal tip of the pen in Higgins Eternal ink, and wrote directly below the last entry in a clear, fine hand, 10 April 1943, Leadbetter Point Base Camp. In her head she saw again the falcon gyring among the wigeons, his silhouette against the evening sky so terribly graceful and fluent.

It was her brother Tom, ten years older, who had started her in the business of collecting birds' nests, Tom who had taken her into the woods and fields, a small child, and told her the names of flowers, birds, trees, how to catch and mount butterflies and insects. They sat under the oaks behind their parents' Napa Valley house, and Tom taught her to voice the acorn woodpeckers—their strange squawks and purrs—while he balanced a sketchbook in his lap and drew the woodpeckers in every careful detail.

Some of his professors were still listing the double barreled shotgun as an essential tool of identification; Grinnell himself had been inclined that way. But Tom's generation, coming into the field in the 1920s, had begun the shift from taxidermy toward studying the behavior of free-living birds. Sight identification in the field was challenging—there were few published guides, none very complete—and Tom intended his sketchbook to help her with it. "You're a girl, so you'll have to prove you're better than the boys." This wasn't a joke; Tom never had teased her in that way. "Universities don't mind teaching girls," he told her, "they just don't like to hire them. By the time you finish your studies, you'll need to know more birds on sight than anybody else."

In the summer of 1933, when she was twenty, an undergraduate at Stanford, and Tom a field biologist for the Berkeley Museum of Vertebrate Zoology, he joined a mapping and scientific expedition to the Arctic. The expedition had been plagued with bad luck. His letters, coming in bunches sent out with whalers and fishing boats encountered in the Bering Sea, reported a minor fire in the galley, the death of the ship's cat, expedition notes and specimens spoiled by an overturned lamp. Then came months of silence. Then a letter in an unfamiliar hand. *So sorry to convey sad news, Tom a bright mind and a boon pal, yours in sympathy &cetera.* The expedition had been plagued not by bad luck but by one of its members—perhaps mad with syphilis or anarchism—methodically practicing mischief. A fire set in the ship's radio room had spread to the boiler, and when the vessel sank to the bottom of the Spitsbergen estuary, Tom had been among the seven drowned. The survivors were months in lifeboats and starvation camps in the archipelago, had been at the verge of death themselves when finally rescued by a Norwegian sealing vessel.

She left her university studies and went home to St. Helena to console her parents, and be consoled by them. She had been a late and unexpected addition to their lives, a "caboose" they doted on, but it was Tom who had represented all their best hopes. It was assumed that a woman who went to university would eventually marry, and thereafter carry her knowledge of the world like a secret pearl in her apron pocket, but Tom's keen scientific mind and great ambition had seemed to promise public accolades and prizes. Now his parents wondered if their expectations had somehow weighed him down and been the cause of his drowning.

When Tom sailed for the Arctic, he had left his field guide with her—by then it was a thick book, fifteen years of careful drawings he intended someday to see into print. But for a year, more than a year after his death, she hardly carried it into the fields at all. She played Patience, sometimes for hours at a time, turning over the cards quickly, reshuffling the entire deck whenever the play became difficult. She read cheap romance novels and mysteries and failed to answer letters. She might have married—there was a suitor, a boyhood chum of Tom's, evidently attracted by her melancholy air—but when he pressed his suit she became suddenly awake, and desperate for meaning in her life. She gave up card playing and wrote a plea for readmission to the university which was denied on the first letter but granted on the third. Tom had warned her that only the most extraordinary women were advanced or promoted in the scientific disciplines, and she meant to be one of them. Employment opportunities would disappear completely if she were to marry, and therefore she would never marry. Her life as a scientist would be her own; but also, she felt, a tribute to Tom.

The weather was unsettled and wet; she dressed every day in waterproofs whether or not the sky promised rain. When she hiked out to the point in the early morning, birds rose up singly and in flocks all around her, veering off across the pale sky. She settled into an island of arrowweed out in the salt marsh, or into a swale at the edge of the jack pines, and pulled onto her shoulders a cape made of netting and bits of yarn having a rough resemblance to marsh grasses. Then she found a relatively comfortable position and became motionless, and in a little while the birds returned and resumed their ordinary business.

These early weeks in spring the peninsula was crowded with tens of thousands of birds, a hundred species and subspecies jostling together as they passed through from their southern wintering grounds to their northern breeding grounds. She was well acquainted with the peninsula birds—all the usual species of the summer breeding season—but the mixed flocks of the spring migration were another matter. She kept Tom's field guide open in her lap and referred to it frequently. If a bird was not already illustrated there, she opened to a blank page and sketched it quickly herself, drawings she would have to refine later—Tom had been the better artist—and then compare to specimens in the Stanford natural history collections in hope of discovering the name.

At high tide, or whenever rain flooded the hollow she was sitting in, she slogged across the point to the driftwood beach, made herself comfortable among jumbled driftlogs, and took up scrutiny of the gulls and little plovers and sandpipers along the surf line. When the huge old howitzers at Fort Canby twenty miles to the south let fly their practice rounds, the dim booming echo sent the shorebirds into the sky in a great rippling cloud.

At the end of April a heavy storm arriving in the night lifted and belled the walls of the tent, drove rain through the waxed canvas, brawled and thrashed in the heavy-limbed firs. For hours, a strange green lightning flared almost continuously, and thunder followed in tremendous explosions—she imagined this must be the sound of a battlefield under a barrage. She lay awake listening to the shriek and groan of falling trees, the crash of breaking limbs. In the last hour before daybreak the bombardment at last slackened, and although the wind was still howling she dressed in waterproofs, put specimen sacks in the pocket of her coat, took a flashlight, and went out into the storm. She kept to the rain-flattened grass at the edge of the foredune, away from driftlogs and the high, huge, booming surf. The wind was beating in from the northwest; it rattled and shook the rain clothes, drove cold and wet through seams and gaps to bare skin. In other weather, she had watched gulls walk the beach at night, breakers rushing in ranks of yellow-green flame, the wet sand alive with tiny stars. Now a leaden surf rolled out to a black sky, and she felt herself to be alone at the edge of the known world.

The beach was empty of birds—all but the dead. The sand was littered with hundreds of bodies of water-soaked gulls, short-billed dowitchers, pelicans, puffins. Among them were storm-petrels, albatrosses, shearwaters—pelagic birds who spent their lives at sea, and came to land so rarely that she had seen them only in taxidermy. She took several corpses into her specimen sacks.

She climbed over the dune and waded a mile of salt marsh to the bay shore. The curved point was completely flooded, the tide flats and sand shore drowned under feet of water. The headland, four miles north across the bay, was indistinguishable in the darkness—no lights shone from Tokeland—but the North Cove lighthouse swung a red beam and then a white one through the storm every half minute or so, the brief streak of light glimmering with tiny sparks, bits of haloed flotsam falling with the rain.

To keep from the flood, she broke a path a dozen yards inland through salt grass and scrub, her legs whipped by willow branches. At her feet, in the dim cone of the flashlight, drifts of bluish chaff floated on the puddles. She took some into a specimen sack—bits of sodden feather, maybe, from an elegant tern, or a mew gull.

She ate a cold breakfast back at the tent, and when the darkness thinned she autopsied a dead albatross and recorded her findings on a fresh page in Species Accounts: *No bones broken; dark streaks of something viscous—not oil—in the anterior and posterior air sacs; death from obstruction of the airway?* Or from causes unknown.

The small bits she had collected from the wind-roughened puddles were not feather, as she had thought, but something like flakes of ash or thin scales of paint, blue to her eye, even now in daylight, but colorless under the lens—motes as clear and insubstantial as breath. She wrote, *I do not know what they are.*

In late morning she walked out to the ocean again. The sky was lurid—utterly black in the west, veined with great streaks of orchid purple and emerald green. The wind was squally and cold, the beach in flood tide awash with the bodies of dead birds. She stood and looked and then hiked across to the bay.

From the edge of the marsh, she could hear a dog howling, a terrible prolonged wailing of pain or fear, and when she came out on the mud flats a wet black dog was pacing back and forth, lifting its muzzle every little while in a long, loud, doleful cry of anguish. She called to it without coming very near— she knew nothing of dogs, and thought this one might be rabid. The dog went on pacing and crying, looking out across the bay where an oysterboat rolled and heaved on the swell. Several men on the deck of the boat appeared to be casting and retrieving a drag net without recovering anything. The water was too choppy to see what it was they cast for—a man overboard, she feared, and then realized he must already have drowned—that they were casting for a body—or their efforts would have had more urgency. This was not something she could think about for long.

While she stood watching they brought up something heavy and dark, something like a waterlogged stump. The oystermen had seen her watching from the bay shore, and when they had the thing aboard they hoisted it up and displayed it for her, lifting and spreading the arms wide, lifting up the heavy head until the mouth fell open to white teeth, a red tongue. The bear's thick, sodden pelt streamed with salt water. The dog pointed his nose at the sky and suddenly raised a new wail—it seemed to her a sound of terrible bereavement. One of the men on the boat shouted something, but she could not make it out against the chop of waves on the muddy shore.

Several times in the years since his death she had been visited by Tom, or rather Tom's ghost. Once, just at dusk, she had seen him sitting below an oak tree alive with acorn woodpeckers, and when she called to him he turned and grinned and made the purring sound a woodpecker makes in greeting its fellows. She came upon him suddenly in the narrow aisles of the Stanford library stacks, where he smiled slightly as if embarrassed and then turned into another aisle without speaking. On the peninsula, where heavy rain could turn the meadows and fields into an archipelago of islands, the houses and barns afloat in their yards, she had seen Tom crossing through the flooded tombstones of the Ocean Park cemetery, not walking on water but wading in his heavy hiking boots, raising a white surf that slapped against the stones. When she spoke to him he glanced back with a soft expression but did not reply.

None of this, of course, was real. A moment afterward, the person sitting under the oak was Claude Gerald who lived uphill from her parents' house in St. Helena. In the library stacks, it was Benjamin Morse, a student in her botany class whose dark hair brushing the collar of his shirt was so much like Tom's. The one she had seen crossing the flooded churchyard was a young man who sold oysters on the pier at Nahcotta—she did not know his name—on his way to the feed store in Ocean Park.

After Tom drowned in the Spitsbergen estuary, but during the months when she had still believed him to be alive, she had been visited by vivid dreams of him, dreams that slipped away in the morning, beyond retrieve. It seemed to her that glimpses of Tom's ghost must be fragments of those dreams, dreams she had thought irrecoverable, and a separate, nameless loss. She wrote down each sighting at the back of the Journal in Species Accounts, on the page set aside for uncommon birds, the page titled Incidental, Accidental, Rare.

The birds had mostly gone to ground or been driven inland by the storm, so in the afternoon when the rain briefly slackened she took the sand trail to Oysterville to replenish groceries and post her letters. She walked quickly, holding down her hat. The sky in the west was still black, but now rippling every little while with silent green lightning. Dry blue flakes of ash or dust—she was at a loss what to call it—lifted and fell on the wind, and gathered at the outer edges of puddles in a stiff rime.

Oysterville's prosperity had failed decades earlier with the failure of the San Francisco oyster market, the village by now reduced to a few dozen weather-battered houses and barns scattered between the upland woods and the mud flats. The post office occupied space in Mulvey's Store, and the storekeeper, whose name was not Mulvey, and who served also as postmaster, remembered her from previous years.

"It's you, is it, come back to look for your strange birds." He meant this in a neighborly way. She was by most standards an odd woman, one who dressed in trousers and tramped about in wild territory that was home to bears; a woman known to carry a pistol, and whose behavior and study could not properly be called "bird-watching." But he had known her sort in North Carolina as a boy—"yarbs" who sold leaves and snake venom as curatives door to door, and lived out wild in the woods; and he was himself eccentric enough to think well of her.

It crossed her mind to tell him the correct term for a strange bird was incidental, or rare; but she smiled slightly and said, "Yes, it's me," and handed him several letters to post.

While he rummaged for any mail that might have come for her, he said, "Well, that was a storm we had, wasn't it, I never seen a sky like that, never have, nor such lightning."

She agreed that it was a terrible storm.

"A tempest, my mama would have called it, but no, I never seen it like that, which I wonder if it wasn't those fellows over to Fort Canby, shooting off some sort of ordnance, which they claim not. Or else the Japs, but if so they have got poor aim, they hit nothing but trees." He brought out two letters, one addressed in her mother's hand and the other in her father's. "Now what else can I do you for, miss?"

She gave him a short list—flashlight batteries, chocolate, a piece of smoked ham—and she bought a copy of the weekly

Chinook Observer, its bold headline announcing "Yanks Shoot Down Yamamoto." She stowed everything in her knapsack and swung the sack to her shoulder, but did not immediately take the trail to camp. On the lee side of Mulvey's porch she found a bench and sat to read her letters. Her parents each gave much the same mundane report comprised of errands and weather and neighborhood gossip. "They have shot down Yamamoto," her father wrote, which was his only reference to the war.

While she was skimming the front page of the newspaper a young girl ten or eleven years old came through the yard, and when she saw her there she veered across and stepped up onto the porch. "Is your name Miss Kenney? Are you the woman looks for birds?" The girl was in rubber boots and a brown sweater. Her fair hair was unevenly cut, held back with bobby pins under a hat decorated with fishhooks and bird feathers.

"I am Barbara Kenney," she said. And then—this is what Tom would have done—she told the girl, "I am an ornithologist, which is a scientist who studies birds. Are you interested in science?"

She considered her answer. "I wonder about things, if that's science."

"It is."

The girl ran her tongue across her chapped lips. "I wonder about some birds I saw. I could show you them."

"Do you know the species name? Or can you describe them to me?"

"They're oystercatchers."

On the peninsula, she had only ever seen oystercatchers on the rocks below the North Head lighthouse a good twenty miles to the south, prying mollusks out of coastal rocks with their long, tough, bright orange bills. She said, "Where did you see them? Are you certain they are oystercatchers?"

"They're over on the mud flats"—the girl pointed vaguely—"which is not where I ever have seen them. And most of them dead on the ground."

She could not think what the girl's story might mean, or how to measure the truthfulness of it. But she thought of the albatrosses and petrels dead on the Leadbetter beach. She put away her newspaper and stood. "Well, all right, show me."

The girl led her south on the tarred plank road toward Nahcotta. There were jack pines on both sides of the road, and the wind made a sound in them like the rattle of pebbles in a jar. A splintered windmill on the roof of a house made a faint whine, spinning its few intact vanes. In the west, the black sky was shot through every little while with flutters of silent, virid lightning.

After half a mile, they turned east and walked on the criss-crossing dikes of a cranberry farm and then the girl stepped down onto one of the bogs and headed straight across it. The field was soggy but not flooded, and the vines had not yet begun to bloom. The girl stepped with care, not to break the twiggy branches.

At the far edge of the bog they passed through a small woodlot and came onto a secluded part of the bay shore. There were dozens of black oystercatchers dead and dying on the wet mud. The birds not yet dead beat their long wings weakly against the ground and made faint yelping sounds, ghostlike and plaintive. Their golden eyes seemed to study the sky through milky film.

She knelt and examined several of the dead birds. She lifted wings and spread feathers and felt along the bodies for shotgun pellets, but the birds were unbloodied and intact.

The girl, watching her, said, "What made them fall? How come they died, do you know?"

"We have had such a fierce storm," she said after a moment. "I imagine it had something to do with that. There were a great many dead birds on the beach this morning—seabirds we don't see on the land. It may be the unusual weather drove them ashore. And brought down the oystercatchers."

The girl pulled at the hem of her sweater with grimy hands and glanced toward the dark sky in the west. "I went over to Klipsan this morning and there were a lot of whales that drove up onto the beach. We get them sometimes, one or two, but there's so many I couldn't count them all. Maybe a hundred, they're laying all up and down the sand for most of a mile, just laying there waiting to die I guess. Is that on account of the weather too?"

"I don't know. It may be." She said nothing about the dog, the bear.

"You'd think a big storm would make them swim down deep, not come out on the beach," the girl said, which was perhaps not a question.

Barbara wrapped two dead birds and then a living one in sheets of newspaper and put them in the knapsack. The live bird rustled the paper and cried weakly.

"Will you cut them open to see what killed them?" the girl asked her.

"Yes. Sometimes an autopsy can work out the cause of death."

She walked among the birds still on the ground, quickly twisting the necks of those still moving. The girl watched this in silence. Then she said, "I live at the Whalebone Inn. Will you come and tell me if you work out what killed them?"

She knew the Whalebone Inn, a boardinghouse in Nahcotta. "Yes, I'll come and find you if I learn anything."

They walked back together across the cranberry fields. When they came out on the road, the clouds were huge above the tops of the trees, violently bruise-colored, rippling with that strange lightning. They looked at the sky in silence. A dry blue rain had begun to fall again; it collected in fine drifts on the brim of the girl's hat.

"I am camped at Leadbetter Point. Will you come and tell me if you find any more dead birds in numbers like that, or where they aren't usually seen?"

The girl nodded, and after a hesitation she said, "Do you know the real name for an oystercatcher?"

"Do you mean the species name? The black ones here on the peninsula are *Haematopus bachmani*. Bachman was a friend to Audubon, and there are several birds named for him."

"Have all the names been given out by now?"

"Do you mean, have all the birds on the earth been discovered and given a name? No, no, every year some new ones are found. If we were in South America we might discover one—there are more species of birds there than anywhere. I don't imagine all the species on the earth will ever be known and named. People are always finding new mushrooms and insects and fish."

The girl cast her a sidelong look. "Are any birds named for a woman?"

"Yes, a few." She considered how much more to say—how much Tom would have said. "But most of those are named for queens or goddesses, or for the daughters or wives of scientists, not for women who are themselves scientists." She did not say that in the winter just past she had taken work as a poorly paid assistant to a prominent male professor, trapping birds and preparing their skeletons for his outdated study of the mechanics of bird flight; or that the winter before, she had resorted to teaching children at a grade school in Calistoga. She did not say: Universities are willing to educate women, but not employ them.

"Are any birds named for you?"

"No." She did not smile. "Not yet."

Overnight, as blood will clot in a wound, the clouds thickened and hardened, and in the morning what remained was a black flaw stretching out of sight to the north and south, a long, shifting vein of darkness, glossy and depthless.

The storm had battered the coast for hundreds of miles, from Vancouver Island to Bandon, and inland as far as Spokane and Boise. Fishermen cutting through her camp on their way to the beach told her the widespread belief: that a new and terrible weapon detonated over at Hanford or at one of the secret sites in Canada had brought on the unnatural storm and left that huge black pall in the sky.

A woman she met on the beach was of another mind. God, she said, had opened a portal into heaven and shortly would raise up all the believers.

In the following days, extraordinarily high tides gnawed at the beaches and mudflats; roads and paths disappeared; fifty-year-old houses built on bluffs above the sand fell into the sea. Rafts of dead fish floated in on the next tide and the next, and their decaying bodies littered all the salt marshes and the sand beaches. There were so many fin whales and gray whales decaying on the beach at Klipsan that when the wind blew northerly she could smell the stench from her camp almost ten miles away.

Her notebook became a record of casualties and losses. Thousands of plovers, the subjects of her summer study, had been scattered, driven away or killed in the storm. She posted signs to warn people away from the nesting grounds—this was a crucial time for the few hundred pairs who remained—but the beach had been reduced to a narrow strand, and the Coast Guard horse patrol came up and down it twice a day, heedless of the birds' shallow nests. And in the days after the storm, beachcombers from the tourist cabins, as well as peninsula natives from Oysterville and Nahcotta, walked over the dunes and through the plover nesting sites or drove onto the beach and parked above the high tide line. From the open sand, the black rift seemed to hang just overhead, almost within reach, and on clear nights it was a starless streak through the firmament. People sat on blankets on the sand, or on the fenders and the running boards of cars, and stared up at it.

She watched it too, from driftlogs above the nesting grounds. One day she watched a single heron, then nine pelicans, then a pair of horned grebes rise through the sky and vanish into the blackness. Methodically, she wrote down the time of day, and the numbers of the birds, their names. She tried to think what else to say, and finally wrote, *Gone*.

She had come to the peninsula for the first time in 1927, on a month-long summer holiday with her parents. She was fourteen years old. They rented a board-and-batten cabin on the beach side at Ocean Park, and she spent her days roaming the sand hills, the woods and shorelines. She went to the beach at low tide and came back with her pockets full of shells and agates, her bare legs wet and sandy to the knees. She hiked the oyster-shell road a mile and a half to the bay shore, collected feathers and shells along the edge of the slack water and rummaged in the spruce woods for empty nests and birds' eggs. The pungent carcass of a ninety-foot whale had washed onto the beach near Ocean Park and she drew its detailed likeness in her letter to Tom, beneath a long list of the ducks and pelicans she had seen on the bay, and shorebirds observed on the surf beach. Several times that month she hiked out to Leadbetter Point. There were tens of thousands of snowy plovers nesting there and raising their young, the broad bare sand dimpled with uncountable numbers of their shallow scraped nests. *A boy was flying a kite,* she wrote to Tom, *and wherever it crossed overhead the little birds would rise up in a panic. Do you think a paper kite looks to a plover very much like a hawk?*

She and her mother dug razor clams at low tide, shucked them, and fried them in cornmeal. At night her father built great driftwood bonfires and the three of them sat on the sand watching showers of bright sparks rise into the darkness. She was used to the Napa Valley, where the normal weather in summer was stiflingly hot, and a dry wind rattled the oak leaves. In August, weather on the peninsula was often cool, and she was astonished by the clarity and depth of the sky when the fog cleared out in the afternoons. Walking the bay shore two miles from the ocean, she could hear the breakers as a low continuous throb when she stood still and listened for it.

One week it rained every day. Salt hardened in the shakers and green mold bloomed on the window sills, but she found this kind of weather—days and days with a great drumming of rain on the roof, a lowering slate gray sky, a tremendous wet wind tearing through the trees—oddly exciting. She put on a rain coat and walked across the sand hills to the ocean where she stood under her streaming hat watching the surf breaking high and brown, clear to the horizon, tossing great logs like balsam chips. In the morning, before the wind picked up, before her parents stirred in the other room, before the barest gray light began to signal the day, she lay in bed and listened to the gabble of thousands of geese feeding on the tidewater marshes. *It's wonderful here,* she wrote to Tom.

The woman who came to the door at the Whalebone Inn was not someone she recognized, though the woman seemed taken aback and said, "Oh! It's you!" as if they were acquainted from long past.

"I'm looking for a girl who lives here, she has a brown sweater and her hair is light in color. I failed to get her name."

"That would be Alice. What do you want her for?"

"I'd like to speak with her, if I may."

The woman, who was Alice's aunt, considered her niece an odd and baffling child—a girl who preferred capturing frogs to playing with dolls; a girl who liked to keep snakes as pets. It was a mild worry of hers, that Alice might grow up to be an eccentric and homely hermit-spinster such as the one now standing on the porch. After a considerable pause to weigh Alice's best interests, she stepped out and shouted, "Alice! Com'ere now, I mean it!"

In a moment the girl came in sight, walking up from the tidal flats. She was barefooted and muddy, in pants raggedly cut off at the knees. Her sweater pockets bulged with shells or agates.

"Hello, Alice, I brought you something."

She walked down to meet the girl and held out to her a small ring-bound notebook with a fresh pencil stuck through the rings. Alice took the book and opened to the first page and then looked up.

"It's a place to write down what you see, and find, and what you wonder about. You must write your name at the top, and the date, on every page, but it's not to be a diary. It's a place to write the names of the birds you see, if you know what they are. Or you can say what they look like, or make a drawing—you write on this side of the page, and make your drawings and maps over on the other side. And write down where you saw the birds and what they were doing, and how many there were. Write in it every day. Later on you will probably want to record your observations in ink in a more systematic way, but I've been keeping books like this one since I was a little girl. I have so many books now, they fill two long shelves."

Alice looked up from the book, pressing her hand in it to keep the wind from lifting and fluttering the empty pages. "There's a coyote I see sometimes, and a porcupine. Should I write those down too?"

"Yes, I shouldn't have said so much about birds. You must be a naturalist, for now, and not a specialist until you are older and decide for yourself what interests you most. So write down everything you see, everything in nature, any animals you see, what the weather is, and what the plants are doing—are they leafing out, are the buds swollen, are they flowering? And if you collect shells and rocks, write down what you've found, what kind they are, or what you think formed them. And write down what you wonder about, but try to be very sparing of sentiment and opinion—the best scientists are impartial, not swayed by their own beliefs." She smiled slightly. "If a woman is to have birds or other creatures named for her, she must be the very best in her field."

The girl tucked her chin to hide her own expression which was not a smile. Then she said, "Is it all right if I think back, and write down what I remember from a while ago? Just to catch up."

"Yes, but you will want to be clear. You could say: 'This is what I remember from last week, or last summer.'"

After a moment, Alice said with a glance, "I want to write down about the oystercatchers."

"Yes. You should do that."

The girl's look shifted toward the sky in the west, the thick black flaw above the tops of the trees. "Did you work out what killed them? The oystercatchers?"

She hesitated. "No. But I hope someone will discover it eventually. You should write down everything you saw around the time of the storm, and afterward. But only what you know or have seen. These things might be important, later, to understanding what occurred."

The woman who had answered the door was still watching from the porch of the Whalebone Inn. Now she called out, "Alice, you ought to be washing up for supper before long." The wind lifted and snapped the front of her apron like a flag.

Alice answered her, "I will," but without moving to do it.

Then, after a silence, Alice said, "I have seen birds going into that hole in the sky. Have you? There's saw-whets and barred owls that live on Long Island and when I was camped over there the other night I saw five of them go up."

She had written that morning: *Fourteen willets—usually*

solitary, have never seen so many fly together—up and gone. She had
seen children on the beach write notes and tie them into the
tails of kites, and when they let go the tethering string the kites
lifted into the blackness and disappeared. She did not say any
of this to Alice.

She said, "You should write down what you saw, the owls disappearing, but Alice, no one knows what it is, so you shouldn't
call it a hole in the sky." Then she said, "Did you row over there
to the island? I would worry. The bay has been very rough."
From the dock at Nahcotta it was at least a mile across Willapa
Bay to Long Island. When she was no older than Alice, she had
used to row a canoe on Clear Lake even in the fall when the hard
easterly winds would blow foam off the choppy waves; but that
was before Tom drowned.

The girl shrugged. "I went at low tide, and it was shoal water.
If I was to overturn, I guess I could have stood up and walked
to shore."

They went on standing together in the yard a few more
moments. Then Alice looked down at the book in her hands
and said, "If it's a hole and the birds are going on through it, I
wonder what is on the other side."

The wind drew a lock of hair across the girl's face and she
pushed it back and hooked it behind her ear. It was late in the
afternoon and the sky had begun to redden above the black
flaw. They both looked up at the hollow barking of gulls overhead, and watched without speaking as a flock of twelve or thir-
teen flew west and disappeared into the depths of the blackness.

From a thicket of arrow grass in the salt marsh she watched a
lumber ship half a mile off the point laboring into the bay, the

white surf booming against the ship's hull and decks. This was dusk at the end of a wet day, and a pair of whimbrels foraging in the mudflats were the only birds she had seen in an hour. Her attention drifted. She looked away and then back, and the big vessel at that moment heeled over suddenly with a terrible shrieking of metal. Two men in bright yellow anoraks, small as the end of her thumb from this distance, slid off the deck into the gray water and disappeared. She drew in a loud breath as if it might be possible to call them back, but the sound that came on the exhale was hollow and wordless.

There were other men staggering about on the ship—yellow warblers moving jerkily from branch to leaf, this is what came into her mind—and there must have been men in the wheel-house far forward on the bow, men standing behind the dark, rain-streaked windows, though she could not see them, could not hear them shouting to one another, she only imagined this. The ship leaned and settled—hard aground, listing onto its starboard side—and waves broke on it in great foaming sheets.

She stood up numbly and threw off the marsh cape, took the pistol from her coat pocket and fired it three times into the sky. In a few minutes, someone on the ship shot off a signal flare, its blurred yellow streak wobbling upward, arcing toward the black flaw and disappearing into it. The ship's horn blared, blared again, and a third time.

With the last of the daylight failing, she began hurriedly to gather driftwood and pile it onto one of the mud islands in the marsh. Beach bonfires had been forbidden since the beginning of the war but this was all she knew to do, it was what peninsula people had done in the days when shipwrecks were common, bonfires on the beach to illuminate the darkness for any crewmen who might be able to swim to shore. The wood was sodden, too wet to light, and she was standing there in her mud-caked shoes, breathless with effort, thinking about the can of kerosene half a mile away in her camp, when something like a rumble of thunder shook the ground. The ship in the channel had gradually become invisible but for marker lights drowned intermittently by the breaking seas, but when she looked toward it a leaping glare lit up the whole mouth of the bay. For a startled moment she thought the wet driftwood had ignited, but it was something belowdecks on the ship—covert munitions, she would think later, carried with the lumber—that had begun to burn. The ship was very low in the water, leaning hard on its keel now, and swells were breaking over the upper deck, smothering it completely in gray foam and solid water. The fire shot up higher after every flood, and flames followed the oil out onto the glossy water and lifted upward in a yellow curtain.

She stood and watched men holding to the railings around the wheelhouse let go and drop and disappear into the water. Someone threw a Jacob's ladder over the lee side and men began climbing down it. One of them was Tom—she knew him by his plaid mackinaw—Tom!—and then a swell broke over the ship in a solid white sheet and he vanished under the cataract. Other men climbed down behind him and were swept off, or jumped from the last rung and sank in the burning water. All of this occurred in silence, or seemed to, as the wind, and the roar of the flames, deafened her.

People living in Oysterville four miles away, and in hermit cabins along the bay shore, must have seen the burning ship—it lit up the sky. They began to walk out of the darkness onto the firelit marsh, singly and in pairs, wading through the flood in their gum boots, until there were a dozen or better standing around her, staring and silent, or talking quietly. Someone asked what she had seen, and she shook her head, unable to speak.

After a while, a Coast Guard double-ended rescue boat came laboring out of the darkness into the glare. There was a lifesaving station near the North Cove lighthouse. She had only ever visited the station in summer—young men in white trousers, tight knit tops, white seamen's caps, running rescue drills for small crowds of admiring tourists—but on the walls of the station house there were photographs of wrecked clipper ships and of rescue boats breasting enormous crashing waves, photographs captioned "Heroes of the Surf," and "Storm Warriors." The Coast Guard boat, very small against the hugeness of the firestorm, came within a few hundred yards and then held off, rolling and pitching on the heavy sea. Several men came out of the forward cabin and shot a line across the water that fell short. They tried again, and a third time, a fourth, and then stood and watched the ship burn. The fire rose up in a great column of vivid orange and writhing black, and the wind took it all west into the starless hole in the sky.

After midnight, when the fire had burned down somewhat, the Coast Guard boat began to motor back and forth across the heavy swells, evidently searching for survivors or bodies in the water near the wreck. The tide, someone said, would likely take the bodies up the Naselle River to Raymond or South Bend, but nevertheless a few people began walking the bay shore in case any might wash up along the Point.

She searched in the arrow grass and picked up her things from where she had dropped them—binoculars, notebook, the camouflage cape—and waded back across the marsh into the trees and found her tent in the darkness and lay down, shivering, in her wet clothes. When the night began to thin toward grayness, she put her notebook and Tom's field guide in the knapsack and walked through the dark trees to the ocean beach.

Fog obliterated the headlands and the surf, but in the half-light of dawn the flaw in the sky seemed to hang just overhead, a satiny black ribbon she felt she might stand on tiptoe and touch with an outstretched hand.

It was high tide, but there was a long black sedan parked on the beach. It seemed to her that the car would be lost to the ocean in the next quarter hour, and that the man who had driven it there was either unaware or unconcerned. He crouched behind a driftlog out of the wind and fiddled with a small piece of machinery—a toy rocket ship, she thought, or a Roman candle.

She walked down to him through a dimpled field of plover nests. There were no more than a few dozen birds still remaining on Leadbetter beaches, and the nests on this part of the strand were unpopulated, empty of eggs. The man glanced up but said nothing, intent on his work. He had not shaved in recent days and his graying stubble—he was a man nearing sixty—was bright with beads of rain. She sat near him and opened the field guide to a blank page at the back, where Tom had drawn a few rare and incidental species, and she began to sketch the machine, which was not a toy: it stood like a white egret on tripod legs, its neck and bill pointed upward.

The surf came in around the man's big car and lifted it and carried it west a few yards and dropped it. The motion caught his eye, and belatedly he woke to the situation and shuffled to his feet. By then the tires had already settled half a foot into the wet sand. He stood there, considering, and then shook his head and said, "Hell's bells," in a tone of disgust, and crouched down again with his machine.

In a short while he took a piece of paper and a pencil from his pocket, wrote a note, spindled it, and slid it inside the narrow beak of the egret. She had come to the beach with an uncertain plan—had thought she might build a fire on the sand and send something—a letter? the field guide?—in ash and smoke up to Tom. But now she tore a page from the back of the notebook and wrote a few lines. *Tom, the world is hard*, she wrote. *But everything lives on. Even love. Even loneliness.*

She folded the paper very small and held it out to the man. He barely glanced at her, took it without speaking and pushed it tightly into a cavity in the nose cone. Then he struck a match and lit a short piece of fuse and said offhandedly, "You should probably get farther back," and they both stepped away fifteen or twenty feet. The rocket made a low grating or rasping noise—the sound certain gulls make, though she had not seen many gulls in recent days—and shot straight up, trailing white smoke and red sparks. They watched it rise through the gray sky and arc slightly and disappear through the rupture in the roof of their world.

ACKNOWLEDGMENTS

Many of these stories owe their existence to Richard Butner, who now and again invited me to Sycamore Hill, but insisted I had to bring an unpublished story with me if I wanted to attend. And certainly the present form of these stories is due to the careful, insightful reading and critique I received there, from the various writers who attended. I want to call out C.C. Finlay especially, for his most excellent suggestion for the ending of "The Presley Brothers."

FIRST PUBLICATION

"Joining." *Fantasy and Science Fiction Magazine*. June 1984.

"Interlocking Pieces." *Universe 14*, Terry Carr, editor. Garden City, N.Y: Doubleday & Co., 1984.

"Seaborne." *Fantasy and Science Fiction Magazine*. December 1984.

"Wenonah's Gift." *Isaac Asimov's Magazine of Science Fiction*. July 1986.

"Little Hills." *Northwest Magazine*. March 22, 1987.

"Personal Silence." *Isaac Asimov's Magazine of Science Fiction*. January 1990.

"Lambing Season." *Asimov's Science Fiction*. July 2002.

"Eating Ashes." *Lady Churchill's Rosebud Wristlet*. November 2002.

"The Visited Man." *Eclipse Three*, Jonathan Strahan, editor. San Francisco, Calif: Night Shade Books, 2009.

"Downstream." *The Grove Review*. Spring 2010.

"Unforeseen." *Asimov's Science Fiction*. April/May 2010.

"The Grinnell Method." strangehorizons.com. November 3/10, 2012.

"The Presley Brothers." interfictions.com. November 2013.

"Dead Men Rise Up Never." *Catamaran Literary Reader*. Summer 2016.

ABOUT THE AUTHOR

Molly Gloss is a fourth-generation Oregonian who now lives in the Portland area. She is the author of six other novels: *The Jump-Off Creek*, *The Dazzle of Day*, *Outside the Gates*, *Wild Life*, *The Hearts of Horses*, and *Falling from Horses*.

Her awards include the Oregon Book Award, the Pacific Northwest Book Award, the PEN/Faulkner Award for Fiction, the James Tiptree Jr. Literary Award, the Theodore Sturgeon Memorial Award, and a Whiting Award for Fiction, and her short story "Lambing Season" was a finalist for the Hugo and Nebula Awards. Her work often concerns the landscape, literature, mythology, and life of the American West. Visit the author at mollygloss.com or on Twitter at @mollygloss.